DANCING DEAD

By James Robert Fuller

A Myrtle Beach Crime Thriller

Book VI

Dedicated to:

All Front-Line & Health Care Workers, who, during the Covid-19 pandemic, put the country's welfare ahead of their own well-being.

Thank you, all.

THE MYRTLE BEACH CRIME THRILLERS

By *James Robert Fuller*

Paradise: Disturbed – Book I
The Scale Tippers – Book II
The Falano Findings - Book III
The Combo – Book IV
The Dispatcher – Book V
Dancing Dead – Book VI

Book VII
Coming for Christmas 2021

FOLLOW THE SERIES AT:
MYRTLEBEACHTHRILLERS.COM

Contact the author at:
RONWING44@GMAIL.COM

READERS' COMMENTS

Paradise: Disturbed

Much to our collective delight we finished reading "Paradise Disturbed." Wonderful twists and turns with the backdrop visits of the murderer to some of our favorite golf courses, tourist attractions and restaurants. This is a must read for any murder mystery fan, especially locals familiar with Myrtle Beach. What a plot! Weaving a diabolical serial killer into a golf course theme, along with the Alligator Adventure scenario, is a stroke of genius. Plus the repartee that goes on between the two FBI agents adds just the right touch of humor!... Bob and Judi Kiernan.

I enjoy the dialogue between FBI agents, Ron Lee, and Tim Pond. The constant ragging on each other makes me laugh. Great characters... John Coughenour

Poor Ernie! I loved that character...and I loved the book!... Bill Jackson

I just finished Paradise Disturbed, which I had a hard time putting it down. I thoroughly enjoyed the story. I can't wait to start The Scale Tippers... Tere Harper.

I'm having a hard time putting this book down! I absolutely love it!... Linda Bolt

Paradise Disturbed was so much fun in a terrifying way, that I read it almost in one sitting and immediately passed it on to a golfer friend. These books are great for escaping from the pandemic for a few hours... Nancy Bracken.

I have read Paradise: Disturbed and love the fast pace you set. The two agents are great together and the creep factor was really good on this one - can't wait to get to the next one... Mary Patten.

The Scale Tippers

All I can say is I really enjoyed the 1st book of your new series... and then, the second was even better. I had to throw away a couple of shirts due to salivating down the front of myself while reading all of Agent Ron Lee's donut adventures... Joe Saffran.

The books are gripping, I can't put them down. Everything stops until I finish. My wife is still waiting for me to mow the lawn...when is the next one?... Gary Whittaker

Lay off the donut comments!... Ron Lee

I have read the 2nd book and thoroughly enjoyed it. I can't wait to read The Falano Findings. They are great!... Tere Harper

I have read all four of the Myrtle Beach Crime Thrillers and Scale Tippers is my favorite. I know the locales used in the story and I love stories that involve the Mafia!... Tim Graham

The Falano Findings

I just finished The Falano's Findings and all I can say is... I loved it! Looking forward to whatever comes next!... Tere Harper

*Loved all three of the Murder Mystery Series! The Falano Findings, brings you savage, intense, brutal, murders; however softens the tone with wit & humor brought on by the antics of the donut toting, I.R.S. Special Agent Ron Lee, and his partner Agent Tim Pond. A real page turner...*Joe Saffran

I read "The Falano Findings" and was hooked immediately and couldn't put it down.. I can't wait for "The Combo". I am an Horry County and Myrtle Beach native and J.R. Fuller really brings life... AND DEATH to the area... Sig Buster, III

"Falano Findings" was his best yet. Looking forward to the next one. Now my favorite author!... Gary Whitaker

I'm not much of a reader, but I couldn't put Paradise Disturbed down and read it in record time. Same thing happened with Scale Tippers and The Falano Findings. They pull you in and won't let go! I can't wait for the next one !!... Paul Reilley

The Combo

Been waiting for "THE COMBO" ever since I finished "FALANO." When it finally arrived it didn't disappoint. It took off where "The Falano Findings" left off and the race was on for the rest of the book. Now I'm waiting with bated breath for "The Dispatcher"… Sig Buster, III

All four in the Murder Mystery series have been enjoyable to read ! The Combo, like the others grabs you and won't let go until the end. If you think you know how the book will end, you better keep on reading because you will be wrong! Can't wait for the next book to come out ... Paul Reilley.

"Loved it!" … Joe Saffran

"Quite a storyline! The Mamba was a great character and the twist in the story was perfect." … Alex Harvey

"That cartel is never going to let up, is it? Loved the story and I love Ron and Tim. Keep those donuts coming!" … Agnus Cosart

The Dispatcher

"Loved reading how the cantankerous detectives skillfully worked their way around the Myrtle Beach area to solve the murders with grit and humor." … Pat Gurley

"All of J.R. Fuller's thrillers have kept me on the edge of my seat and the Dispatcher was no

different. I can't wait for my copy of "Dancing Dead." …Sig Buster

"Don't try to figure out the endings of these books as I tried and was wrong each time !! Very difficult to put the books down once you start. Enjoyed all the previous books and looking forward to the Dancing Dead !!" … Paul Reilley

"Despite the fact that we were thoroughly knocked off, or should I say dispatched, "The Dispatcher" was a gem. It got me through the few days of mild COVID 19 in quarantine. Judi also could not put the book down. She now supports OPEN CARRY. You are a diabolical master of twists and turns. The whole series is great reading." … Bob and Judi Kiernan

DANCING DEAD

A Myrtle Beach Crime Thriller

Book VI

Authored by

JAMES ROBERT FULLER

FIRST EDITION

May 2021

ISBN: 979-1-6780-7310-7

PROLOGUE

State Trooper Sergeant Harvey Little, with his cruiser parked in the exit lane of Long Bay's gated community, poured a cup of coffee from his thermos. He was working the midnight to 8:00am shift, and he had just gotten comfortable to enjoy his 4:00am coffee break. Everything was going fine until he spotted a cube truck, with only one headlight, heading west on Route 9.

"The driver may not know he's missing a light," muttered the trooper, as he started his vehicle and pulled out onto the highway.

Little followed the truck for a half-mile. Turning on his blue lights, he pulled into the left lane to wave the truck over, but as he did, the truck swerved into his path.

Little avoided the collision by slamming on his brakes and steering his cruiser into the soft grassy median strip where he came to a full stop.

The truck continued on, leaving Little stuck in mud. He radioed his situation to troopers in the vicinity. Within minutes a roadblock, five miles up the road, was in place.

Seeing the roadblock up ahead, the truck came to an abrupt halt 200 yards short of the roadblock. Three men, all carrying firearms, leaped from the cab, and raced toward the woods bordering the road.

Trooper Little, having freed his vehicle from the mud, arrived at the scene as they were running.

Seeing the trooper, the gunmen turned their AK-47 weapons on him and sprayed his cruiser with multiple volleys. The state police would later announce they found 68 bullet holes in Little's cruiser. How Little escaped death, much less even being struck, was a miracle.

1

Moments before the trooper's windshield exploded into a thousand pieces, Little fell out the driver's door and onto the Route 9 pavement. He scurried on hands and knees to the rear of the vehicle while dodging the fusillade of hot lead directed his way.

Seconds later, as Little lay hunkered down, he realized he was no longer under attack. The gunmen's attention had turned elsewhere.

Hearing the cracks of sniper rifles, he knew the other troopers, seeing he was under attack, were retaliating.

A sniper's first shot took out the gunman closest to the woods. Snipers cut down the two remaining gunmen, ending the conflict.

When the gunfire subsided, Little made his way to meet the other officers.

As he approached them, Corporal Ben Wilson asked, "What is this all about, Harv?"

"I don't have a clue, Benny."

He took a half-dozen steps toward the truck, but stopped, asking, "Do I hear music?"

The gunmen had been listening to a CD when they abandoned the truck. Playing was a haunting Latino ballad, called *"No More Boleros."*

"It's coming from the truck, Harvey," yelled a trooper who had checked out the cab.

Little motioned to open the truck's rear doors.

"Let's see what the hell they have inside the truck which is so damn important they found it necessary to get themselves killed."

The officer swung them open.

Inside, encased in a thick white shield of frost, hung a dozen bodies of men and women impaled on hooks attached to the truck's ceiling.

"Omigod!" whispered Little.

The bouncing beams from a half-dozen trooper flashlights turned the truck's interior into something beyond surreal.

The truck's violent stop had some frozen bodies swaying and twirling, while others just rocked back and forth. It was too macabre for words.

"They look like ghosts dancing to the music, Harv."

"Yeah, they do," agreed Little. "Dancing dead."

A quarter mile away, a car pulled off the road and killed its lights. The two occupants, Chuck Delgato, and Murphy Bortelli, watched the shootout between the truck's occupants and the State Troopers. They continued to watch as the troopers opened the truck's doors.

"We'd better head back to tell Brett the bad news."

"He ain't gonna be happy, Chuck."

"Can't say I blame him," responded Delgato as he dialed a phone number on his cell.

"Yeah."

Chuck gave a one word command. "Abort."

TUESDAY - SEPTEMBER 17, 2019

It was 6:12am when Ron Lee's phone rang. Still in sleep mode, Ron rolled over, retrieved his phone from the nightstand, and seeing the caller's name, answered, "Yes?"

"You're reinstated," said Braddock as if his mouth was full of dog shit. "Be at the office within the hour."

Click.

Ron called his partner, Tim Pond.

A groggy Tim answered.

"Did you get a call?"

"Yeah, I did."

"See you in an hour. Oh, and Tim."

"Yeah?"

"Don't forget the donuts."

CHAPTER 1
PAPER FOR GOLD

4 MONTHS EARLIER - MAY 2019 - JUAREZ, MEXICO

Juan Pablo Amarillo, the leader of the Juarez Cartel, was enjoying a breakfast of fresh fruits when handed a note by Jorge Ortiz, one of his most trusted lieutenants.

It read, *Nice try, Juan.* Colonel Ron Lee's signature followed.

"What does this mean, Jorge?"

"The hit squad failed, senor."

"They are all dead?"

"The mortuary received four body bags from the Federal Ministerial Police."

"Four? I sent five."

"We received only four. They found the note inside Alejandro Lopez's body bag."

"Alejandro was one of our best men!"

"He was that, Juan Pablo."

"The two FBI agents?"

"Alive and well."

"Damn! What about our operations?"

"Shut down!"

"We have a lot of money invested in the area."

"Over two billion in cash, Juan Pablo."

"Where is it?"

"Driscoll stored it everywhere," answered Jorge, referring to the former, now deceased, head of operations in South Carolina and Georgia.

"Do we know these places?"

"We do. Driscoll sent a list of the locations where he stored the cash."

"Safely, I presume. I don't want our money rotting in the ground. They estimate Pablo Escobar lost $2.1 billion a year, much of it eaten by rats."

"Driscoll didn't bury your money in the ground, Juan Pablo," said an assuring Jorge.

"Get me the list, Jorge, and call Luiz Beltrán. I need to see him, now!"

Beltrán was Juan Pablo's financial advisor and the man he most trusted.

An hour later, Juan Pablo and Beltrán were discussing the approximate $2 billion in cash stashed away in Myrtle Beach, South Carolina.

Beltrán held the list of locations where they had hidden the money.

"How much space is $2 billion taking up, Luiz?"

"I'm assuming, according to this list, most of it is on pallets in various storage facilities."

"Si," answered Juan Pablo. "Driscoll did not keep all of his eggs in one basket."

"That was wise of Mr. Driscoll, may he rest in peace."

"I don't share your sympathy, Luiz. The man blew our operation in Georgetown. It's why I had him killed."

"He ran a good operation, Juan Pablo. Perhaps you could have been more lenient."

"Si, but hindsight is always 20-20, Luiz."

"So true, my friend. But getting back to your question. A million dollar bundle weighs 22 pounds. I'm estimating if you stacked 50 million dollars on a pallet, it would weigh around 1100 pounds. Therefore, it would take about 40 pallets to hold two billion dollars in hundred-dollar bills. If, however, 20s, 10s, and 5s comprise a good deal of the cash, which I suspect they do, then you're talking 500 or more pallets."

"Based on the size of the list, Luiz, 500 is closer to the truth."

"Yes, Driscoll has at least 60 storage locations on his list," concurred Luiz.

"What a mess," moaned Juan Pablo.

"Si, it is, but may I offer a suggestion?"

"But of course, amigo."

"Convert the cash to gold. Gold would require minimal storage space, and there would be no deterioration. Plus, the gold's value would increase!"

"How could we do this, Luiz? We can't walk into a bank with $2 billion in cash and ask to exchange it for gold!"

"No, you cannot, Juan Pablo, but you can buy gold from online bullion dealers who ask no questions."

"Luiz, you are a genius!"

"Maybe so, but I pale when compared to you, Juan Pablo."

"True, true," replied Juan Pablo, as both men laughed at themselves.

"Listen to me, Juan Pablo," said a serious Luiz. "This job will require a small army of workers, temporary of course, and a calculating leader."

"When you say, temporary, Luiz, you mean throwaways?"

"I do. You don't want any loose ends, amigo."

"You're right. We'll need someone special to handle what needs doing. I believe I know just the man."

"Oh? Who might that be?"

"His name is Brett Cardone. He grew up in Juarez but gained American citizenship a few years ago. He's smart, ruthless, and lethal. His father, gunned down in a raid by the Federales, worked for me as a soldier. Brett, at 18-years-old, exacted his revenge by killing the captain who led the raid."

"He sounds dangerous, amigo."

"Oh, he is much more than dangerous, Luiz. He soldiered for me for a year. During that brief span, he killed 31 men and women. But I knew it was a waste of talent. He was much too smart for a dead-end position. I brought him in and trained him how to run an operation. He's running our Northwest operations out of Portland. I'll have him come here for a meeting."

"I look forward to meeting him."

"Tell me about the gold, Luiz."

"It comes in various size bars, ranging from an ounce to 500 ounces."

"What would you suggest we buy?"

"I suggest you purchase the 400 and 500 ounce bars but mix in $300 million in 1, 10, and 20 ounce bars."

"Why the smaller bars, Luiz?"

"You can use them like cash, but without the bulk."

"Yes, I see," whispered Juan Pablo.

"It would give you about 2300 ingots in the larger weights and about 500 bars in the lesser weights."

"How many pallets?"

"Well, eighty 400-ounce ingots weighs a ton. If you wanted to have each pallet hold a ton, it would require somewhere in the neighborhood of 28 pallets. The smaller bars would need a single pallet."

"From a possible 500 pallets and a possible 60 storage units to 30 pallets and a half-dozen storage units! Genius!" cried an elated Amarillo. "I'll have Cardone here tomorrow evening, Luiz. ᴾlan on having dinner here."

Luiz's *'genius suggestion'* would be the death knell for scores of innocents and the not-so-innocent.

CHAPTER 2
REINSTATEMENT

The first twenty seconds was a staring contest. No one spoke. There was barely breathing.

Braddock broke the silence, saying, "If it were up to me, you'd still be in your beds."

"Apparently wiser heads prevailed," remarked Ron, ensuring the ice would forever go unbroken.

"Here are your badges and weapons," hissed Braddock as he opened a drawer in his desk and withdrew the two agents' hardware, tossing them onto his desk.

"I see you kept them nice and clean for us, Captain," remarked Tim with a grin.

"Okay, Captain, tell us what's going on," said Ron sternly. "You didn't get us out of bed to do desk work."

Braddock, leaning back in his chair, snorted a laugh, then said, "I wish it was the reason. But it is not. There's a truck parked out on Route 9, about six miles past the Long Bay Golf Club."

"What's in the truck?"

"Bodies. Hung like meat."

"How many bodies?"

"A dozen was the latest count. We also have three dead hombres who tried to make a run for it. State Police snipers nailed them all."

"Maybe they should have wounded one," remarked Tim.

"So what do you think it's all about, Jim?" asked Ron.

"I don't know. If I were to make a guess, I'd say they could be mules who outlived their usefulness."

"That's a good guess, I suppose. Human trafficking also comes to mind. So this is our case then?"

"Yes, it is, but I want daily reports. Daily! You got it?"

"It gets busy out there in the field, Jim. Sometimes it's necessary to place incidentals on the back burner."

"Well, Colonel, if you want to keep those badges, you boys had better hand in a daily report or else I'll have you resuspended."

"Really, Jim? And who issued that threat? Was it the guys who brought us back? No, I doubt they would say something that stupid. You'll get a report when we have something to report. If that's not satisfactory, then I suggest you assign the case to other agents. But, I doubt you have the balls."

Braddock, enraged, stood, and keeping his voice just below a scream, said, "Get out of my office! Go do your damn job! And try not to kill everyone you run into!"

"Yikes!" said Tim. "This may be tougher than I thought, Ron. There's a chance we may go to court."

"Not a chance, partner."

CHAPTER 3
GRAVE FINDINGS

SEPTEMBER 17, 2019 - 8:30AM

Arriving at the crime scene at 8:30, Sergeant Little greeted them as they stepped from their vehicle.

"I'm Sergeant Little, fellas."

"FBI Special agent Ron Lee, and this is my partner, Agent Tim Pond."

"We expected you fellas to be here much earlier."

"It's a long story, sergeant."

"Oh. How long?"

"Two months and one day," quipped Tim.

"Fill us in, sergeant," ordered Ron.

Little described his attempt to pull over the truck, through the subsequent shootout.

"How about the truck, sergeant? Have you traced the VIN?"

"Stolen last week from a meat supply warehouse, which accounts for the hooks in the ceiling."

"Is the truck refrigerated?"

"It is, and it was working full force."

"Is the coroner here?"

"Yes, sir. He's inside the truck."

"Well, I guess it's time we have a look," sighed Ron, not overly eager to climb into a refrigerated truck containing a dozen bodies.

Reaching the rear of the truck, Tim asked, "Are we climbing, Ron?"

Not wanting to mingle with the corpses, Ron replied, "No." Instead they stood, staring upward at the now stilled bodies.

A moment later, Robert Edge, the county coroner, appeared from somewhere in the truck.

"Morning, Robert." greeted Ron.

"What's so damn good about it, Ron? If the troopers had set up the roadblock three miles further on in the next county, I'd still be in my damn bed!"

"Nice to see you too, Bob."

"They took you guys off suspension to handle this case, did they?"

"Seems that way," replied Ron.

"Well, good luck, fellas."

"Any thoughts as to the cause of death, Bob?"

"I'm not sure, Ron, but I suspect poison."

"Sounds like a murder case to me," said Tim with a shit-eating grin.

"Still at the top of your game, I see, Agent Pond."

"I'll take it as a compliment, Bob."

"I bet you will," retorted Edge.

"Find anything unusual, Bob?" asked Ron.

"Maybe, but I can't be certain. We need to defrost the bodies so I can do a more thorough examination."

"What is it you're uncertain about?"

"It's their hands, fingers to be exact."

"What about them?" asked Tim.

"Their thumbs are so worn their fingerprints are almost indistinguishable."

"What's your thoughts?"

"Can't say right now, Ron. But I will say, whatever it was wearing down their fingerprints, wasn't something with a rough texture. I'll know more after we get them back to the lab."

"Okay, Bob. Give us a heads-up as soon as you have something."

"Will do, Ron."

Turning to Sergeant Little, Ron said, "Let's have a look at the villains, sergeant."

"They are still where they fell, Agent Lee. Still dead too."

Both Ron and Tim grinned at the trooper's wisecrack.

Upon seeing the bodies, little doubt existed the gunmen were former residents from somewhere south of the border.

"Any ID's, Sergeant Little?"

"No IDs, sir."

"Did you find anything of consequence?"

"This guy had a pack of matches on him. They have the Heather Glen Golf Club insignia."

"He doesn't look like someone who plays golf," quipped Tim.

"No, but maybe he worked there. Take a picture of his face, Tim. We'll stop there to see if anyone knows him."

"Do you think this bullet hole in his face might affect our identifying him?"

"I doubt it. It's not like he was a movie star."

"Anything else, sergeant?"

"The fella lying over there had this picture in his otherwise empty wallet."

Examining the photo, Ron saw a good-looking Latin girl with a beautiful smile.

"Nice-looking girl," muttered Ron.

"There's an inscription in Spanish on the back, sir."

"What does it say, Ron?" asked Tim.

Ron flipped the photo and read the inscription aloud, saying, "To José with all my love, Anita."

"Hell, that should be easy to track down," joked Tim. "What would you guess? A thousand José's and a few hundred Anita's, statewide?"

"We'll show it around, maybe get it in the paper. Someone might recognize her," suggested Ron.

"Did you find anything on the victims, Sergeant Little?"

"Someone stripped the bodies, Agent Pond. No jewelry, no IDs, nothing."

"What about in the cab?" asked Ron.

"A candy-bar wrapper is all we found. Oh, and a piece of paper with the number 26 written on it."

"I wonder where they were taking the bodies?" uttered Tim.

"Does the truck have a trip odometer, Sarge?" asked Ron.

"I don't know. Let's have a look-see."

Walking over to the truck, Ron opened the driver's door, and seeing the key in the ignition, climbed in, and started it up.

A moment later, he announced, "It has a trip odometer. It's reading 20.4."

"What are you thinking, Ron?"

"Well, partner, it's a longshot, but maybe their destination was 26 miles from where they started. Any thoughts, sergeant, on what's six miles up the road?"

"It's really a desolate area up that way. It's dominated by the Juniper Swamp all the way to the Green Sea community. I can't think of anything. Sorry, sir."

"No problem. Tim and I will take a ride and see where it leads us. Hell, this piece of paper could mean a lot of things or it could mean nothing."

As they got into their car, Ron said to Tim, "Let's map what is 20.4 miles back from this spot."

"You realize they could have gotten onto Route 9 from a dozen different locations, don't you?"

"That's true, but if you were told to travel 26 miles on Route 9, chances are you would set the mileage indicator when you reached Route 9."

"I have to admit, it's what I would do."

"Let's take a drive up the road, Tim. Maybe, we'll get lucky."

Eight minutes later they had traveled 5.6 miles. Ron pulled the car over to the shoulder of the road.

"Sergeant Little wasn't kidding when he said it was desolate," remarked Tim.

Using a set of binoculars, Ron said, "It looks like a dirt road up there about a quarter mile. Let's have a look."

Reaching the road, Ron once again pulled off to the shoulder.

Tim, checking his map, announced, "This is SC-26-140."

To the right, they could see a half-dozen shacks. To their left, there was nothing.

"Let's try the left side, Tim."

They drove two miles when they came upon mashed down brush leading into an overgrown field.

"Looks like something big drove in here, Ron."

"Yeah, let's take a walk into this field."

Exiting their car, the two agents followed the flattened brush for about 400 yards when they came to a dirt covered area measuring 50' x 10'.

"What are you thinking, Ron?"

"I'm thinking mass grave."

"That was my first thought as well."

"You can see tire tracks where, what I'm guessing might be a payloader moved back and forth pushing the dirt into the hole."

"You think there's something buried here?"

"I'm betting this is where they planned to bury the bodies in the truck. They must have had a chase car following the truck. When they saw the truck overtaken, they notified whoever was here to get out. Before leaving, they filled in the hole."

"Hey, Ron, look over there, about a hundred yards."

"Yeah, what about it?"

"The brush isn't as high as it is here."

"Let's meander over there, Tim-o-thy."

Although the two areas were equal in size, in this new area, weeds and grasses had taken hold.

"Looks to me like these weeds can't be over six-inches high."

"Agreed," murmured Ron. "I'd bet a dollar…"

"Don't say it, Ron, until you actually buy a friggin' donut. To finish your thought, yeah, there's something buried here."

"If it's another load of bodies, then the question is: Why is someone killing what appears to be migrants and burying them in mass graves?"

"Hey, Ron."

"Yeah?"

"When they dig this up, I don't want to be within ten miles of it."

"It could be fragrant, partner. There's no doubt about it."

CHAPTER 4
BRETT CARDONE

4 MONTHS EARLIER - MAY 2019 - JUAREZ, MEXICO

"Juan Pablo, Brett Cardone has arrived."

"Ahh, good, Jorge. Send him in and notify Luiz."

A moment later, a tall, tanned-skinned man, with dark wavy hair, and deep brown eyes entered the room.

"Brett, it is good to see you, my friend."

"Juan Pablo, it is my honor, sir."

"How are things in Portland?"

"All is running smooth, sir. We are exceeding expectations."

"That is good to hear, Brett," replied Juan Pablo, already knowing the expected answer.

"What brings me back to Juarez, sir?"

"We'll discuss that as soon as Luiz Beltrán… ahh, here he is now."

"Juan Pablo, I see our guest has arrived."

"Luiz, I would like you to meet Brett Cardone."

"Glad to meet you, senor."

"Likewise, Mr. Beltrán."

"Luiz is my financial advisor, Brett. Together we have come up with a plan to solve a serious problem involving two billion dollars."

"Two billion! That is a serious problem!" exclaimed Cardone.

"Yes, it is, Brett. It's why I am picking you to manage the solution."

"Anything you ask, Juan Pablo. How can I be of service?"

"I want you to take over the dormant South Carolina operation."

"Doesn't Cameron Driscoll run that operation?"

"He did. We retired Mr. Driscoll," answered Juan Pablo, not needing to detail his reply.

"I see," Cardone muttered under his breath.

"Here's the situation, Brett. There is an approximate two billion dollars in cash stored in 60 plus locations along the Grand Strand. Our plan is to convert the cash into gold and reduce storage locations by 90% or more."

"It will take a lot of personnel, Juan Pablo. Sorting, counting, and packaging all that money will take… weeks, or more likely, months."

"You have a clear vision of the logistics, Brett. I'm glad I picked you for this job."

"Thank you for your confidence, Juan Pablo. Now, it's my opinion we will need to import the labor. We don't want locals knowing about this operation, and we don't want our people doing a mindless job."

"Correct," agreed Luiz. "However, when finished, you will need to…"

"Eliminate them," said Cardone, knowing, without being told, what needed doing.

"I think he has the gist of it, Juan Pablo."

"He's a smart man, Luiz."

"Brett, each time you accumulate and package $60 million dollars," explained Luiz, "contact us and I will make the arrangements to transfer the money to the bullion dealers."

"That means you plan on thirty-some transfers."

"You're good in math, Brett. I calculated there will be a need for 34 transfers."

"It's only a guess, but it might take five days to count out and package $60 million. If I'm right, we're talking… 160 days to do all two billion."

"I must admit, five months is more than expected," Luiz replied in a disappointing tone.

"Although it will lengthen the time to complete the task, it would be wise not to exceed more than a dozen workers," explained Brett.

"What makes you say that?" asked Luiz.

"More than a dozen will stretch us too thin, Senor Beltrán. Besides housing and feeding them, they'll need watching day and night. That takes staff. If someone were to escape, well…"

"We will not tolerate an escape," warned Juan Pablo, giving Cardone a look that spoke volumes.

"I agree, Juan Pablo. That's why it is imperative we don't stretch our security."

"Good point, Brett."

Brett, after an appreciative nod to Juan Pablo, continued, saying, "This will take some time, Juan Pablo. The work will be tedious. The workers will grow restless and non-productive in a short amount of time. I can see replacing them every 2-3 weeks."

"Do what you must, Brett. We will send you the workers and anything else you need."

"I see a need to buy an entire storage facility, Juan Pablo. I can house the workers in it and process the money when it arrives."

"How much will you need?" asked Luiz.

"The cost of the facility might exceed a million. Then there will be beds, food, and appliances like refrigerators, stoves, etc. I think two million will cover it."

"Do it," said Juan Pablo, with a firm voice.

"I have two men in Portland who I need on my team. They are well-versed in elimination procedures."

"Fine. What about the Portland operation? Who will handle that in your absence?"

"My wife."

"Does your wife have the respect of the people in the organization?"

"She does."

"Can she make the tough decisions, should they arise?"

"She will."

"You understand there can be no foul ups without repercussions."

"I do. She can do the job, sir. Lisa has my complete trust."

"I sincerely hope so, Brett," said Juan Pablo, with another look Brett could read loud and clear.

"When will Myrtle Beach be operational?" asked Luiz.

"I'll need two weeks to locate a facility, and another two weeks to secure it."

"That sounds reasonable," said Juan Pablo.

"We'll need a few days to set up the living quarters for our staff and the workers. Once we're situated, we'll need time to train the staff. When we complete those tasks, we'll be ready to bring in the money and the first group of laborers. I'm saying we'll be ready by… mid-July."

"That means, if your estimate of 160 days is close to being correct, you will complete the count by Christmas."

"Give or take," nodded Cardone.

"I'll give you to Christmas Eve, Brett. Get it done."

"Yes, sir, Juan Pablo."

"We have completed our business here, Brett. Thank you."

Brett was ready to leave when Juan Pablo said, "Wait. There is one other thing."

"What's that, Juan Pablo?"

"The FBI killed my nephew in Myrtle Beach."

"Yes, I heard. My condolences, sir."

"Listen carefully, Brett. Your number one job is to get our money collected so we can convert it to gold. But, if you should cross paths with FBI agents Lee and Pond, take them out by any means possible! Don't go out of your way, Brett, but if the opportunity presents itself… kill them!"

Cardone, nodding his understanding, stood, said a word to Luiz, and headed toward the doorway. As he walked, he could feel the piercing eyes of Juan Pablo on his back. The pressure was already mounting. He understood failure was a death sentence.

CHAPTER 5
MUSTARD AND THE END

TUESDAY - SEPTEMBER 17, 2019 - 4:00AM

A black 4-door Toyota Camry was trailing the truck. Two men occupied the vehicle, both trained killers.

They were a half-mile behind the truck when they saw the headlights of Trooper Little's cruiser pop on. Watching from a distance, they saw him pull onto Route 9 and turn in the truck's direction.

They were less than a quarter-mile behind the trooper's cruiser when they saw the blue lights flashing.

"Hey Mustard, why do you think he's going after them?" asked the driver, Charles Delgato.

He had directed the question to his partner, Murph Bortelli, better known as Mustard. It was a strange nickname for sure, but well earned.

Both men were west-coast mobsters who Cardone hired to keep his Portland operation running smooth. Their job was to eradicate anyone who got out of line, and they were lethally proficient at their trade. When they did a job, Bortelli always added a flourish. Thus the name, Mustard.

Delgato also had a well-deserved nickname: The End. It didn't come from playing football. It derived from the finality of the man's work. When ordered to eliminate someone, for that someone, it was "the end."

"I don't know, Chuck. They weren't speeding or driving wild. Stay back. Let's see how this plays out."

Minutes later they saw the truck swing into the path of the trooper and force him off the road.

"What are those dumb-fucks doing!" screamed Mustard. "That stupid move just brought half the troopers in the county into play."

They glanced over at the cruiser now sitting in the median as they passed.

"He's stuck in the mud, Chuck."

"Yeah, but you can bet your sweet-ass he's called some of his friends. This ain't gonna end well, Murph."

"If the cops don't kill them, we'll wind up killing them," voiced a knowing Bortelli.

"I don't think we need to worry about them, Murph. Those assholes just narrowed their choices to one. They are going to die."

Three minutes and four miles further up the road, they saw the roadblock.

"Told ya," muttered Chuck.

Delgato, looking into his rearview mirror, announced, "I think the trooper stuck in the mud, got himself unstuck. He's coming up behind us at warp speed."

"Pull over and let him pass, Chuck. Let's just sit here and watch. If I'm right, this won't take long."

Mustard was right. They watched their crew get taken out by a sniper. A few minutes later, they witnessed the troopers open the rear of the truck.

"Let's go inform the boss."

"He ain't gonna be happy, Chuck."

"Hell, can you blame him? You know what this means, Murph?"

"Tell me."

"It means the FBI is going to get involved. It means our operation, known to no one, is now in jeopardy."

"This is a hick town, Chuck. I doubt the FBI staffs this branch with any Sherlock's."

"We can only hope, Murph."

CHAPTER 6
ELIMINATION

It was 5:10 when they rang his doorbell. Although there was no immediate answer, they knew not to ring a second time.

Cardone would answer, but not until he vetted the caller as someone he knew.

They saw lights come on inside and knew the door would open within seconds.

Almost on cue, the door swung open and Cardone, wearing a white robe and slippers, asked, "What's wrong?"

"Our truck was pulled over. The crew challenged the law, and the law won. Snipers picked them off one by one. They had no chance. The truck's cargo is now in the hands of the law," explained Chuck.

"Why did it get pulled?"

"No idea, boss. They were doing the speed limit, driving with caution, and 'boom' out of the blue, they're being blue lighted by a trooper. They forced the cop off the road, but a roadblock was waiting for them. There was a shootout and…"

"Damn! Now the damn FBI will have their noses stuck up everybody's ass."

"Yeah, but maybe they ain't sharp, boss, this being a small town and all," suggested Bortelli.

"Wrong, Murph! They have two guys who killed Juan Pablo's favorite nephew, broke Driscoll's operation, and wiped out an assassination squad sent to kill them. I'll bet they're dragging their asses out of bed as we speak."

"What do you want us to do, boss?" asked Mustard.

"Did our dead crew have friends who might know something?"

"I know the kid, José, was head-over-heels in love with a girlfriend. I think her name is Anita. She works on the Big M casino boat."

"What about the other two?"

"They both worked at the Heather Glen golf course, doing course maintenance. There are two other Mexicans working there. I don't know if there was any camaraderie among them."

"We can't afford to take any chances, now can we, Mustard?"

"No, sir, we can't. We'll take care of everything before noon."

"Let's make it… before ten, why don't we?"

"Yes, sir. Before ten."

"Get back to me as soon as you've cleaned up."

"Will do, boss."

As they climbed into their vehicle, Mustard asked, "Do you know the guys at Heather Glen who we need to deal with, Chuck?"

"I've seen them once or twice. If we hurry, we can catch them in the parking lot. They'll be reporting for work at 6:00."

"Let's give it a shot."

"How about two shots," joked The End.

****

It was 5:48 when they pulled into the Heather Glen parking lot.

"The employees park at the rear of the lot, Mustard, which makes it ideal for us. It's a distance to the clubhouse and there are lots of trees between each lane of parking. Since the sun doesn't rise until seven, it will still be pitch-dark."

"I'll bet they come together in one vehicle."

"That's a good bet, Mustard. We can only hope."

"Okay, let's back into a parking space and await our two Mexican friends."

As they waited, they screwed silencers onto their Glocks.

"I wish I had a cup of joe to wash these down," said Mustard as he unwrapped two Ho Hos.

"Damn, Murph, how many Ho Hos do you eat in a day?"

"I don't know. Maybe six or eight."

"They're full of chemicals, you know," said Chuck. "Those things are going to kill you someday."

"Thanks for worrying about my health partner, but at least I'll die happy."

It was 6:11 when an old Ford Ranger pickup pulled into the parking lot. It parked in the first parking space at the very end of the lane.

The hitmen's Camry was just twenty feet away.

They waited until they heard both of the truck's doors slam shut. Although it was dark, they could see the outline of both men. They were short in stature, and on the thin side.

Chuck called out, "Amigos!"

The two men stopped and, looking in Chuck's direction, answered, "Si, senor?"

"Do you know Raul and Juan?"

Not understanding the question, but knowing the names, one man answered, "Si, Raul and Juan."

"Let's go," whispered Mustard.

Both men exited the Camry and, tucking their Glocks into their pants, walked toward the two workers.

"Hola!" said Chuck.

"Hola," answered the two men in sync.

Once they were within five feet of the two men, they pulled their weapons. A pull of the triggers sent the two workers to the promised land.

As they lay there, Mustard stood above them and shot them both in the eyes.

With an unreal calmness, the two killers returned to their car and drove off.

"The Big M doesn't open until 5:00, Mustard."

"The boss said to complete all business by 10:00. We'll go to her home, but first, let's go have breakfast."

"Great idea, partner!"

CHAPTER 7
SPEAKING SPANISH

TUESDAY - SEPTEMBER 17, 2019 - 11:00AM

Ron and Tim hung around the assumed burial ground until an FBI forensic team arrived.

"What do we have here, Ron?"

Asking was Joe Lagrange, the head of the Myrtle Beach Forensic Division.

"Well, Joe, we're not positive, but we believe we're standing atop a mass grave. There may be another filled-in grave over there," said Ron, pointing toward their original find. "We think they intended to fill it with the folks who got waylaid on Route 9."

"That's a bad one, Ron. My other team is working that situation."

"Dig up both spots, Joe, in the event we're wrong about the one over there."

"Will do. We'll check the surrounding area for any more spots like this."

"I'm curious how old the growth of these weeds might be, Joe."

Bending down, Lagrange pulled several weeds and grasses from the ground. He examined the roots and the plant for a few minutes, then said, "I'd estimate 2-3 weeks."

"Hmm, two to three weeks. Well, keep me informed, Joe."

"Will do, Ron."

As they walked back through the field to their vehicle, Ron's phone rang. It was Bill Baxter, head of the Myrtle Beach State Police.

"Hey, Bill. What's up?"

"Congratulations, fellas. I'm glad to see you back on the job. How did you enjoy your two-month hiatus?"

"Thanks, Bill. Glad to be back. The paid leave wasn't hard to take. Why the call?"

"We may have a connection with the shoot-out on Route 9."

"Connection? A connection to what, Bill?"

"We found two Mexican workers murdered at the…"

"Stop! Let me guess. At the Heather Glen golf course."

"Yeah! How did you know?"

"It's a two plus two thing, Bill. What time did this happen?"

"The coroner says around six this morning."

"They're killing all potential connections," mumbled Ron.

"Who are you talking about, Ron?"

"Who's ever behind the truck full of bodies."

"Any ideas?"

"Not a clue."

"The hit on the two Mexican workers looks professional, Ron."

"Oh, I bet it was. There's a big-time operation going on somewhere. Big-time operations call for professionals on every level. I have a gut feeling there are going to be more professional hits coming soon. There are tracks that need covering, Bill."

"Are you going to stop at Heather Glen?"

"We're thinking there's a young woman targeted for death, if, in fact, she isn't already dead. We need to find her… now!"

"Who would she be?"

"Her name is Anita. José was in love with her."

"Who the hell is José?"

"He's nobody any more, because he's already dead."

Ron, hanging up without saying goodbye, turned to Tim, saying, "C'mon, we need to find Anita."

"Okay, but where do we start?"

"Great question, partner. Might you also have a brilliant answer?"

"Let me see the photo, Ron."

Tim examined the photo for a minute, then handing it to Ron, said, "She's wearing a vest, Ron. Could it be the uniform where she works? Look at her vest. There's a partial emblem showing on the left side. Do you recognize it?"

Taking the photo, Ron perused it for a minute, then said, "It looks familiar but I can't place it."

"Take a photo of it and send it to the office. Heather can run it through a program and maybe find a hit."

Ron did as Tim suggested and then called Heather.

"Heather, I sent you... What? Oh, yeah, last night was super. Listen, I sent... What? Tonight? Again? So soon?"

A long pause followed, then Tim heard Ron say, "Okay, okay. I'll give it my best. Now listen to me. I sent you a photo of a woman. She's wearing a vest with a hint of an insignia or emblem. We think it's where she works. Run a scan on it and see if you get a hit. I'll wait."

During the pause, Tim asked, "So you were great last night, eh?"

"Don't go there, Tim," scolded Ron.

Tim gave him no mind, saying, "So you're a regular Don Juan, eh?"

"I said don't go there!"

"Were donuts involved?"

"You're an asshole," Ron said, smiling.

Tim was about to say something, but Ron, hearing Heather's voice, put his phone to his ear, saying, "The Big M casino boat! Got it. Thanks. Yeah, I'll be around about 8:00. Goodbye."

"I heard," said Tim, as he performed a U-turn to head back to Route 9.

"We need to fly, Tim."

"Can we call them?"

"Who?"

"The Big M."

"Another great idea, Tim-o-thy!"

"Send them her picture. They'll be able to tell us where she lives."

"You're not as dumb as you look, Tim-o-thy," said Ron as he looked up The Big M phone number.

"That's because I use makeup, Ron."

"I thought you looked different. Nice job on the rouge."

"Gracious."

"Ahh, you speak Spanish."

"I'm surprised, being the decorated FBI agent you are, you didn't know I was fluent in the Latin languages. Let me impress you as I rattle off some examples: taco, burrito, enchilada, fajita, margarita, Corona. Should I go on?"

"No. You have already blown me away."

Ron dialed the number and heard, *"Big M."*

"Hello. This is Special Agent Ron Lee of the FBI. I was wondering if I send you a photo of one of your employees, might you tell us where she lives?"

Whoever was on the other end of the phone spoke and Ron answered, "It's a photo of a girl whose first name is Anita."

More talk on the other end resulted in Ron saying, "Okay, I'm sending it now."

Ron sent the photo.

A moment later the voice on the other end confirmed receiving it.

"I need to show it to other staff members, Agent Lee. I'll call you back."

"Please hurry. Her life is at stake."

"They are going to call back, I take it," said Tim.

"Si," said Ron.

"I see you have expanded your Spanish vocabulary, Ron."

"Si."

Tim had covered most of Route 9 while driving at 85 miles per hour. He had just passed through the intersection of Route 9 and 57 when Ron's phone rang.

"Hello!"

There was a pause while Ron listened to the caller.

"Got it! Thank you!"

"What's the scoop?"

"Her name is Anita Lopez, Tim. She lives at 716 Landing Road in Little River."

Tim hit the navigation button of the dash and voiced the woman's address. Directions to the Lopez home flashed on the screen a second later.

"We're three miles out, Ron."

Ron glanced at his watch and saw it was high noon.

"Push it, Tim."

Unless Tim could reverse time, it didn't matter how fast he went. They were already three hours too late.

CHAPTER 8
ANITA

"She lives just up the road, Mustard," said Chuck, wiping egg from his face and swallowing the last mouthful of his black coffee.

Having finished their large breakfast at the Sunny Side Up Grill, they were now ready to attend to business.

The business at hand was eliminating a young girl who, unbeknownst to them, knew nothing of her dead boyfriend's extracurricular activities.

It didn't matter to them, however. Their marching orders were to dispose of potential threats, and that's what they would do.

"Pick up the check, Chuck. I got it last time," said Mustard with a grin.

"Why you lyin' bastard! The last bill you ever picked up, you cheap prick, was Bill Fedonia, who we tossed in a dumpster back in Oakland ten years ago."

"Was it just ten years ago? I was thinking it might have been more like fifteen."

"It's a damn good thing your gun isn't where your wallet is, Mustard. You'd be the slowest gun in the west."

"I'll get it next time, Chuck. I promise."

"Yeah, and I'm Peter Pan."

****

It was 9:10 as they knocked on Anita Lopez's door. Opening the door, she said, "Yes, may I help you?"

"Anita Lopez?"

"Yes, I'm Anita. Please excuse my appearance, I'm cleaning the house."

She had answered dressed in jeans and a Coastal Carolina sweatshirt. Her hair was askew, and she wore no makeup.

Even though she looked like a charwoman, they could not deny her beauty.

"No problem, miss," said Mustard. "May we come in? We have news about José."

"José! Has something happened to him?"

"We'd rather talk about it inside, miss," insisted Chuck.

"Who are you? You're not the police."

"No, we're not. We are co-workers of José," lied Mustard.

She stepped aside, and both men entered, each taking a half-dozen steps inside.

"What has happened to José?" she asked, her eyes widening with a knowing fear.

"There's been an accident, miss."

"Where? At the golf course?"

"No, there's been an altercation on Route 9."

"Wait! What do you mean, an altercation? You said there was an accident."

Seeing the woman was becoming wary, Mustard decided they were wasting time. Turning to Chuck, he said, "Let's get on with it."

Both men pulled their weapons and pointed them at the woman.

Anita's look of fear had Chuck realizing she knew nothing of José's involvement in nefarious affairs.

"Move!" shouted Mustard. "Get away from the door. Is there anyone else in the house?"

"No. I li..li..live alone," stuttered Anita, as she moved away from the door.

"Where's the bathroom?" shouted Mustard.

"Down the hallway," Anita answered, while nodding her head in the room's direction.

"Lead the way!" directed Mustard.

Anita walked the short distance down the hall and turned right into the bathroom.

"Get in the tub!"

"Why?" asked the now hysterical girl.

"Just do as I say. Get in the tub!"

As Anita stepped into the combination shower/tub, she asked, "What have I…"

She didn't finish the sentence. Mustard shot her in the forehead, leaving her brains and blood drooling down the shower wall. Her body slid downward, leaving a smeared blood trail on the tiled wall.

"You didn't fire, Chuck. Why not?"

"I felt sorry for her, Mustard. It's obvious she didn't know a damn thing about José's activities."

"Maybe not," replied Mustard as he stepped forward to shoot Anita twice more, once in each eye. "But it's a chance we don't dare take."

"I know you're right, Mustard, but I couldn't bring myself to do it."

"Chuck, we've been together the better part of twenty years and I love you like a brother. Now listen to me, partner. If you ever again show softness, I'll put a bullet in your head. Do you understand me?"

"Yeah, I understand, Mustard. It won't happen again. I promise."

Mustard pulled the shower curtain closed, and they left the house.

As Chuck drove, Mustard called Cardone.

Two rings later, he heard, *"Yeah?"*

Hearing Cardone's voice, Mustard said, "It's done."

"Excellent. Now find us another disposal area. We still have thirteen weeks to go."

Click.

"He would like us to find a replacement disposal area, Chuck. Do you have any ideas?"

"Yeah, I do. I've been thinking."

"And?"

"Ovens."

CHAPTER 9
WELL PAST RIPE

Having received no reply to their ringing of the doorbell or their pounding on the door, Ron and Tim busted it down.

A quick check found the girl in the tub.

"Why shoot a dead woman in both her eyes, Ron?"

"I'm guessing it's the work of a sick-fucking-whacko, Tim."

"I doubt you're wrong, partner."

"Call it in, Tim. I have a call on my cell."

It was Joe LaGrange.

"Joe. What's up?"

"Thought you'd like to know what we found, Ron."

"Tell me."

"We dug up the hole you thought might be empty."

"And was it?"

"No. We dug down six feet and found nothing, but then I dug another six."

"How many, Joe?"

"We found a dozen bodies. Well past ripe. I'd say three weeks."

"What about the short grass area?"

"We found a double grave. A dozen bodies in each layer."

"Any idea how long they've been in the ground?"

"I'd estimate the top layer… a month. The bottom layer, six to seven weeks. They covered all the bodies with lime to speed up the decomposition. The bodies in the second grave were beyond recognizable as human."

"Did you find any other potential gravesites in the area?"

"We scoured the area but didn't find any others. We'll keep looking though."

"Okay, Joe. Keep me informed."

"Will do, Ron."

"What was that all about?"

"Joe found 36 bodies buried in those spots we located. Three graves with twelve bodies in each grave. He estimates the oldest grave in the neighborhood of six to seven weeks."

"What the hell is going on, Ron?"

"Not sure, partner. It seems someone is hiring migrants to do two or three weeks of work. After which they eliminate that batch and replace them with a fresh batch who also have a limited lifespan."

"What kind of work would require less than a three-week turnaround?"

"I don't know, Tim, but we better find out. Chances are another dozen migrants have less than three weeks to live."

"I'm thinking if we're to crack this case, Ron, we need to know what the hell these dead migrants were doing."

"That, my friend, is a definite bingo!"

"Any ideas?"

"Maybe Robert Edge can provide a clue."

"You're thinking about the worn fingers. Right?"

"That I am," replied Ron. Then, taking another look at the body of Anita Lopez, he said, "Call Baxter."

"And say what?"

"Ask him if the two Mexican golf course workers had their eyes shot out."

As Tim dialed Baxter's number, the forensic team, headed by Laura Powell, arrived.

"Afternoon, Special Agent Lee."

"Hello, Laura. Not much doubt about what happened here."

"I dare say, today has been the busiest day in our history. Route 9, Heather Glen, the field gravesite, and now this."

"Now you know why they pay us the big bucks, Laura."

"No one should have to make a living doing this shit, Ron."

"You'll get no argument from me."

"Any ideas why someone would kill this little filly?"

"Yeah, I do. Her boyfriend was on the wrong side of the shootout on Route 9."

"For that she gets mutilated!"

"It gets worse, Laura, and it's going to get even more so."

"I feel for you guys having to deal with this."

"Feel for her, Laura, not us."

As Laura ended her conversation, Tim appeared.

"What did Baxter say?"

"They shot both men in the eyes."

"They?"

"Baxter said the two slugs that killed the workers were from different guns. All four eye shots came from the same gun."

"Well, it looks like we have ourselves a pro who likes to embellish his kills. Have the office check the files for similar killings around the country."

"I already called Heather and gave her the heads-up."

"Good job."

"By the way, she asked me if this might detain you tonight?"

"And what, I hate to even ask, did you tell her?"

"I told her I didn't think so because you were planning on having a couple dozen raw oysters for lunch. She responded, and I quote, 'Oh, my!'"

"You want to know something, partner?"

"What's that, Ron?"

"You are an honest to God prick!"

CHAPTER 10
MICHAEL CARTER

FOUR MONTHS EARLIER – June 1, 2019

Brett Cardone arrived in Myrtle Beach with a small entourage of five others, including his men from Portland, Chuck "The End" Delgato and Murphy "Mustard" Bortelli.

After renting a car for each individual, they checked into the Oceanfront Villas at the Grand Dunes. Cardone paid the bill in full for a five-month lease on five villas.

After everyone got squared away, they gathered in Cardone's villa for a meeting.

Brett opened the meeting by announcing, "We need a warehouse. It needs to be big enough to hold 100 pallets, house 25 people, have plenty of work space, and accommodate a minimum of two vehicles."

"I'll take care of it, Brett," volunteered his top aide, Mike Carter. "What's the budget for a warehouse?"

"I trust you'll do a good job finding something suitable. As for cost, we can't have it traceable, Mike."

Mike knew what that meant.

"When will you have a bank account set up for us, Mike?"

"As soon as this meeting is over, I'm heading to the Wells Fargo. We have accounts in Portland with them. I'll set up an account here."

"No! I want nothing connected to the business in Portland. Set up something new, Mike."

"Okay, Brett."

"Now, once we have the warehouse, I'll need it secured. Cameras, alarms, the works."

"I'll handle it, boss," replied Chuck Delgato.

"Thank you, Chuck. We'll also need furniture. Things like beds, dressers, ovens, refrigerators, lights, tables, desks, and linens."

"That's right up my alley, boss," said Marcia Cole, his wife's top aide, who Brett borrowed for a few weeks.

"We'll need clothes for the workers and the pantries stocked with food. I want these people well fed, well dressed, and comfortable. Don't forget medical and cleaning supplies."

"I'll handle those also," offered Marcia.

"Are you sure, Marcia? That's a heavy load."

"I can handle it, Mr. Cardone."

Cardone gave her a smiling nod, which she returned.

Marcia knew she'd be spending a lot of time in Cardone's villa, especially in the evening hours. Everyone else in the room knew it too, but none dared to acknowledge it.

Cardone continued, saying, "We will need a truck to haul the money from the storage units."

"I'll handle that, boss," announced Bortelli.

"Rent the truck, Murph. Change it out every two weeks. Rent from different rental companies."

"Gotcha."

"There's a forklift in one of the storage facilities. Find it!"

"I'll find it, boss," declared Luiz Patrone, one of the other two men Cardone brought along to organize the workshop and train the workers.

"Okay then, let's get to work. We have to be ready by mid-July."

****

Michael Carter, a close member of the Cardone organization, acted as Cardone's personal secretary, but he was much more than that. He was in charge of the money.

All the money.

Although Carter himself never administered strong-arm techniques, he, whenever it became necessary, was never shy of calling on those who were proficient with that side of the business.

It's why Chuck Delgato accompanied him on all one-on-one meetings. Delgato knew his place: observe, listen, and most of all, protect. He also knew to never speak while Michael carried on business.

Carter had always been a shrewd wheeler-dealer.

His instincts were always spot-on, and he used those to his advantage to out-maneuver his opponents. When the deal closed, and all papers signed, his opponents received only what Michael wanted them to have.

The renting of a warehouse was a prime example.

The warehouse on Oak Street in downtown Myrtle Beach had 35,000 square feet of space. It was big, but not too big. The owner, James Henry, offered to lease it for $3500 a month but required a minimum of a three-year lease.

"If my math hasn't failed me, Mr. Henry, 36 months at $3500-a-month comes to $126,000. Correct?"

Mr. Henry, knowing his lease rates, nodded his head. "That is the number, yes."

"The people I represent won't be needing the warehouse for three years, sir, so let's negotiate."

"I'm listening."

"We'll pay you double what you're asking, plus we plan on making some renovations which will increase the value of your property. That's $7000 a month for six months, which is $42,000. The renovations…"

"What renovations?"

"We plan on putting in a state-of-the-art security system, sir. When we leave, it stays."

"Hmm, what will you be doing in here requiring state-of-the-art security?" asked Henry.

Knowing the owner would ask, Carter answered, "We are distributors of classified medical materials for the U.S. Military. That's all I can tell you, Mr. Henry."

"What happens to these medical materials? And why six months?"

"We ship them to our military installations all over the globe. Why six months, you ask? Many criminal and foreign organizations would like to get their hands on our revolutionary medical materials. We feel it is in our best interest to not stay in one place too long."

"In that case, I think a $100,000 would be more appropriate, Mr. Carter."

Carter, expecting such a reply, answered, "That's a big jump, Mr. Henry. Let's make it $75,000."

"$100,000."

"I see we are at an impasse. It seems as if we must look elsewhere. Thank you for your time, Mr. Henry."

As Carter made his way toward the doorway, he heard, "$80,000!"

Carter turned, and extending his arms in an apologetic pose, replied, "I'm sorry, but 75 is the limit the government has given me. Goodbye, sir."

"Okay, $75,000, but you have to be out by December 31st!"

"It won't be a problem, Mr. Henry. I'll meet you back here tomorrow at 1:00 with the $12,500 in cash."

"Cash?"

"Yes, sir. This, being a covert operation, the government frowns on checks. If you can't handle cash, I suppose…"

"No, no. Cash is fine."

"You'll receive an equal payment on the first of each month. Is that satisfactory?"

"Yeah, that will work."

"Did I mention it is tax free, sir?"

Knowing it to be the case, Henry answered, "No, you did not. I'm guessing it has to be that way because it's a covert operation."

"Correct, Mr. Henry. Now, I need to inform you about a non-disclosure statement you're required to sign."

"A non-disclosure statement? What the hell is that?"

"If you reveal our contract to anyone, including registering the lease with the city, there will be a penalty."

"What kind of penalty?"

"You will repay all monies over your regular rate of $21,000 for a six month rental."

"Ahh, now that won't be a problem, Mr. Carter."

"Good. I'll be here tomorrow at 1:00. Please don't keep the U.S. Government waiting, sir."

"I'll be here, sir!"

"I'm sure you will, Mr. Henry."

As they were leaving the building, Carter whispered to Delgato, "Find out everything about this guy, Chuck. Where he lives, family, friends, everything."

"Will do, Mike."

CHAPTER 11
"LIVE DEAD BODIES."

WEDNESDAY - SEPTEMBER 18, 2019 7:30AM

Ron was perusing Joe Lagrange's forensic report when Tim entered the office carrying coffee and a bag of donuts.

"Ahh, ain't it great that we're back to old times, partner," voiced Ron with an increasing grin crossing his face.

"Oh, yeah. It's great, all right. Donuts went up about ten cents apiece, and coffee went up a quarter. Seeing I limit myself to a $10 budget, your donut consumption is being limited to just four per day."

"Hmm, I feel violated," mumbled Ron.

"Violated?"

"Sort of."

"Gosh, Ron, I'm sorry. If only I knew you'd feel this way… I would have done it months ago!"

"I guess, to fill the void, I have to eat a bigger breakfast."

"Oh, and what is your current typical breakfast?"

"Three eggs, over easy, 4 or 5 slices of bacon, extra crispy, a few slices of toast…"

"A few?"

"Three or four, heavy on the butter, of course."

"Oh, of course. Is that it?"

"No. I have juice and coffee, and a small dessert."

"Dessert? For breakfast?"

"Yeah. You know, a sweet roll or a danish."

"You're kidding. Right?"

"It's what I had this morning. Sometimes, when it's cold out, I'll have oatmeal."

"In place of the eggs?"

"No. In addition."

"What time do you eat breakfast, Ron?"

"I get up early. I eat around 5:30," replied Ron as he inhaled a crème-filled donut.

"Gee, you mean you go almost two hours without eating before the donuts arrive. I don't see how you do it," said a mocking Tim.

"It's a struggle. It's why I get upset with you when you come strolling in at 8:30 or 9:00," responded Ron, while licking the residue of a chocolate éclair from his fingers.

"You're disgusting," said Tim, ending the conversation.

"I take it you're offended."

"You got that right! What are you reading?"

"The forensic report on the mass graves. Joe sent photos."

"Damn!" exploded Tim. "Are you telling me you're looking at photos of those disgusting decaying bodies, while woofing down donuts?"

"Yeah, what's wrong with that? Hey, look at what the maggots did to this guy's chest cavity."

"You're beyond disgusting."

Ron smiled at his partner's display of feigned revulsion before saying, "As soon as we finish these donuts…"

"Donut. I only have a single donut, Ron."

"As I was saying, when we finish our donuts, we're heading to the morgue."

"You must have a stainless steel stomach. First you eat an entire buffet for breakfast. Then, as you inhale donuts, you peruse a bunch of decomposed bodies, and you want to follow that by rushing off to the morgue to see live dead bodies. Incredible!"

"Did I hear you say, 'live dead bodies?'"

Tim, thinking back on what he said, mumbled, "Maybe."

They were on the road to the County Morgue in Conway by 9:15.

"Well, tell me, partner, did you and Heather hook up last night?"

"A gentleman never tells, Tim."

"That may be true, Ron, but I was asking you."

"We may have had some time together. Yes."

"I take it she takes top."

"What! Why would you say that?"

"Because I know you can't do a single pushup. That implies you taking top is out of the question. The fear of you falling on her, ruins the moment. I can see the headline: Murder under the rotundum."

"We're not talking about this, partner. I don't ask you about your love-making techniques."

"Only because you know I can do forty pushups."

"There are many ways to skin a cat, Tim-o-thy."

"I'm thinking Heather has to be very athletic."

"I'm afraid to ask, but why you would say that?"

"Even if she's on top, she'd have to be a contortionist to position herself under that donut-filled gut of yours."

"I must admit, she is flexible for her age."

"I'm guessing she greases your body, then sits on your stomach, and slides downward until she bumps into 'little Ron.' How's that for analysis?"

"It may be your best detective work, partner. We'll discuss this even more during your annual review."

Ten minutes later, they walked into the morgue and made their way downstairs to where Robert Edge was plying his trade.

Walking through the swinging doors, they entered the lab to see a line of gurneys, each with a toe-tagged body lying on it.

"Morning Robert," called out Ron.

"Good morning fellas," greeted Robert Edge. "The twelve victims died by asphyxiation."

"Asphyxiation?"

"Yes. Death occurred after ingesting an enormous amount of strychnine, which causes the strangulation of the air passages."

"Strychnine?"

"Aged, but dependable."

"All these people ingested it, Bob?"

"Yeah. It makes you wonder how they pulled it off, doesn't it?"

"It does," conceded Ron.

"Well, how about a picnic?" suggested Edge.

"Say what?" exclaimed Tim.

"They filled their stomachs with the same Mexican foods: burritos, enchiladas, tacos, rice, chicken, beef, shrimp, and lots of tequila."

"A going away feast," murmured Ron.

"That was my thought too, Ron," stated Edge.

"Gives new meaning to a goodbye dinner, that's for sure," uttered Tim.

"How soon for the strychnine to take effect, Bob?"

"It depends on the dosage, Ron. Might take anywhere from 15 to 60 minutes. This kicked in closer to the 15 minute range."

"What makes you say that, Bob?"

"More than half of them died with their heads on their plates. We found food plastered to their faces, up to their hairlines and beyond."

"Anything else, Bob?"

"Ron, do you remember my saying they had worn their fingerprints down by something with a semi-rough texture?"

"Yes. What have you come up with?"

"We found ink under their fingernails."

"Ink? What color ink?" asked Tim.

"The color of money."

Ron stood digesting Robert's statement for a moment, then said, "They were counting money. Let me correct myself. It's more likely they were sorting it, so machines could count it."

"Yes, Ron," agreed Edge. "Mucho dinero."

"Drug money, Ron?"

"That's my guess, partner."

"It means the cartel is back in town," added Tim.

"Seems so."

"If we're right, then I see a lot more blood in our future."

"Yeah, so do I, Tim. Let's make sure it isn't ours."

CHAPTER 12
"...just a band-aid..."

While Ron and Tim were at the County Morgue, the cartel was busy covering their tracks.

Knowing it wouldn't be long before the FBI realized the cartel was back in town, Brett Cardone called in his crew to discuss how to delay the FBI finding them.

Carter did the talking for the group.

"Chuck has an excellent idea involving a pet crematory," reported Mike.

"Oh? Let's hear it." said Brett.

"It will reduce chances of being caught disposing of bodies to near zero. Although it will take longer, the result leaves nothing to trace."

"Sounds good, Mike. What else?"

"I believe we have some details needing attention."

"For instance?"

"The FBI found the graves. It won't be long before they beat the bushes for private contractors who rent heavy equipment. They'll find our guys, and make no mistake, the FBI... will... find them. And when they do, those guys will talk," Mike added with a forceful tone of certainty.

Nodding his head in agreement, Brett turned to Bortelli, asking, "Murph, can you manage the situation?"

"We'll have it done by nightfall, boss."

"What else, Mike?"

"The bodies in the truck, along with the Feds finding the mass graves, will lead them to some solid conclusions, Brett."

"Which means?"

"They'll be checking Driscoll's holdings to see if he had a building of this size. When they find out he didn't, they'll start checking recent sales or rentals."

"I thought we didn't register the lease with the county."

"We didn't," replied Mike.

"So what's the problem?"

"If Mr. Henry did any business with his other holdings since May, the FBI will knock on his door."

"Meaning?"

"He might crack."

"So we take him out. No big deal."

"That may be just a band-aid," quipped Mike.

"A band-aid? What do you mean a band-aid?"

"We can make him disappear, Brett, but that won't stop the FBI from knocking on his door. When he doesn't answer, they might look into his holdings. They'll find this building and, even though Henry didn't register the building as leased, they may stop by just out of curiosity. If they do, it's game, set, match."

Brett sneered at Mike's tennis analogy but agreed with his conclusion.

"Got any ideas, bright boy?"

"One."

"Yeah, well, please, Mike, enlighten me."

"We have to make it disappear, Brett."

"Make what disappear? The building? What? Are you thinking we should call in David Copperfield? I know he made the Statue of Liberty disappear. Making a warehouse disappear should be a piece of cake."

Everyone laughed at Brett's sarcastic reply. Even Michael, the target of the snide words, managed a grin.

"No, not the building itself, Brett. We need to make the fact it even exists, disappear."

"Sorry, Mike, but you're not making any sense," voiced Brett. "I'm smart, but not on your level. Say what you mean. Okay?"

"Sure. Sorry, Brett. I didn't mean to be ambiguous. What I'm saying is, we need to hack into the city's computers and remove this building from the records."

Brett's eyes widened at Mike's proposal. "That's ingenious, Mike! But, can we do it?"

"None of us are capable, Brett."

"Then who?"

"It has to be an inside job. We need someone who has access to property records and to the county's computers. He or she must know how to manipulate information."

"Okay, tell me how we find this person, Mike, and after we find him, how do we convince him to do our bidding?"

"The second part of the question has a straightforward answer: money. The first part, however, not so easy."

"You've given this some thought, haven't you?"

"Yes, I have."

"Let's hear your thinking."

"We identify people who have hands-on access to the records system. We determine who is the weakest link and approach that person with a proposal."

"What if they balk?"

Mike gave Brett a *"What do you think"* look before saying, "We need to get this done as fast as possible."

"Okay, Mike, so how do we do it?"

"Let me handle this, Brett. I'll need Marcia's help, but that's it."

"You have my blessing, Michael. Don't screw it up or else we'll all be dead."

"Amen, Brett. Amen."

CHAPTER 13
REPARATIONS

WEDNESDAY - SEPTEMBER 18, 2019 11:50AM

After having spent most of the morning at the morgue, Ron and Tim returned to their office a few minutes before noon.

"I guess it's time to give Braddock an update," voiced Ron.

"I'm surprised Buttock hasn't beaten a path to our door demanding some input."

"We need to cut him slack, partner."

"You getting soft on me, Ron?"

"Neg-a-tory, partner. But he is our superior and deserves to know what we know. If I were him, I'd expect the same."

"I'll buy into that, Ron, but he needs to understand that we do whatever is necessary to get the job done."

"So that's why we break all the rules?" Ron asked with a grin.

"Hey, they make rules so someone can break 'em."

"Can I quote you on that, partner?"

"You can, and while you're at it, you can buy lunch."

"Oh, really? And where did that come from?"

"It came from 1200 donuts purchased at my expense over the past four years."

"Does that include the coffees too?"

"No. We will discuss coffee another day. Right now, the subject is donuts purchased, and lunch paybacks."

"Oh, it's lunches now, is it? How many lunches are we talking about?"

"I'm glad you asked, Ron. Here's how I figure it. A decent lunch might run twelve bucks. With donuts running around two bucks each, a decent lunch equates to a half dozen donuts. I calculate the 1200 donuts I've bought over the years equals 200 half-dozen donuts."

"So you're saying I need to buy you 200 lunches?"

"Give or take. Yeah, that's what I'm saying."

"Don't try comedian as your next career, Tim. They will laugh you off the stage."

"What's that supposed to mean!"

"It means you'll be going lunchless if you expect me to buy."

"All those goddam donuts I bought you and you won't buy me lunch!"

"Not 200, I won't."

"Okay, then how many?"

"Let me ponder on that."

"Ponder, my ass. You don't plan on buying a single damn lunch, you cheap prick!"

"No name calling, please. I don't say nasty things about your lack of verticality."

"Oh, this coming from the white Charles Barkley."

"Meaning?"

"The Round Mound of Rebound!"

"Cheap shot."

"That's the way us short guys operate."

"Okay, just to shut you up, I'll agree to buy lunch every Friday."

"Monday, Wednesday, and Friday sounds better."

"I'm sure it does, but it ain't happening. Friday is the offer."

"Include Mondays and we have a deal."

"You gonna keep the donuts coming every morning?"

"Only if you also buy on the third Wednesday of every month."

"And if I don't?"

"No éclairs, no crème-filled, no sourdough, no jelly, and no coffee."

"This is damn blackmail in its rawest form!"

"I hate to stoop so low, but you've forced me to go deep into my reservoir of dirty tricks."

"You stooping low isn't much of a challenge. You're already three-quarters of the way there."

"This from a man who needed a downward-pointing arrow tattooed on his belly so he could locate an otherwise lost digit-like body part."

"Now that was low, Tim."

"I can go lower if needed."

"We can trade barbs all day, but it would only waste time. After deep consideration, I agree to buy lunches on Mondays and Fridays, if you continue morning donuts and coffee."

"You forgot the third Wednesday of each month."

"You're pushing your luck, Tim-o-thy."

Tim started singing, *"No more éclairs, no more crème-filled, and no more jelly in Ron's belly."*

"I never realized what a devious little prick you were until now."

Tim kept singing.

"All right! Third Wednesday of each month too."

"Great! I agree to continue buying donuts and I'd like to point out today is the third Wednesday of the month."

"Why, you little shit!"

CHAPTER 14
FORCED ATTRITION

"Afternoon, Jim."

"I expected to hear from you sooner," answered Braddock, as his return greeting.

"We had to get our facts together first. No sense reporting conjecture."

"I'll buy that. By the way, men, you did excellent work locating those mass graves."

"Thanks," the two agents replied in unison.

"Okay, so what's the deal now?"

"The cartel may be back in town, Jim."

"What makes you think they ever left?"

"I believe after we removed Driscoll from the picture, they went dormant," replied Ron.

"So why do you think they've returned?"

"More gut than anything else," replied Ron.

"Well, that makes it pretty substantial," quipped Tim.

"Cut the cuteness, Agent Pond," barked Braddock. "Explain, Ron."

"It's about the bodies found in the truck and in the mass graves. Each mass grave contained twelve bodies, as did the truck."

"What does it tell us?" asked Braddock.

"I'll answer that in a minute, Jim."

"I can wait. Please continue."

"The coroner could only autopsy the bodies found inside the truck," Ron explained. "Bodies found in the mass graves had advanced decomposition, due in part to the copious use of lime."

"I saw the photos," said Braddock. "Disgusting."

"Edge found ink embedded in the victim's fingers. The ink matches that used to print money. We estimate for the skin to absorb that much ink, they were handling an extreme amount of money."

"So you're surmising only the cartel could have that much money lying around."

"I am."

"What's the back story?"

"Good question, Jim. I'm guessing Driscoll had money hidden throughout the county, and the cartel has returned to collect it."

"That makes sense, but why the bodies? What's the connection?"

"I've been pondering that, Jim, and to answer your earlier question about the twelve bodies per grave, I think it's a matter of forced attrition."

"Forced attrition?" asked a confused Braddock.

"I'll explain," said Ron.

"Please do."

"We believe there is, at a minimum, a billion dollars involved. Separating and counting that amount of money would require a considerable workforce."

"Absolutely," agreed Braddock.

"The job would also become both time-consuming and tedious."

"No doubt about it," remarked Braddock.

"Wouldn't you agree, Jim, whenever those two variables occur, losing productivity is inevitable?"

"I would agree," nodded Braddock.

"Therefore, to continue a high level of productivity, they rotate in new personnel every few weeks. However, they can't afford to let the previous group go home. A security breach would be devastating. They solve the problem by throwing a poison-laden going-away dinner for the workers. They then load the bodies in a truck and carry them out to where a mass grave awaits."

"Inhumane," whispered Braddock.

"That it is," agreed Ron.

"What's your estimate on the amount of money the cartel has hidden?"

"We're guessing somewhere between one and two billion, sir," answered Tim.

"Damn! That's a lot of cash!"

"Yes, it is," agreed Ron. "And I'm thinking most of it is in small bills."

"Which means?"

"They have a shitload of storage units holding boxes filled with money."

"My guess," said Tim, "is they're gathering the money and shipping it out of state. Maybe putting it on boats to take someplace like the Caymans."

"That's a good thought, partner. How come you didn't mention it earlier?"

"I guess I must have been thinking of what I would order for lunch."

"What the hell are you talking about, Pond!" asked an incredulous Braddock.

"You won't believe it, Jim, but Ron is buying my lunch today, and every Monday and Friday for the rest of his life."

Braddock looked at Ron, saying, "What's the matter, Lee? Lose a bet?"

"Oh, no, sir," interrupted Tim. "We are talking reparations."

"Did you say reparations? What's the hell are you talking about, Pond?"

Ron tried to answer, but Tim butted in with, "It's payback for the 1200 donuts I've bought him over the past four years."

"You guys are nuts. Enough about lunch, donuts, and reparations. What's your next step?"

After giving his partner a long, hard stare, Ron turned to Braddock, saying, "We have a few leads to chase down, Jim. First, we're going to contact local contractors who have payloaders. Maybe we can find the guys who dug the mass graves. They might lead us to those who hired them."

"What else?"

"If the cartel is gathering their money for consolidation, they'll need a sizable building to hold the estimated hundred or more containers being held in storage units."

"I assume you're planning to check out all recent purchases, rentals, or leases of buildings which might fit their needs."

"Correct."

"There's one other thing we need to consider, Ron."

"What's that, Jim?"

"The strong possibility the cartel wants to reclaim their lucrative drug operation."

"Your point being?"

"If true, I expect to see the independents who took over their territories, dying of unnatural causes."

"I'm not sure the cartel is here to reclaim their drug business, Jim."

"What makes you think that, Ron?"

"The mass graves."

"What about them?"

"Those bodies have been in the ground anywhere from three to ten weeks, Jim. Maybe longer," explained Ron.

"True," agreed Braddock.

"Yet, during that time, we've had no action on the streets. If the cartel wanted the independents dead, they'd be dead, and sharing a grave with one of the dirty dozen."

"Nice phrasing, Ron," interjected a grinning Tim.

"Jim, I think their focus is only on the money they left behind. I agree, that could change, but for now, it's all about the money."

"I can't disagree with you, Ron. However, I feel certain when they finish whatever they are doing now, they will go about the bloody business of reclaiming their drug territory."

"If we do our job, Jim, there won't be anyone around to reclaim territory. We'll make sure of that."

Braddock, knowing exactly what Ron meant, shuddered when hearing his words.

CHAPTER 15
LOGAN AND BUBBA

FOUR MONTHS EARLIER

Business for Logan Equipment Rental had been lagging leading up to the day Michael Carter and Chuck Delgato walked into the office trailer and asked to speak with the owner.

"You'd be lookin' for John Logan," said Bubba Graves, whose face, tired and worn, had mercifully seen better days. "He's over in the shed working on a piece of equipment. I'll go fetch him. You fellas make yourself at home. We got us a soda machine if you be needin' a drink."

"We're fine, but we would appreciate talking to your boss."

"Yeah, of course. I'll be right back."

Three minutes later, the trailer's door opened, and a man resembling a brick wall entered. He stood well over six-feet and if his body had an ounce of fat, neither Mike nor Chuck could see it. A shake of his hand had Mike wincing.

"I'm John Logan, fellas. Bubba said you needed to see me."

"Mr. Logan…"

"Please, call me John. We aren't none too proper around here."

"Thank you," replied Mike, while massaging his hand Logan had squeezed. "I'm Michael Carter and this is my associate Charles Delgato. I'd like to make you an offer."

"Nice meeting you, Mike," then with a nod and a smile, added, "Nice meeting you, Chuck. You mentioned an offer, Mike. What kind of offer?"

"I'd like to contract two pieces of equipment to be on call whenever we need them."

"Two pieces. Which would those be?"

"A payloader and a bulldozer."

"We have both, Mike, but to have them at your beck and call? Now, that's something I can't promise."

"Could you, if I paid you a $40,000 retainer each month for... let's say, five months?"

Logan's tongue almost fell out of his mouth and hit the floor. His legs buckled and his right hand reached for a nearby chair for support.

Bubba, hearing the offer, grabbed his chest while his eyes bugged out to the size of silver dollars.

Logan, regaining his composure, cleared his throat to ask, "What would you be doing with my equipment?"

"It's a question you need not ask, John. Just have both pieces of equipment ready for us when needed. We'll give you a 24 hour notice."

"Do you need operators?"

"No, we have experienced people. We'll need them on a carrier though."

"$40,000 a month, you say?"

"Correct, Mr. Logan. I'm prepared to pay you $40,00 right now... in cash."

"You have that amount with you?"

"I do, John. If you accept the offer, you'll receive $40,000 in cash on the first of each month."

"Damn," hissed Logan.

"We guarantee you $200,000. If we exceed five months, we'll pay you $20,000 for each additional week."

"Cash! Is this legal, Mr. Carter?"

"Now why would you ask, John? All you're doing is renting me equipment. What could be illegal about that?"

"Not a damn thing!"

"We do, however, expect the knowledge of this transaction never leaves this room."

"Yeah, of course," uttered Logan. "When you're not using the equipment, can I rent it?"

"We demand, that when we call, the equipment is ready for pickup, and in good working order. It would not be in your best interest if it were not."

John Logan wasn't a college graduate, but he needn't be to realize Mike had threatened him. And make no mistake, he knew it was life-threatening.

"They'll be ready any time you call, Mike."

"Good," said a smiling Carter. "Oh, there's one other thing I'd like to mention."

"What's that, Mike?" asked John.

"It's no big deal, but I prefer being addressed as... Mr. Carter."

The message came across, loud and clear.

WEDNESDAY - SEPTEMBER 18, 2019 4:30PM

The unexpected windfall that came John Logan's way allowed him to pay off his mortgage. Bubba received a $1000 a month raise and John upgraded the office trailer by adding an awning. Whenever business was slow, he and Bubba would often sit in the awning's shade and play cards.

Business was slow when the black Camry drove up the driveway and stopped fifty feet short of the table.

Recognizing the driver as Chuck Delgato, Bubba turned to John, saying, "Why is he here? They returned the equipment last night. Might they need it again already?"

"I don't know, Bubba. Who's the guy with him? That's not the Mr. Carter, fella."

"Never seen 'im before, John," answered Bubba, laying his cards on the table while grabbing his soda bottle and taking a long swig.

"Afternoon, Chuck," greeted John. "Who's this fella you brought with ya?"

"This is Mustard."

"Mustard? How d'you come by that name, fella?" asked Bubba.

"I could explain it to you, mister, but it would be easier to show you."

Before Bubba could reply, both men drew weapons from inside their sport jackets and shot John Logan dead where he stood.

"What the…"

"Now watch," said Mustard as he stood over Logan's body and shot the corpse in each eye.

"Omigod!" cried Bubba.

"Got any last words there, Bubba?"

"Aaaaaaaaaaaaaa..."

"That's quite the vocabulary," said a sneering Mustard, as he and Chuck shot Bubba multiple times.

Although hit five times, Bubba, still alive, lay on the ground just feet from his dead boss, spurting blood from his mouth like a geyser.

Although he couldn't speak, he could see. To Bubba's ultimate horror, the last thing he would ever see was the barrel of Mustard's weapon pointing at his right eye. In that moment, he felt his bladder emptying.

A split second later, all went black.

CHAPTER 16
"... NO CHEF-BOYARDEES..."

"Damn, Ron, we've been to six of these businesses today and we got nothing," complained Tim.

"There are two more on the list, partner," replied Ron, who was driving. "What's the next one?"

Tim, looking at the hand-written list attached to a clipboard, answered, "Logan Equipment Rental. They're on Route 707, near the library."

"I know where it is. I've seen it many a time when traveling Route 31."

It took twenty minutes to make the drive from Pawleys Island to the Logan Equipment rental entrance.

As Ron drove up the long driveway, Tim reported, "The last one on the list is Jordan's Heavy Equipment in Conway."

As Ron made his way around a curve which brought the Logan office trailer into view, he muttered, "It looks like traveling to Conway won't be necessary, partner."

Tim, looking up from the clipboard and seeing the two bodies lying on the ground 50 yards ahead, quipped, "Don't be so quick to judge, Ron. They might just be taking a siesta."

"They're lying in a pool of blood."

"Hmm, it appears we're too late."

"Yeah, it sure does. Call it in."

They were standing over the bodies when an FBI Forensic Team, led by Joe LaGrange, arrived.

"Damn," mouthed Joe. "What kind of sick bastard shoots the eyes out of people already dead?"

"That's a damn good question, Joe. We have reports of this sick shit going back ten years."

"How long ago do you think this happened, Joe?" asked Tim.

LaGrange, after examining the bodies, answered, "Based on the coagulation of the blood, and the limited lividity of the bodies, I'd say, two, maybe three hours ago."

"Son-of-a-bitch!" yelled Ron. "They might still be alive if we made the stops in the reverse order."

"You can't beat yourself up over it, Ron," said Tim. "It was just bad luck."

"Yeah, I know," said Ron with a nod, "but…"

"Let's look inside the trailer, Ron. Maybe we'll find something to help us out."

"Yeah, okay."

Turning to Joe, Ron suggested Joe check the equipment for soil residue that might match last night's digging.

"Already on my to-do list, Ron. However, these guys filled with bullet holes, tells us with reasonable certainty, this be the place."

"Yeah, no doubt about it," replied Ron, as he made his way toward the trailer.

As they stepped into the trailer, they saw a desk in the right-hand rear corner, and next to it, a half-full water cooler. A search of the desk found nothing but empty invoice forms.

Two well-worn couches sat on either side of the doorway. A half-filled soda machine, over-populated with Mountain Dews and Dr. Peppers, occupied the wall in front of them.

To their left, a doorway led to a small kitchen. The kitchen featured a sink, fridge, microwave, and a small table with two non-matching chairs.

A search of the fridge found a half-dozen jars of condiments, a half-eaten tuna sandwich, four bottles of Bud Light, and a container of milk, well past its expiration date.

"It appears these boys weren't no Chef-Boyardee's, Ron."

"They lived the simple life, that's for sure."

Ron, noticing a small door next to the fridge, asked Tim to open it.

Tim pulled it open and announced, "We have us a bingo, Ron, but someone, I suspect the killers, beat us to it."

Ron made his way across the kitchen to where Tim stood holding the pantry door open. Staring at them was an open safe where inside a stack of money lay untouched. Papers, apparently unimportant, littered the floor in front of the safe.

Conspicuous by its absence was any sign of a records book.

"It's a waste of time, I'm sure, but we need to collect the papers lying on the floor, Tim. You never know what we might find. What's the old saying? One man's trash, is another man's gold."

"It sounds familiar."

"How much cash in the stack?"

Tim withdrew the stack and began counting it.

While Tim counted, Ron scooped up all the papers off the floor and began perusing them.

"Twelve thousand, Ron. All in hundreds."

"It seems twelve thousand is nothing but chump change for whoever did this."

"People have called me a chump," said a smiling Tim. "A nibble of this can buy a lot of those ten-dollar lunches."

"Don't get any stupid ideas, Tim-o-thy."

"You are no fun at all, partner."

"There's nothing suspicious in these papers," Ron said while ignoring Tim's harmless insult. "I'm sure they kept a ledger, but I'm betting it's now in the hands of the cartel."

Joe LaGrange barged through the doorway, interrupting their checking of the trailer.

"What's up, Joe?" asked Tim.

"I'm sure you're not surprised to learn the caliber of bullets used for the eye shots match those in the girl and in the two golf course workers."

"We're hoping one of us gets to return the favor to that prick," growled Tim.

"Maybe we can take turns?" suggested Ron.

"I'd have no problem sharing, partner."

"Anything else, Joe?"

"We found a dirty payloader out back. We took dirt samples. I'll have it tested. There's not much doubt it will match the soil samples taken from the mass graves."

"No doubt in my mind at all," muttered Ron.

"I have one other thing, Ron."

"Talk to me."

"We found some tire prints out by the bodies. They are well-defined, so we shouldn't have a problem identifying the brand. It ain't much, but who knows?"

"Print this entire trailer, Joe. I doubt these guys were sloppy, but maybe we'll catch a break."

"Where you guys going from here, Ron?"

"We're going home to get a good night's sleep. I suspect sleep will be a scarce commodity over the next few weeks."

"What's going to happen if you guys can't solve this?"

"It's simple arithmetic, Joe. For every two weeks that pass, twelve people will die."

CHAPTER 17
HORACE LEDBETTER

FRIDAY - SEPTEMBER 20, 2019 9:00AM

Upon hearing about the compromised disposal phase of the Grand Strand Project, Juan Pablo knew the FBI would get involved, and would soon look into recent occupation of warehouses.

He, like Brett, upon hearing about Michael's plan to hack the city's computer and deleting the property from records, considered it genius.

"It should give you enough time to meet your goal," he told Brett.

"How much money will you need for a bribe, Brett?"

"I think it might take a half-million, Juan Pablo."

"I think half of that would suffice."

"Okay, I'll inform Mike of your suggestion. If it's necessary, do we have permission to go higher?"

"Of course, but start low, Brett. If you're working in sales, they tell you, 'Start high because you can always go down.' It's just the opposite in the bribery business," Juan Pablo said with a snicker.

"Should I pay the money with the cash we have on hand?"

"Yes, that will be fine."

"Is there anything else, Juan Pablo?"

"Have you come up with an alternate solution for disposal?"

"We have. In fact, Michael is negotiating a deal for what we need, as we speak."

****

The car, with three male occupants, turned onto Ledbetter Road, named after the road's sole occupant.

Seven miles later it pulled into the driveway of the 92-year-old house. Old was an apt description, although decomposing was far better.

Leaving their car, the three men climbed five barely passable steps to a porch that had seen much better days.

Michael pressed the doorbell.

It didn't work.

Michael knocked, aggressively.

The door had three glass panes at eye level. Michael could see the old man approaching. When he opened the door, Michael asked, "Mr. Horace Ledbetter?"

"You're talking to him," answered the aging man. He wore a pair of worn jeans, along with a flannel shirt that looked older than he did. "Can I help you fellas?"

"We hope so, sir. My name is Michael, and these are my two associates, Murph and Charles. We're here to talk to you about your business."

"My business building be located out back. Do you wanna see it?"

"We would, sir," answered Michael.

"Well, come through the house then. We'll go out the back door."

While making their way through the musty smelling house, Michael asked, "How long have you owned the business, Mr. Ledbetter?"

"My daddy built it back in '71. I took it over in '86 when he passed."

"Is your equipment in good operating condition?"

"I believe so. Why you askin'?"

"We would like to purchase your business, sir."

"Buy it? What makes you think it's for sale?"

"We're willing to make you a substantial offer, Mr. Ledbetter. One that will sustain you through your entire retirement."

"I ain't ready to retire. What's this all about, fellas?"

"Our line of work needs this type of business."

"And just what kind of work requires an animal crematorium?"

"Turkey farm, sir."

"Oh? Since I'm not all that familiar with raising turkeys, might you explain the need for a crematorium?"

"There is quite a bit of loss in the turkey business, sir. We need the crematorium to dispose of those losses."

"How come you don't follow standard procedures in disposing of dead birds?" asked the all too curious, Ledbetter.

"How's that, sir?"

"Well, I know of some turkey farmers up in North Carolina, who, when losing birds, bury them, under the scrutiny of the state's Agricultural Department."

"That's true," replied Michael, who had done some research on turkey farming, "but we feel cremation is safer and more efficient."

"Your right, but it's far more expensive."

"We realize that, sir, and that's why we need our own crematorium."

"That makes sense," agreed Ledbetter. "Okay, let me hear your offer."

"Do you own the land, sir?"

"I have a mortgage on the land, but the business is clear."

"How much is your mortgage, Mr. Ledbetter?"

"Not much. I'd say around $40,000."

"We'll pay off your mortgage and pay you a sum of $250,000."

"Hmm, it seems like I should have gotten into the turkey business."

Michael, smiling at Ledbetter's reply, asked, "Could we see the ovens, sir?"

"I prefer the term *chambers*, sir. It's a more comforting term to the pet owners."

"Ahh, then can we see the chambers, sir?" asked Michael with a congenial smile.

"Yes. Follow me."

A few moments later they entered a barnlike building, only smaller.

"I have two chambers. One holds multiple bodies, the other, much smaller, is used to cremate a single animal. I use the smaller one when people request their pet's ashes."

"Would you be kind enough to show us how to operate the ovens, oops, I'm sorry, the chambers, Mr. Ledbetter?"

"Not a problem. I use natural gas. The chamber temperatures can be as high as 1800 degrees."

"Is that the same temperature used to cremate a human?" asked Chuck.

"Same type of chamber, same temperatures," answered Ledbetter.

They watched Ledbetter start the ovens. He left the doors open so they could see the fierceness of the flames.

"How many birds would this chamber hold for a mass cremation, Mr. Ledbetter?"

"Turkeys, I couldn't say, but I've cremated eight to twelve dogs, depending on size, at one time. If I had to guess, maybe 15 to 20 birds. Maybe more."

"How long does it take, sir?"

"With dogs, it can take anywhere from one to three hours. It just depends how much meat you want to pack in there."

"Well, I think you have answered all of our questions, Mr. Ledbetter. Have you given thought to our offer, or is it something you'll discuss with your wife and children?"

"Got no wife. Got no children. The wife died three years after we married, back in '86. I give no thought to marryin' again."

"I see," Michael said with a nod. "Well, have you given thought to our offer?"

"I have, sir. I apprcciate your offer to pay off the mortgage. That's something I didn't see coming. However, the payout you offered, after pondering on having to buy a new house, doesn't seem to be enough to get me through retirement, as you suggested."

"I see your point, Mr. Ledbetter. Do you have a number you have in mind, sir?"

"Well, I guess I do. It seems unreasonable, and I don't want you to get upset. You've been real charitable with your offer."

"Let's hear your number, sir."

"Well, being 78 years of age, I'm thinking maybe $400,000 would last me to the day I enter the promised land."

"$400,000, you say. I was thinking we'd top it off at $300,000, plus paying off the mortgage."

"That's right kind of you, sir, but I'm afraid I'll need $400."

"Well, Mr. Ledbetter, if that's your bottom-line number, then maybe, just to satisfy our curiosity about your equipment, we should experience a real cremation."

"I'm sorry, but I don't have any animals here to cremate. Business has been kinda slow."

"Don't worry, Mr. Ledbetter, we have our own backup plan."

Michael gave Mustard a nod and then turned away while his henchman put a bullet in Mr. Ledbetter's brain.

"Put him in the oven, fellas, and fire it up. Let's get a live demo, no pun intended, of our new business."

Ninety minutes later, Michael called Cardone.

"Talk to me, Michael."

"We are in the cremation business, Brett."

"And how much did it cost us?"

"I'm not sure, Brett. What's the going rate for a single bullet?"

CHAPTER 18
"THE CARTEL."

FRIDAY - SEPTEMBER 20, 2019 7:00AM

Two hours before Juan Pablo and Brett Cardone discussed business, and three hours before Horace Ledbetter took his last breath, Ron and Tim were enjoying donuts and drinking coffee in their office.

They had spent the previous day with local officials and law enforcement agencies, reviewing the case.

****

They had gathered the usual lawmen and county officials in the FBI conference room. Their purpose: brief them on a recent case, which had sent shock waves up and down the Grand Strand.

Ron opened the meeting by saying, "There's not much I can tell you, that you don't already know."

"Tell us what you have, Ron," encouraged Captain Bill Baxter, head of the South Carolina State Troopers in Horry County.

"We had a shootout on Route 9 a couple nights back. When the smoke cleared, three bad guys were making their way to hell. They had been driving a truck with a missing headlight when a state trooper, Sergeant Harvey Little, tried to pull them over. They resisted by forcing his cruiser off the road. State troopers set up a roadblock. When the truck reached the roadblock, a firefight broke out. Snipers sent all three occupants of the truck straight to hell."

"Corporal Len Coupling, my nephew, was one of those snipers," added a proud Baxter.

"We found a book of matches from the Heather Glen Golf Club. We also found a photo of a young woman. Thinking the matches might lead us to someone who knew the deceased, we sent state troopers to the golf course to locate anyone who might have known them. The troopers found two employees, both Mexican, lying dead in the parking lot. We identified the young woman and went to her home, but Agent Pond and I were too late. We found her shot to death in her bathtub."

Rumbles of shock spread through the room.

"Wait," said Ron. "There's much more."

"I doubt it would be an exaggeration to say that what you've told us already is unsettling," said Myrtle Beach's assistant Chief of Police, Marty Brown.

Ron, nodding his head in agreement, continued.

"When they opened the truck, they found a dozen bodies, hanging from hooks. The victims all appeared to be of Latin descent. We concurred they were being taken to a burial site."

"My God," voiced Sam Addleson, a local councilman. "Who would do such a thing?"

"Give me a few more minutes, sir," said Ron.

"I'm sorry to have interrupted, Agent Lee."

"My partner, Tim Pond, and I were lucky enough to find the burial site, where three other burials had already occurred. Each of those burials contained 12 bodies."

"They all died from being poisoned," added Tim.

"It took heavy equipment to dig the mass graves," Ron continued. "We searched for small-time contractors who had that type of equipment. We found them, but, too late, we found them dead."

"Damn!" yelled Marty Brown.

"Now, I ask you, gentlemen. Who would kill 48 innocent people? Who would kill the friends of the men driving the 'body' truck? And finally, why kill the owners of the equipment that buried the bodies?"

"There's only one obvious answer," said Tim. "The cartel. To cover their tracks."

"Cartel!" shouted a dozen of the room's inhabitants.

"We believe they have returned to claim what they left behind."

"And what would that be, Special Agent Lee?" asked Addleson.

"We're estimating between one and two billion dollars."

Hearing Ron's answer, silence cloaked the room.

"What leads you to that conclusion, Agent Lee?" asked Brown.

"The coroner performed autopsies on the bodies hanging in the truck. He found ink embedded into their fingers and hands. He concluded it is the same ink used to print U.S. currency."

"And?"

"We believe the cartel is bringing people in from Mexico to sort and count money for packaging."

"Packaging? What for?"

"We haven't determined that as yet."

"Why not hire locals?" asked an officer sitting at the end of the table.

"Family and friends would miss them. The cartel wouldn't want the local law looking for missing people. No one, however, will miss people imported from across the border."

"You said one to two billion, Ron," voiced Joseph Hill, the head of the Horry County Sheriff's Department. "How in the hell did you arrive at that vast amount?"

"The bodies."

"What do you mean, the bodies?"

"These people aren't working an eight-hour shift. More like a 10 or 12. They aren't going home to their families at the end of the workday, nor are they getting weekends and holidays off. Counting or sorting large amounts of money for weeks at a time gets tedious. Productivity takes a dive. People, being prisoners, begin thinking of escape. Escaping is a no-no."

"Your point being, Ron?" asked Baxter.

"The cartel has put a number on when they should turnover personnel. We think it's somewhere between two and three weeks."

"So if you're correct in your assessment, this has been going on between eight to twelve weeks," calculated Baxter.

"That's correct, Bill."

"So where do we stand?" asked Mayor Beverly Boswell, who had been quiet up to this point.

"To tell the truth, Your Honor, we have nothing, other than conjecture."

"What kind of conjecture, Agent Lee?"

"We know that the previous head of the Carolina's cartel, the now deceased Cameron Driscoll, hid money all over the county."

"Go on," urged the Mayor.

"We think the cartel is consolidating their money for reasons we don't know. But, wherever they are consolidating, it has to be, in terms of square footage, expansive."

"Why is that, Agent Lee?"

"Well, ma'am, they not only need a lot of space to hold pallets of money, but they also have to house the staff to sort and count it. That means makeshift living quarters for a minimum of a dozen workers. Then add the management and security people. If I'm right, I'm guessing the living quarters has to accommodate 24 or more."

"So what's your next step, Agent Lee?"

"We look for a building that can accommodate the cartel's needs."

****

"Where did you get the donuts, Tim?"

"A place called Ducks Donuts. What do you think?'

"They are delicious. I'm partial to the Boston Cremes."

"I'm glad you like them. Say, Ron, might I need to remind you that today is Friday?"

"No, you needn't remind me. Where would you like to have lunch?"

"I'm thinking of a fish fry at Greg's Cabana."

"Greg's? The Greg's on 17 Business in Garden City?"

"That would be the place, partner. Their fish fry goes for ten bucks."

"Yeah, but I bet it doesn't include a drink."

"No, that's another two bucks, but I'm worth it."

"Really? Since when?"

"Since I did all the warehouse background work."

"Well, damn! That's your job!"

"Good point, Ron, but it ain't my job to find you the finest in donuts! From now on, I'll bring in those packaged frosted donuts you find at the checkout counter. I think they cost two bucks a bag for two dozen. If you're lucky, they'll be fresh."

"Okay, I'll buy you a damn drink, you little dickhead."

"Ahh, there you go again, repeating those exact words Wilma used on our honeymoon."

"Well, there's one thing you can say for Wilma."

"Oh, what's that?"

"Nothing wrong with her eyesight."

"Ha-ha. Let's get back to business. What do we have from forensics?"

"Joe sent over a report on those tire tracks. He identified them as Michelin Primary MXM4, P225/45R18."

"Assuming our killers are riding around in style, what car manufacturer puts those on their cars?"

"He says they are high-dollar premium tires. Toyota puts them on certain cars, like the Lexus and the high-end Camry."

"It shouldn't take us long to track down two million cars fitting that description."

"He also found a shoe print, near the tire print. Shoe size 11."

"Make and model?"

"No such luck, Tim-o-thy."

"Well, let's hit the road, Ron."

"How long is the list?"

"I checked for rented, leased, and sold going six months back. We have 42 structures to check out."

"Where will we start?"

"There are two places between Garden City and Pawleys Island."

"How convenient for you. Greg's is down that way."

"Oh, so it is," replied Tim, with his usual shit-eating grin.

CHAPTER 19
THE TRYST

"How are things progressing?" asked Brett Cardone, of Luiz Patrone, the man he put in charge of overseeing the counting of the cartel's drug money.

"No hitches. We passed the $900 million mark yesterday, boss."

"That's excellent! That leaves us in the neighborhood of $1.1 billion to go," remarked Cardone.

"This batch of workers is the best we've had," commented Luiz. "We'll have another $80 million ready tomorrow. That's only four days versus the normal five."

"How did you manage that?"

"I've upped the hours to 14 a day. Told everyone they would get a large bonus."

"Great idea, Luiz. What's your projection to finish the job?"

"Well, we've done $900 in two months. But, if we maintain the $20 million a day pace, I'm estimating 55 days which will take us into late November."

"Damn, that's incredible, Luiz. At that rate, we would finish four weeks earlier than expected. Try to do $25 million a day. We'd pick up more 10 days."

"I'll do my best, boss."

"Have you seen Marcia?" asked Brett, having something other than work on his mind.

"I saw her leaving this morning. I think she was meeting a real estate agent who works in the city offices."

"Yeah, that's right. Where is she now?"

"I think she's being entertained by a member as we speak."

Luiz was right, Marcia was being entertained by a member. Luiz had used the right word, but it was the definition he had wrong.

****

She was on top. As Marcia's head rolled back, her eyes closed, and her breathing became heavier. Her mouth, with the tip of her tongue protruding, was emitting guttural moans. She rode his member like it was a bucking bronco. Her ample breasts heaved while in the clutch of his hands and nibbling of his warm mouth. Her moans became louder, her thrusts faster. Then came the eruption.

She cried out, "Yes! Yes! Oh, yes! Omigod!"

Low moans followed those emphatic cries of ecstasy as the orgasm subsided, but the small aftershocks were still reverberating when he exploded inside her.

While looking into his eyes, she smiled at his labored-breathing. She felt his shrinking member striving in vain to penetrate deeper into her. Then she watched his face surrender to the futility as he went limp inside her. His ride of ecstasy ended as a deep breath escaped his lungs, and his body slumped into momentary exhaustion.

She bent down and kissed him before rolling off to lie at his side.

"Nice," she whispered.

"Oh? I hadn't noticed."

She punched his chest.

They both laughed.

They had checked into the DoubleTree Hotel. Their room overlooked the ocean and the beach below. But they hadn't checked into the hotel room for its scenery. They were there purely for lust. It wasn't their first tryst, and it wouldn't be their last.

As they snuggled under a blanket, she asked, with unmistakable fear in her voice, "What will happen if he catches us?"

His hand, mimicking a gun, emerged from under the blanket. The thumb cocked the imaginary hammer, while his merged index and middle fingers moved to a spot between her eyes. He pulled the imaginary trigger while making a soft *pop* sound. Adding an embellished finish to his charade, he blew away imaginary smoke from the end of his fingers.

"I doubt it will be that painless," she sighed with a nervous giggle.

"I was trying to be kind."

"If his wife discovers he sleeps with any woman having a willing vagina, and rapes those that don't, she'll have the rotten prick killed. She's a real bitch, far more dangerous than he is."

"That's hard to believe. I've seen his work. He had a carwash guy pulled apart by two trucks just for leaving water spots on his Mercedes."

"I'll admit that's bad, but his wife, who I'm sure has hair on her chest and a pair of balls, beat that."

"Oh? Let's hear it."

"A woman, working in their kitchen as a cook, overcooked a rack of lamb Mrs. Cardone was planning to serve to a large contingent of guests."

"Oh-oh, not good," murmured Mike.

"You got that right," agreed Marcia. "After saying good night to her guests, she ordered two of her henchmen to take the cook outside. While the cook's husband watched, they disemboweled her in the backyard. They shot her husband six times in the head when he moved to save her."

"Nice," said Michael, shaking his head in disbelief.

"That's not the end. The cook, with her guts spilling out onto the ground, somehow screamed, 'you son-of-a-bitch' at Lisa."

"And?"

"Lisa, takes a shotgun, puts it in the woman's mouth, pulls the trigger, and blows the woman's head into the next county, or so it seemed."

"Hmm, remind me not to get on the wrong side of Mrs. Cardone."

"You only have to worry about Brett, Michael, whereas I must keep watch over both my shoulders."

She glanced at the clock radio sitting on the bedside night table. It read 11:45.

"I have to go," she said, throwing the blanket aside.

"Where?" he asked, pulling her closer with a restraining grab of her arm.

"The Tax Assessor's Office. Why are you asking me that? You're the one who came up with this plan."

"I did, but I didn't give you a deadline, did I?"

"Your point being?" she asked, although she knew the answer. In fact, as his hand ran up the inside of her right thigh, she could see his point gaining rapid strength.

"I believe I may have some deeds to consider."

"Dirty deeds, I'm sure," she replied with a knowing smile. "You're up to no good."

"Oh, but to the contrary, my love. All is on the up and up!"

"So I see," she said, as her left hand surrounded his stiffened manhood. "I swear I put it through its paces just a few minutes ago."

"Oh, no. That was just a prototype."

"You don't say! Well, what are we waiting for? Bring on the real thing!" she said, while mounting him.

"Uh-uh. It's my turn to take top," he said, as he rolled her over.

"My, my, Mr. Carter, you seem to have a way with the ladies."

"You're no lady, Miss Cole, but you are one incredible woman."

"So you say, Michael."

"Would I lie, Marcia?"

"Shut up, Michael, and show this lady a good time."

"I think everything is in place."

"Oh my, it sure is!" she exclaimed, as he filled her void with a series of slow thrusts. "You have remarkable recovery abilities, Mr. Carter. I think I might enjoy this."

"Well, I'm sure this beats going to the office of deeds."

"I'll be the judge of that... but I'm betting... you're right... again," she moaned.

****

Parked in the DoubleTree's parking lot was a black Toyota Camry.

In the driver's seat, eating his bag-lunch and watching the ocean, sat Chuck Delgato, fulfilling his secondary, but less-lethal, role as Michael's chauffeur.

Although Chuck understood what the couple was doing, he felt it was none of his business. But he also knew that if caught, Brett would have them killed, regardless of their importance to the mission.

He liked Mike and Marcia, but if told to kill them, he wouldn't delay.

It was also a given that if Brett discovered Chuck knew of the couple's indiscretions, Mustard, his partner of twenty years, would kill the three of them.

The thought of Mustard killing him did not sit well with Chuck. Even more disconcerting was visioning Mustard shooting him in his dead eyes.

Chuck, after giving that indisputable scenario some thought, came up with a contingency plan.

Satisfied with his plan, he continued to eat his lunch and watch the waves breaking on the beach.

CHAPTER 20
"... stepping on roaches."

"Just where the hell are we on this damn case?"

"Not far," replied a resigned Ron. "Up to now, all we have is supposition, although I think it's solid."

They were in their office washing down donuts with hot coffee while waiting for an 8:30 meeting with Jim Braddock.

"So our angle is the cartel is back in town."

"Correct."

"But we don't know where."

"Correct again!"

"We don't know why."

"Another bingo."

"And we don't know who's running the show."

"That seems to sum it up, Tim-o-thy."

"Well, whoever's in charge, is a cold-hearted son-of-a-bitch."

"Couldn't agree more, Tim. He seems to be Satan himself and he has two demon-angels who feel killing is comparable to stepping on roaches."

"Our theory has the cartel coming back to consolidate all the money that Driscoll left hidden somewhere."

"That's the current thought," agreed Ron.

"Fair enough. I'll buy into that. However, we also have heard nothing on the street about renegade dealers having to give up their business."

"That's a fact, Tim."

"Although unfortunate, over the past four months, we have found no street criminals in dumpsters with a bullet in their head and their scrotum in their mouth."

"You're right. It is quiet out there, at least on that point," agreed Ron.

"I know it's unfathomable to even think it, but is the cartel relinquishing its business in these here parts?"

"Possible, but I doubt it, Tim."

"Then what the hell is going on?"

"That's why they pay us the big bucks, partner. We're supposed to find out and stop this shit."

"What's this 'us' shit. Maybe you're getting paid big bucks, but not me."

"Wait a minute, Tim. Let me fetch my violin so I can provide background music to your whining."

"Screw you! After my mortgage and car payments, I have just enough left to keep you in donuts."

"Yeah, but I'm saving you big bucks by buying your lunch a couple times a week."

Tim didn't know the money Ron spent on Tim's lunches wasn't coming out of Ron's pocket. He was adding the cost of those lunches to his monthly expense account, which no one ever questioned.

"I take it you have noticed I don't eat lunch on the other days? Reason being? I can't afford it!"

"Oh, I noticed. I just thought you were dieting," Ron said as he finished his second of three chocolate éclairs.

"I'm not the one in need of a diet, partner."

"Was there an implication there?"

"You know that old saying, 'His eyes were bigger than his stomach'? That doesn't apply to you."

"I pay little attention to those old sayings, partner, except for the one that goes, 'stay in your own lane.'"

"That's obvious. Tell me, Ron, is there a raise in my future?"

"Until just a minute ago, maybe, but now it's under further review."

"Bullshit!" mumbled Tim.

"Gosh, a positive changes into a negative, in the blink of an eye," said Ron. "Who'da thunk it?"

"Dickhead!"

"Oops! Now it's on a back shelf."

"Double dickhead."

The phone interrupted the vacillating.

Tim answered, listened, and saying nothing, hung up.

"Wrong number? Robot call?" snickered Ron.

"Braddock will see us now. I'm told someone from the F-A-T-F, whatever the hell that is, will join us."

"It's the Financial Action Task Force."

"Oh? So what's their purpose?"

"They come up with policies to deal with protecting the global financial system against money laundering and terrorist financing, amongst other things."

"Hmm, you thinking what I'm thinking?"

"I'm thinking real hard about this third unfinished éclair. But, I'm also thinking the FATF's presence may have a definite connection to our case. Let's go find out."

"You have large portions of éclairs one and two, clinging to your face, Ron. I suggest you wipe off the chocolate before we leave."

"Are you implying it's not a good look?"

"No, it isn't. But, even cleaned up, it's nothing to write home about."

"I'm sorry, but were you asking about a raise?"

"Did I ever mention, Ron, that you have an uncanny resemblance to Paul Newman?"

"Now you're talking!"

CHAPTER 21
"... playing with fire..."

The FAFT meeting wasn't the only meeting in town. A second meeting, held at the warehouse, involved Brett Cardone and Murphy Borelli.

"Where's Delgato?" asked Cardone.

"He's with Mike."

"Doing what?"

"I don't know. He didn't say."

"Okay. You can fill him in when you see him."

"Fill him in on what?"

"It wasn't a priority, but Juan Pablo asked, that if we ran into a certain pair of FBI agents while we were in town, that we make them disappear."

"Kill FBI Agents! Damn, boss, that's like playing with fire while holding a damn can of gas."

"I know, but it's what Juan Pablo wants. Would you like to argue with him, Mustard?"

"I'll pass," answered Murphy, with a weak smile.

"Good answer."

"Have we crossed paths with these FBI agents?"

"According to my sources, Special Agent Ron Lee and Agent Tim Pond are working the case. They are the two agents responsible for the death of Michael Garcia."

"Who in the hell is Michael Garcia?"

"Juan Pablo's most-favored nephew."

"Oh, now I understand why we are being tasked with killing these two agents."

"I'm glad I didn't have to spell it out for you, Mustard," replied Brett, with a crease of a grin.

"Might you have any thoughts as how we can fulfill Juan Pablo's wishes, boss?"

"I do. We set a trap. My source tells me Agents Lee and Pond have determined the Juarez cartel is back in town, although they have no definitive proof as yet."

"I'm guessing finding 48 bodies is a good indicator," interrupted Mustard.

"Yes, I would think so," agreed Brett. "They are correct to believe we are here to retrieve cartel money. They are assuming the bodies found in the mass graves were of people we used to sort, count, and bundle the money."

"Two plus two thinking," remarked Mustard.

"Very smart are these agents, although they know nothing about the gold. I understand now how they took down Driscoll. I don't plan on being another success story for the FBI."

"So how do we rid ourselves of these two guys, Brett?"

"I'll meet with you and the others tonight at 8:00 in my villa. I'll lay it all out."

"Are there any special requirements we'll need for this job, Brett?"

"No, Mustard. We already have them."

"Good. I hate shopping for stuff."

Brett, taking a moment to smile at Murph's comment, added, "They don't know it, but if I were FBI Agents Lee and Pond, I'd be getting my affairs in order."

CHAPTER 22
THE FATF

MONDAY - SEPTEMBER 30, 2019 10:00AM

Braddock had summoned them to the conference room. When they arrived, they saw twenty others seated around the table. Most were familiar FBI personnel, but there were also two unfamiliar faces sitting on either side of Braddock.

Braddock, seated at the head of the table, upon seeing the arrival of his two renegade agents, stood, and addressed the room.

"I believe we now have everyone expected in attendance. I'd like to introduce to you Mr. Nicolas Jonas from the international organization of the Financial Action Task Force and Mr. Carl Snell, our U.S. representative of FATF. They have some disturbing news to share."

Braddock gave a nod to the man, who, a moment earlier, he had introduced as Carl Snell.

Standing, Snell cleared his throat and began speaking.

"Good morning, Agents. Mr. Jonas, who is from France, has asked that I do the talking as his English, he admits, goes wanting."

Some polite laughter and smiles greeted Snell's opening comment.

"We have come to Myrtle Beach to warn of a potential terrorist attack."

"What signaled an attack may be in the wind?" asked Braddock.

"There's been some unusual movement in the money markets."

"A movement? Can you provide some details? What type of movement would cause a terrorist alert?" asked a woman seated four seats away from Snell.

"Reports are coming in about unusual activity in the gold market."

"Define unusual," stated the same woman.

"The purchases have all been in the sixty-million dollar range. Purchases of that size are not unusual, but there's a definite pattern."

"What is the pattern?" asked another agent.

"These $60 million purchases occur every five days."

"What's the total amount?" asked Ron, while doing the math in his head. "Wait! Let me guess. Might it be somewhere in the neighborhood of $850 million?"

"Not another word, Agent Lee!" yelled Braddock, who took an abrupt stance. "Everyone clear the room!"

Ron and Tim, understanding Braddock's order did not pertain to them, stayed seated as the room cleared.

Moments later, the room had emptied, leaving only Braddock, his two agents, and the FATF agents.

Braddock took his seat, saying, "Let's continue."

Somewhat unsettled by the abrupt emptying of the room, Snell pulled his chair closer to the table, and responded to Ron's question.

"If the pattern holds true, that's the projected amount come Wednesday."

Jonas, silent until now, leaned forward in his chair, and staring quizzically at Ron, asked, "How did you know. Agent…?"

"Lee. Special Agent Ron Lee. This is my partner, Agent Tim Pond."

"How did you know it was $850 million, Agent Lee?"

"Sirs, I have an idea who is buying the gold. I can't say whether they are buying gold to fund a terrorist attack, although I doubt it."

"Let's hear your story, Agent Lee," suggested Snell.

"As Captain Braddock can confirm, my partner and I have been working on a mass murder case. It kicked off when a truck, loaded with dead people, got involved with state police after refusing to pull over for having a single headlight."

"I read about that in the Washington Post," Snell voiced. "Do you think there's a connection to the gold purchasing?"

"I do," replied Ron, "although we knew nothing about gold until just a few minutes ago. We believe the Juarez cartel has returned…"

"Returned?" asked Jonas.

"The Juarez Cartel?" posed Snell.

"We ran the cartel out of town 9 months ago. It's believed they left around two billion dollars behind. I'm of the opinion they sent a team back to claim it."

"Two billion!" exclaimed Snell.

"That's just an estimate, Mr. Snell, based on their activity in the area over the past ten years. We don't know the exact figure."

"It's your assumption, Agent Lee, the cartel has returned to reclaim two billion dollars, but you have no definitive proof to back it up."

"That's correct, Mr. Snell," admitted Ron.

"Well, we believe gold is being funneled to terrorists."

"Do you have any proof?" asked Ron.

Snell gave Ron's question some thought and with sagging shoulders, murmured, "None."

"Don't feel bad, Mr. Snell," replied an empathetic Ron. "I must concede, we also lack the definitive proof needed to say, with any certainty, that this slaughter is the doings of the cartel."

"Do I see a 'but' coming?"

"You do, sir," Ron answered with a nod to the FATF agent. "Saw it coming, did you?"

"It was more than obvious, Agent Lee. So let's hear it."

After handing the FAFT agents a half-dozen photos, Ron continued his argument.

"As I mentioned a few moments ago, we also have no definitive proof. We do, however, have 36 bodies in a mass grave, and 12 more, destined for that same mass grave, dangling from ropes in a truck."

Ron hesitated for a moment after seeing the horrified looks on the two FATF agents' faces. The details of the photos had taken them aback.

"Please continue, Agent Lee," said Jonas, in a heavy French accent.

"If you are ready," said Ron.

"We're ready, Agent Lee. Let's hear the rest."

Nodding, Ron resumed, "We also have two dead golf course workers and a dead girlfriend. We attribute their deaths to their connections with the men who were driving the bodies to the mass gravesite. In addition, we have the two dead contractors whose heavy-duty equipment was used to dig the mass graves."

"I can see where you would conclude…"

"Let's discuss the deaths of those last five individuals I just mentioned," said Ron, as he handed the two men three additional photos.

"We know there were two shooters. Each victim, except the girl, had wounds from two separate guns. All had two post-mortem bullet wounds in both eyes."

"My God," uttered Jonas, appalled by the photo of the dead girl.

"I have to ask, Mr. Snell," said Ron. "Does the brutality of those acts sound familiar to you? Do they resemble the ruthlessness those folks from south of the border might inflict?"

"After hearing your arguments, Agent Lee, I must concur that your suspicions have merit. How, may I ask, are you handling it?"

"That, sir, is the proverbial $64,000 question. We know, in our gut, the cartel is the culprit. However, that's based on nothing but supposition."

"I understand," replied a nodding Snell.

"We realize their operation requires considerable manpower and a substantial amount of space," explained Tim.

"We also know the previous regime had no such property in their possession," added Ron.

"Which means?" asked a memorized Jonas.

"Which means," explained Tim, "they have had to either, buy, rent, or lease a building to house their operation. We are checking into anything that fits that mold."

"There's one other detail I think is worth mentioning, which I haven't shared with Agent Pond." said Ron with a coy look at Tim.

"Oh! And what's that?" asked Braddock.

"What are you holding back on me?" chirped Tim, his curiosity mixed with a smidgeon of anxiousness.

"Since the two of us have a history with Juan Pablo Amarillo, head of the Juarez cartel, I think it's safe to say, we, again, have targets on our backs."

"Oh, shit," moaned Tim.

CHAPTER 23
LISA CARDONE

It was an old farmhouse sitting back from an unpaved country road. The Northwest weather, with years of rain and snow, had taken its toll on the wooden structure.

Fifty yards behind the derelict-looking house stood an equally beaten-down barn.

Passerby's seeing the two structures had to wonder how they remained standing.

Looks, however, can be deceiving.

Although the barn's exterior looked as if the structure were on its' last legs, its interior, with rooms and decors rivaling that of five-star hotels, told a different story.

Inside its ramshackle exterior was the heart of a drug operation bringing in millions of dollars each month.

These buildings, sitting on the outskirts of a forgotten Oregon town, housed the headquarters and processing plant of the Juarez Cartel's biggest cocaine operations on the west coast.

Gales Creek, a town dating back to the early 1800s, sat 50 miles from the Pacific to its west and 40 miles from Portland to its east. Being the last stagecoach stop between it and Tillamook, 45 miles to the west, was the town's most notable claim to fame.

Brett Cardone managed the operation, but in his absence, his wife, Lisa, was running the show without a blip. But that was about to change.

Lisa was an impressive woman.

She stood five foot seven and weighed just over one-thirty. Her hair, just two shades away from being black, was a dark creamy brown that hung down to her shoulders. Her eye color matched her hair.

The shape of her face tended toward oblong, rather than round. She had a perfect nose and appealing lips. When she smiled, people would woo. When she frowned, they would cower. Her body bordered on incredible. The breasts were ample and firm, her waist a lean 28, and her hips a perfect 34.

She also had an IQ of 139.

Impressive? Yes.

There was, however, one other number to consider. Her boiling point hovered around 50.

Dangerous? No doubt.

Sitting behind her husband's enormous oak desk, Lisa was reading the morning paper when Brett's secretary, Sheila Evans, entered carrying a freshly brewed cup of coffee.

"Morning, boss," greeted the redheaded Sheila. "Here's your coffee and a danish."

"Thank you," said Lisa. "Anything to report?"

Sheila always came in at 7:00am to meet with the late shift supervisor. He would convey to her that evening's production information or any other topic the boss needed to know.

Lisa was always at her desk by 8:00am. She expected her coffee no later than 8:05.

"When I spoke with Ernie this morning, he said we may have a personnel problem."

Ernie Nivens was the 11:00pm to 7:00am floor manager. He had been with Brett Cardone ever since the Portland operation started up. Having served four tours in Afghanistan as an MP, he had seen a lot of death, much of which he contributed.

"Oh? Let's hear it."

"Ernie heard through the grapevine, that a guy working on the packaging line, is skimming product. He's stealing an ounce or two a night, taking it home, and selling it on the street."

"You don't say. What's this stupid prick's name?"

"Hernando. Hernando Alvarez. He's been with us about 16 months."

"Married? Kids?"

"Married? Yes. Kids? No."

"What about the wife?"

"Name is Carla. She works at a beauty salon in Portland."

"Hmm. Let's have Willie and Stone bring them in. When they arrive, take them to the barn. I'll deal with this myself. Give me a heads-up when all is ready."

"Is there any specific time you want them here?"

"Yeah. Lunchtime."

It was 12:05 when she heard Sheila's voice on the intercom.

"They're here, Lisa."

"Okay. Have them taken to the barn. I'll be there in five minutes."

Closing a ledger she was working on, Lisa opened one of the desk's drawers and removed a Glock 17.

After checking the magazine and seeing she had a full clip, she tucked the gun into the back of her jeans. She fixed her makeup, put a jacket on over her long-sleeved blouse, and made her way toward the barn.

The 50-yard trek to the barn was one Lisa always enjoyed. She liked the nearby countryside, and the smell of the pines that wafted down from the nearby Tualatin mountains to the west. As she reached the barn's doors, she took in a deep breath of the pine-scented mountain air, exhaled, and with a stoic look, entered the building.

She walked past the lines where they packaged the cocaine. The momentary quiet was the result of the 20 workers, all but three being men, enjoying their 45-minute lunch break.

Looking ahead, she saw Sheila with Willie, Stone, and two others, who she knew to be the Alvarez couple, standing just outside the lunchroom doorway.

Lisa said nothing as she walked past the fivesome, who, without a word, followed her into the lunchroom.

The 30' x 20' lunchroom Brett insisted on having built at the rear of the barn wasn't what one would expect at a drug mill. The décor included well-crafted wooden tables, comfortable leather chairs, and four large-screen televisions mounted on each wall. Traditional kitchen appliances lined the back wall.

It reminded her of Brett's, "Happy workers are good workers," motto.

What a fucking waste of money, she thought.

As Lisa entered the room, everyone stopped eating and stood. The workers feared her, for they had heard the rumor of what she had done to her cook.

"Please, sit down," she commanded.

Hernando and Carla stood in the back of the room, sandwiched by the two behemoths Willie and Stone - one black, one white.

The couple looked frightened. They had every reason to be, although Carla has no inkling of her husband's purported transgressions.

Lisa approached within two feet of Hernando. She could smell the fear evaporating off his body. She saw the sweat beads along his hairline.

A smile filled her face. She loved the power she had inherited.

"So, Mr. Alvarez, is it?"

"Si, Senorita Cardone."

"Do you know why you and your lovely wife Carla, are here?"

Hernando didn't answer. He just shook his head.

"No? Well, let me give you a hint, senor. It's about you stealing and selling my cocaine!"

Carla, although knowing only token English, understood most of what Lisa had said. Turning to her husband, her face horrified, she uttered a slew of Spanish from her mortified lips. The last of those words were, *"¿No pensaste en mi?"*

Lisa looked at the husband, saying, "She's right, Hernando. Why didn't you think of her? Look what you've done to this poor innocent woman."

Hernando, knowing and accepting his fate, replied, "I make her a widow. Si?"

"No, Hernando," smiled Lisa, "you make her dead."

Pulling the Glock from her jeans, Lisa shot Carla right between the eyes, scattering Carla's brains against the wall, some six feet away.

The lunchroom erupted with screams. Most stood, wanting to be anywhere but where they were.

"Sit and be quiet!" screamed Lisa.

All sat. Whimpers ceased, but fear gathered in throats and hearts.

"I have done nothing!" insisted the crying Hernando.

Lisa, smiling at Hernando's denial, turned to face the twenty workers, saying, "Hernando has been skimming my cocaine and selling it on the street."

All gasped.

"You cannot take what is mine. If you do, this happens."

Pointing her gun at Hernando's crotch, Lisa pulled the trigger and sent his genitals to manhood heaven.

Witnessing the unthinkable, the lunchroom inhabitants went into chaotic shock.

The greater screams, as expected, came from Hernando.

"Does it hurt, baby," cooed Lisa. "Here, let me take the pain away."

All shrieked as they watched Lisa put the gun in Hernando's mouth and pull the trigger.

Hernando's brains joined those of his wife on the wall.

After taking time to gaze at the bloodied wall, Lisa faced the workers. Pointing at the two bodies, she warned them, "This is you, if you decide to steal from me... and Mr. Cardone."

A nodding of heads ricochet throughout the workers.

"Remember," she continued, "What happened in this room, stays in this room. If not, your brains and those of your entire family will wind up scattered on a wall."

Although they heard her words, it was her facial expressions that had them believing.

"Now," she said with a big smile, "Please, finish your lunch. Bon appétit."

Passing a mortified Sheila on her exit from the lunchroom, Lisa said, "After they eat, have them clean up this fucking mess."

CHAPTER 24
MAKING PLANS

MONDAY - SEPTEMBER 30, 2019 8:00PM

Marcia was the last to arrive. Michael preceded her arrival by only minutes. Their guilty eyes met for a brief second as she sat.

"Where have you been all day, Marcia? I haven't had the pleasure of your company in the past two days."

"I've been doing Michael's bidding, Brett."

"And what bidding might that be?"

"Trying to establish a rapport with someone in the Records Office."

"Any progress?"

"Nothing substantial. I hope to have everything squared away by Wednesday."

"Make it tomorrow, Marcia."

"Why tomorrow? We need finesse to do this right."

"An inside source informed me the FBI is now checking out all warehouses rented or leased since June."

"Calm down, Brett. We knew that was coming," said Michael. "We're good for now."

"Maybe we are," replied Brett, "but I'm having the other situation taken care of tomorrow."

"I'm working a guy who works in the tax office," said Marcia. "He's going to take some persuading though."

"If I may, I'll borrow a line from the *Godfather*, and say 'make him an offer he can't refuse,' Marcia."

"Money is no object?"

"Start at $100K," Brett replied, "but don't be afraid to go higher."

"And if that doesn't persuade him?"

"Use all your powers, Marcia," Brett said with a laugh. "After all, they are quite persuasive."

Marcia, scowling at Brett's remark, flashed a look toward Michael for support, but she knew, considering the circumstances, he could offer none.

She was lucky the look went unnoticed by Brett, but it did not escape Mustard's watchful eyes.

"Okay, let's get down to business."

"Which is?" asked Michael.

"Killing FBI agents, Ron Lee and Tim Pond."

Michael exploded from his chair, screaming, "What the hell are you saying, Brett? We can't kill FBI agents. It will put the mission in jeopardy."

"It's the request of Juan Pablo, Mike."

Mike, hearing Brett's reply, sighed, and knowing any argument would be a waste of time, asked, "I take it you have a plan?"

"I do, Mike, but understand, killing these two men is not our top priority. Our priority remains the money, but, if given the chance, we will kill these two agents. We won't act on this until we near the end of our mission."

"Okay, Brett. Let's hear the plan."

****

Brett was laying out the plan to eliminate Ron and Tim, just as the two exhausted agents stumbled into their office.

Dead tired after visiting ten rented, leased, or purchased warehouses in Horry County, they flopped into their respective desk chairs, laid their heads back, and stared at the ceiling.

Ron broke the silence, saying, "I'll give you permission to shoot me, partner, for not thinking of this earlier."

"Give me a minute or two to get my gun out," responded a dog-tired Tim.

Grinning, Ron answered, "Take your time."

Tim removed his gun from its holster and placing it on his desk, said, "Okay, Ron, go ahead. Tell me why I'm going to shoot you."

Seeing Tim had employed his weapon, Ron said, "You're taking me a bit too literally, wouldn't you say, Tim-o-thy?"

"I've been waiting a long time for this opportunity, Ron. It only knocks once, maybe twice."

Ron, ignoring Tim's remark, said. "I'm thinking the truck was heading west on Route 9. That indicates that the direction it was coming from was behind it."

"God bless, America!" shouted Tim. "That college degree you have is paying off in spades! I never would have thought that an object moving forward leaves the past behind. You are goddamn brilliant, Ron. I don't care what Buttocks thinks!"

"Up yours," Ron replied, while giving Tim a well-known finger gesture.

"Well, now, isn't that classy," admonished Tim.

"What it means is that whatever warehouses you have on the list that are west of Route 31 are unlikely candidates."

Tim, grasping Ron's inference, went down the list of remaining warehouses and saw seven were west of Route 31.

"That leaves us eighteen more to check out, Ron."

"How many south of 501?"

Tim, taking a quick glimpse of the list, showed three remained south of 501.

"Three."

"We can all but discard those."

"Why?"

"The dead tell me so."

"Please explain that idiotic statement, Ron."

"The girl, the two dead golf course workers, and at least one of the truck guys all lived and worked at the north end of the Strand. Chances are the truck's origination point is at the north end."

"That's a bit of a stretch, Ron."

"I think not. Tomorrow will tell the story."

There would be no story. They didn't know it, but they were chasing a dead-end.

****

It was going on 9:30 when Brett ended his meeting.

"Stick around for a minute, Mike. We need to talk."

"What is it, Brett?" asked Mike, trying to stay composed while thinking Brett knew about his affair with Marcia.

"The FBI checking out warehouses, has me worried, Mike."

A relieved Mike softly exhaled, then replied, "Well, they won't find our warehouse as we never registered the lease."

"That's comforting, Mike, but I'd feel much better if we eliminated, sooner rather than later, all possibilities of being uncovered."

Mike, understanding what Brett was conveying, responded, "I'll have it taken care of in the morning."

"That includes all attachments, Mike."

"I know. We'll take care of it."

"Good. I'll sleep much better now."

CHAPTER 25
"... use it for bait."

The phone rang in villa 648.

"Hello," answered Mustard.

Recognizing the caller as Mike, he didn't speak another word until, saying, "We'll be there in five minutes."

Chuck, who had been showering, walked into the living room of their shared villa, drying his hair with one towel while having another wrapped around his waist.

"Who was that?"

"Mike."

"What's up?"

"He wants to see us. He has a job that needs doing."

"A messy job?"

"If I had to guess, I'd say yes. Get dressed. He expects us in five."

They were two minutes late, but Mike didn't mention it. Instead he asked Chuck, "Did you check out the warehouse guy like I asked?"

"Yeah, I did, Mike."

"What did you find out?"

Chuck pulled a small pocket pad from his jacket, flipped it open, ruffled through a few pages, found what he was looking for and began reading.

"He lives in a neighborhood called Prestwick. It's at the south end of the beach, near Surfside Beach."

"Wife? Kids?"

"He married in 2012. It lasted two years. No kids," answered Chuck. "He now has a sweet-lookin' squeeze who goes by the name of Margie Horth."

"Friends?"

"If he has any, I couldn't locate them. Hell, when he plays golf, which he does daily, he either plays alone or with his girlfriend."

"I can see why he has limited friends, based on the interaction we had with him in June."

"More like no friends, Mike," countered Chuck.

"Hmm," Mike muttered. "So he plays golf?"

"Yeah, he plays 18 holes every day. He also plays 'hide the weenie' with Margie three to four times a day."

"Busy fella, ain't he?" submitted Mustard.

"He's a worker, that boy," replied Chuck with a big grin.

"Nice work if you can get it," retorted Mustard.

"The pay ain't too good, but I bet the payoffs are nice," offered Chuck.

"You gotta have some kind of stamina to play 21 to 22 holes a day!" exclaimed Mustard. "That's way past my limit, although I bet I could play those last three or four with no problem."

"Will you two knock it off!" barked Mike. "Now listen. Brett wants him, and anyone who might miss him, to disappear."

"When?" asked Mustard.

"Tomorrow."

"Why tomorrow, Mike?"

"We have an excuse to meet him."

"We do?" asked Mustard. "What is it?"

"It's Mr. Henry's payday. There's $12,500 in this briefcase. You can use it for bait. Bring it back when you're done."

"Do you have a plan for pulling this off, Mike?" asked Chuck.

"No, I don't. I'm leaving it to the both of you. But it has to happen tomorrow."

"Anything else, Mike?"

"Two things. No witnesses, and the bodies must disappear."

"No problem, Mike," said Chuck, with a wide grin. "We were wondering when we'd use our new fireplace."

"Ah, yes, the crematory," nodded Mike. "Good call, Chuck. Let me know when it's done, fellas."

"It's a damn shame though," muttered Chuck.

"What is?" asked Mike.

"That girl Margie is drop dead gorgeous. It's a shame to take her off the board."

"Yes," said Mike, "but it's either her or us, Chuck. I'd rather it be her. What say you?"

"Don't worry, Mike. Tomorrow, she's out of the game."

Chuck and Mustard, as ordered, would dispose of James Henry and his girlfriend, however, the couple's mysterious disappearance would provide the lead the FBI needed to locate the cartel's warehouse.

However, that lead would not reveal itself until weeks later when Bill Baxter, in a chance meeting with Ron and Tim, mentioned the baffling disappearance of the couple.

By then, a dozen new workers had arrived from Mexico. The ashes of those preceding them carried off by the wind.

The same fate awaited these newest arrivals.

CHAPTER 26
"An ambush location."

TUESDAY - OCTOBER 1, 2019 8:00AM

"Jimmy, what are we doing today?"

Asking was Margie Horth, the kept woman of James Henry. She was a 26-year-old, auburn-haired, blue-eyed, tanned skinned beauty, who had been Henry's sex kitten for the past four months. Her sexual appetite was killing him, but he didn't mind it at all.

"I have some work to do in my office, baby. While I'm working, you could go for a swim at the pool."

"The pool has been closed since Labor Day."

"Oh, that's right. I forgot what date it is."

"How could you forget the date? Don't you get paid today?"

"Yeah. They'll call me at 9:00 to set up a meet."

"Since I have nothing to do, can I come along?"

"I'll ask when they call, but I doubt it. They insist no one accompanies me when picking up the payments. Why, I don't quite understand."

"I'm going to take a shower. When I finish showering, would you like to meet me in the bedroom?" she purred.

"It's a nice thought, baby, but not this morning. Maybe later this afternoon we can heat things up."

Prophetic words.

****

Chuck and Mustard had stayed up half the night discussing how they would eliminate the couple.

During that time span, Mustard downed a half-dozen Ho Hos.

"Don't you tire of those things, Murph?"

"Never! When they put me in the ground, I want a box of Ho Hos buried with me."

"They'll melt where you're going, Murph."

Ignoring Chuck's dig, Murph asked, "What time does the sunset tomorrow?"

Checking the paper, Chuck replied, "Seven o'clock. Why? What are you thinking?"

"You said he plays golf every day. Right?"

"That's right. He books 3:00 tee times."

"Would the internet have an aerial view of the neighborhood?"

"Don't know for sure, but I'm guessing it does," replied Chuck.

"Pull it up. Let's have a look."

Chuck had an aerial view up on the screen in less than a minute.

"What are we looking for, Mustard?"

"An ambush location."

"You're thinking of killing them on the golf course?"

"Something like that, Chuck."

Mustard continued to scan the aerial view of the property, using the mouse to move across the landscape.

Satisfied with what he saw, he turned to Chuck, saying, "Tomorrow morning, rent a van that is wide enough and has a ramp to accommodate a golf cart."

"What's the plan, Murph?"

"The plan is to kill two people. This should do the trick."

"Do you mind telling me what you're thinking?"

"Tomorrow, Chuck. It's late. Let's get some sleep. We have a big day ahead of us. It's going to be a killer," he added with a smirk.

CHAPTER 27
Mustard's Plan

TUESDAY - OCTOBER 1, 2019 9:00AM

"Jimmy, don't forget to ask," shouted Margie, upon hearing the phone ringing and seeing it was 9:00.

Jimmy acknowledged her reminder with a retort of, "Okay, Baby," then answered the phone.

"Mr. Henry?"

"Speaking."

"We will hand over your money tonight at 7:10 beside the 5th green at Prestwick."

"What! I'll be finishing up my round on 18 at that time!"

"Change your plans, Jim. Play the back side first."

"I don't know if they will let me."

"We have $12,500 in cash, which I'll hand over to you at the 5th green at 7:10. If you need an idea, maybe you could give the starter a generous tip, for instance."

"I'll do my best."

"Good. Call this number after you leave the 4th green. Got a pencil?"

"Go ahead. I'm ready."

Murph read the number of a burner phone, after which, he said, "See you at 7:10, Mr. Henry."

Click.

Jimmy held onto his phone for a moment while his mind asked, *Why there?*

Margie entered the room, wrapped in a towel, her wet hair hanging down to her shoulders.

"Did you ask them if I could tag along?"

Jimmy, his mind elsewhere, answered, "Sorry, what did you say?"

Margie repeated her question, to which Jimmy replied, "Oh, yeah, I did."

"And?"

"Seems like you'll be with me, Baby."

"Great! Would you like to join me in the bedroom?" she asked, opening the towel to expose her goodies.

"How could I say no to you," replied Jimmy, with little enthusiasm. "I'll be there in a minute."

Jimmy joined Margie in the bedroom, but to Margie's chagrin, Jim couldn't perform. His mind kept wondering why the meeting had to be on the golf course. It was strange because they made all previous payments at his office.

His senses told him to beware, but he shrugged it off as being paranoid. He should have trusted his senses.

CHAPTER 28
"...at least no one got shot."

TUESDAY - OCTOBER 1, 2019 9:00AM

Two hours before James Henry received his call, Ron walked into his FBI office holding a cup of coffee that Heather had made him.

They had made plans to go warehouse hunting at 8:30, but he doubted they would turn up anything of consequence. He had convinced himself the cartel was too smart to allow a leased warehouse to be their undoing.

Opening a file folder he had started for the current case, he began reading through it, hoping something would jump out to lead him to the cartel's operation. After thirty minutes of reading and rereading, he closed the file and took a sip of his now lukewarm coffee.

Almost on cue, Tim walked through the door carrying two cups of hot coffee and four donuts.

"Morning, partner. Your timing is perfect. I was going into donut withdrawal. What did you bring today?"

"I brought you two diet éclairs and two diet sourdoughs."

"Diet donuts! Get out!"

"Just thinking of you, buddy."

Ron took one of the éclairs and bit into it.

"Damn! That is god-awful. It tastes like glue mixed with soap."

"Ahh, mind over matter wins again."

"What the hell does that mean?"

"Diet donuts don't exist. Those, my friend, are your everyday high fat, high calorie, donuts."

"Then why do they taste like crap?"

"Take another bite. I'm sure that taste will disappear. It was all in your mind. You expected bad and your mind made it so. You're just like Pavlov's dogs."

"That's a piss-poor analogy, but I get your point. How about I take you out for a diet lunch?"

"Fat chance that you would get anywhere near diet food. I'm not worried."

"You have a point there," agreed Ron.

"Are you ready to check out some warehouses?"

"Not really," answered Ron. "I'm thinking we're wasting our time."

"You'll get no argument from me, but what other angle do we have?"

"We got nothin'," said Ron, with a bit of anger in his tone. "Hell, I can't even think of an angle we could chase."

"Yeah, well, who's ever running this show, knows how to cover his tracks. Kill fifty-some people and not leave a sniff of a clue. Who could do that?"

"And they aren't close to being done either."

"I concur, partner."

"You know, Tim, there's one option we haven't tried, and the thing about it, it's almost always foolproof."

"What's that, Ron?"

"Follow the money."

"What the hell does that mean? How can we follow the money if we don't know where it is?"

"I don't mean that money."

"Speak English, partner."

"The gold. If the cartel intends to reestablish itself on the Strand, it will need financing."

"Why? Why not just keep some cash?"

"Good question, Tim. I'm surprised you thought of it."

"Screw you!"

Getting a kick out of Tim's reaction, Ron continued, saying, "First off, I'm thinking fewer storage problems."

"Can't argue that point, Ron."

"Second, gold is a better commodity to transact deals. Especially the type of deals in which the cartel takes part."

"Not so sure about that, partner. I think I'd rather carry around a few hundred-dollar bills in my pockets, rather than an ingot of gold."

"And third, I'm guessing they figured out gold increases in value, whereas Ben Franklin's are devaluing."

"So how do we 'follow the money?'"

"We don't, but those guys from FATF can."

"Let's call them."

"No. Let's have Braddock do it. It will make him feel useful."

"What will we do in the meantime?"

"The only thing we can do. It's Tuesday. Right?"

"If yesterday was Monday, today has a good chance of being Tuesday."

"What's our primary objective on Tuesdays?"

Tim's eyes lit up like a 100-watt bulb. "You're a genius, Ron!"

"Where are the Hagan Hackers playing today?"

"Kings North. The first tee time is 10:56."

"Call Hagan. Tell him we're in. And tell him not to pair me with you."

"Why is that? You have something against winning?"

"No. It's your deodorant. It isn't doing the job," replied a smiling Ron.

****

It was 10:36 when Tim and Ron pulled up to the bag drop. Various members of the Hagan Hacker group were in the vicinity when Ron rolled down the window, saying, "Well, hello, boys!"

Al Lowe fired the first volley.

"When the guys heard you two were playing, a half-dozen went home."

"Afraid of the caliber of our game, are they?" quipped Tim.

"Caliber is the operative word, Tim, as in bullets that might come their way."

John Coughenour approached the car, saying, "Well, well, if it isn't the Kryptonite Boys. Who are the unlucky bastards that will be playing with you today?"

"That's a bad rap, John."

"Oh, yeah? Tell that to Ken Hall. Oh, wait, you can't. He's dead."

"That was a case of mistaken identity," said Ron.

"How's that?" asked Coughenour.

"The assassin mistook him for a player. If she knew he played from the ladies' tees, she would only have wounded him."

"Now that was low," said Dave Kessler.

"Now, Dave, " remarked Tim, "you being a card-carrying midget, would know low. Is it true you sleep on a box spring and a mattress because a bed is too high?"

"Screw you, Pond. You're no NBA rebounder yourself."

"True, but I can get into bed without the benefit of a step-stool."

"You boys better stop yakking and get inside and pay up," said Hagan. "You're in the second group."

"Are you telling me we're in the same foursome?" moaned Ron.

"It was that or lose another four guys. We figured if shooting started, it would be best to contain it to a single foursome."

"Who is brave enough to play with us?" asked Tim.

"Tom Daniels and Bobby Joe Gurley," answered John. "I figured one wouldn't hear the bullets and the other wouldn't see them."

"There won't be any fireworks, John."

"I don't care, Ron. I'm in the first group and we ain't looking back if we hear any 'pop' sounds."

"Where's Fred?" asked Ron.

"Beermuender?" asked Rich Freeman.

"How many guys named Fred do we have in this group, Rich?"

"Perhaps," said Rich, starting his reply with his favorite word, "we added a new Fred since you last played."

"Perhaps," replied a mocking Ron. "we didn't."

"He bought a new used car," said Mike Haase. "A Cadillac. He told everyone it was green, but it's closer to a goldish-gray."

"Hell, even Bobby Joe could tell it wasn't green," joked Joe Saffran.

"Yeah, the only green Fred knows is the color of money," quipped Dave Yockey, the group's cookie baker.

"I'll bet after we finish playing, Fred will walk out to the lot, look for a green car and not seeing it, report it as stolen," added Rick Geslain.

Rick's semi-kidding challenge met with a resounding chorus of "No bet!"

After parking the car, Ron and Tim made their way to the pro shop.

Passing the bag drop area, they were about to mount the stairs leading to the Pro Shop when they met Fred coming down.

"Fred! We hear you bought a Cadillac."

"Yeah, I needed a new car."

"Oh, you bought a new one?"

"Yeah, it's a 2019. It has about 28,000 miles on it."

"That." said Ron, "doesn't qualify as new, Fred. New cars have no mileage on them."

"The salesman told me it was new."

"I'm just guessing," said Tim, "but there's a chance he may have omitted adding the word 'once' in front of the word 'new.'"

"I don't think so. He looked honest."

"Honest? Fibbing Fred, are you telling me, the word 'honest' is in your vocabulary?"

"I think I saw it once in a dictionary. Did you know the 'h' is silent?"

"What color is the sky in your world, Fred?" asked Tim.

"Speaking of color," said Ron, "what color is the 'new' car, Fred?"

"Green."

"Light green? Dark green?"

"I'm not sure. The salesman said it was green."

"Are you sure?"

"I heard him say it with my own two eyes."

"That pretty much sums it all up, buddy."

When the round finished, Ron had shot a 78 and Tim shot the same numbers but in reverse order. The team didn't win a thing as they finished a distant eighth.

When asked to comment on the team's poor showing, Bobby Joe said, "We played shitty, but at least no one got shot."

CHAPTER 29
Multiple things happened...

TUESDAY - OCTOBER 1, 2019 7:00PM

Jimmy was finishing up a four-foot putt on the 4th hole when Margie asked, "When are you picking up the money?"

"In about ten minutes. I have to call them. They're meeting us at the next green at 7:10."

"It's getting dark, Jimmy. We won't be able to finish our round."

"I know, baby, but this is how they wanted it."

"Seems like a strange way for someone to pay their rent, Jimmy."

"Yeah, it does, doesn't it?"

Giving thought to Margie's words, Jimmy said, "I want you to stay here. If I'm not back in 15 minutes, I want you to run to the nearest house and call the police. When they arrive, tell them to check the warehouse on Oak."

"Why can't I go with you, Jimmy? What's going on? I'm scared."

"Just do as I ask, Margie. Stay here, I'll be back in fifteen minutes. If I'm not, run to the nearest house and make that call."

****

The reason Mustard had picked the 5th hole to make the kill was obvious.

Links Road separated the 5th hole green from the 6th hole teeing area. Standing in Links Road and looking back toward the 5th hole teeing area, an expanse of manicured grass, sixty yards wide and sixty yards deep lay to the right. Dale Lozier's home sat to the far right of this grassy area.

Twenty yards to the left of the cart path sat a fashionable restroom. Forty yards beyond the restroom stood an occupied home. A large stand of pine trees stood between the cart path and the home, restricting vision in either direction. The trees also buffered sounds coming from the cart path.

Twenty yards from the restroom, and to the right of the cart path, sat a huge sand bunker. The bunker's back side rose to a height of eight feet. Anyone standing behind it had complete cover from anyone approaching the green from the tee.

Chuck would wait until Jimmy drove past in his golf cart. He would then approach Jimmy from behind and kill him.

Mustard, holding the money, would wait at the rear of the van.

****

Jimmy's call came at 7:00, just as instructed.

"I'm on my way to the 5th tee."

"Good," replied Mustard. "Hit your tee shots and I'll be waiting for you up by the green."

Jimmy, upon reaching the par three 5th tee, grabbed a six-iron, walk to the senior tee, and hit his shot onto the green. Returning to the cart, he placed the club back into the bag.

Before climbing into the cart, he unzipped one of the bag's pockets and removed a revolver.

Although he had checked the weapon twice before putting it in his bag, he checked it once more to ensure he had loaded it. He took off the safety and placed it on the seat, snug against his right leg.

Taking a deep breath, he pressed the accelerator and made his way down the cart path toward the 5th green.

Behind him, a fearful Margie, disobeying Jimmy's instructions, made her way to the 5th hole.

****

Driving in circles around Links Road, they were only 500 yards away when the call came. They had plenty of time.

Chuck was driving. Pulling up to where the cart path crossed Links Road, he backed the van down the path about ten yards. Leaving the vehicle, he made his way behind the bunker.

It was as dark as they could hope for.

Mustard exited the vehicle carrying a small duffel bag housing the $12,500. He planted himself up against the van's barn doors and waited.

He heard a ball plop onto the green but didn't hear a second ball.

She must have hit it out-of-bounds, he thought to himself.

Moments later he saw the lights of a golf cart approaching.

Although it was dark, he saw Chuck make his way toward the path after the golf cart had passed the bunker. Chuck was only 20 feet behind the cart when Jimmy came to a stop 25 feet short of the van.

Mustard, because of the cart's lights blinding his eyes, didn't realize the woman wasn't in the cart.

Fact is, he couldn't discern Jimmy until he stepped from the cart and took a few steps past the light beams.

"I have your money, Mr. Henry," he called out, while holding the duffel bag up for viewing. "Hey, could you kill those lights? I can't see."

"Why don't you put the bag on the ground, get in your van, and leave," Jimmy retorted.

Mustard didn't count on the cart's lights being so bright.

"I heard a ball hit the green. I assume that was yours?"

"It was," answered Jimmy. "Now put the money down and leave."

"I didn't hear the lady's ball. I reckon she must have it somewhere other than straight."

"She didn't play today," Jimmy lied.

"He's lying, Mustard," yelled out Chuck. "There are two bags on the cart!"

"Get down the cart path, Chuck!" yelled Mustard. "She's down there! Get her!"

"Noooooo!" screamed Jimmy, turning to fire a wild shot in Chuck's direction.

Mustard, realizing what was happening, pulled his silencer-equipped weapon, took a few steps toward Jimmy, and put a round in the back of his head.

Multiple things happened at that point.

Marcia, hearing a shot, made the mistake of running toward the sound.

Dale Lozier, the neighbor living 60 yards away, was walking his dog on the far side of his house when he heard what he perceived as a shot. Curious about the sound, he made his way to his front yard. Peering through the darkness, he thought he could see a white van parked on the cart path. With his dog yapping away, Dale made his way toward it.

Mustard picked up the dead James Henry and tossed him into the cart. He then pulled the cart forward until it reached the back of the van. Leaving the cart, he opened the barn doors of the van and slid out the ramp.

As he returned to the cart, Dale Lozier arrived, asking, "What the hell are you doing, mister!"

Mustard, without missing a beat, shot Lozier dead, and then he put a bullet in the still yapping dog.

"Nosy bastard!" whispered Mustard as he drove the cart up into the van.

Closing the van's doors, Mustard turned toward the cart path where he last saw Chuck. The darkness was total now. Nothing was visible.

The distance from Margie to where Jimmy had stopped the cart was 153 yards.

Margie, in her quest to find Jimmy, traveled about 45 of those yards, before seeing a figure coming toward her. She stopped, and straining her eyes to see in the darkness, asked, "Jimmy? Is that you?"

"Jimmy is waiting for you, Margie. He told me to come get you," answered Chuck, now just 20 yards away.

"Who are you?" cried Margie.

They were less than ten yards apart when Chuck saw the dark outline of the woman. He didn't hesitate to put two silent .22 bullets into her chest.

He was on her before she fell dead to the ground. Tossing her over his shoulder, he headed up the cart path toward the van.

Still fifty-yards from the van, he heard Mustard call out, "Chuck?"

"Yeah, it's me."

"Did you get her?"

"Yeah. Open the doors."

Reaching the van, Chuck tossed Margie's body inside, where it wedged against the rear wheels of the golf cart.

"Let's get out of here, Chuck. This didn't go as smooth as I had hoped it would."

"No shit, Sherlock."

As they were about to pull away, Chuck caught sight of the bodies of Dale Lozier and his dog.

"What is that all about, Mustard!"

"Some guy and his yappy dog got involved. They were witnesses, Chuck!"

"They? You thought the dog could pick us out in a lineup?"

"He looked like a pointer," Mustard replied with a big smile.

"Let's put them in the back. We'll add them to the cremation. A missing person is better than a murdered person. When Mike gets wind of how we handled this, we'll be in his doghouse."

Contrary to what they thought, it wasn't the Chinese fire drill the two men presumed it was, despite the unexplainable missing neighbor and his dog, and the disappearance of a well-known couple.

A maintenance crew, while performing spring cuttings in March, discovered Jimmy's .38 wedged in the pampas grass lining the cart path on the 5th hole.

The police identified the gun as belonging to a Mr. James Henry, who, along with Margie Horth, had gone missing after driving off to play golf on October 1st.

A ballistics test revealed the gun was clean, having no record of ever being used in any previous crimes.

The trio of Dale Lozier, James Henry, and Margie Horth going missing while on or near the golf course, and finding a gun not related to any crime, baffled the police.

Only after a passing conversation between Bill Baxter and Ron Lee would speculation arise that murder was the culprit.

Although sure of it, the law could never prove murder. Other than pure speculation, the fate of the three would forever remain unknown.

CHAPTER 30
Cremation Talk

"How many bodies should we put in the oven, Chuck?"

"The previous owner said he could fit a dozen dogs in at a time. I think all three, plus the pooch, will fit. What are you thinking?"

"I wouldn't have asked if I had any idea," retorted Mustard, as he slid Lozier's body out of the van. "Help me lift this guy up onto the slab. He's the biggest of the three. Once we get him in, we'll have a better idea."

A couple minutes later, Dale Lozier's body was lying on the slab big enough to hold a horse.

"Looks like they'll all fit, Chuck."

"Appears so, Mustard."

"How long do we cook 'em?"

"I'd guess two to three hours should do it."

Fifteen minutes later they jammed Margie and Jimmy into the chamber, with Lozier's dog tossed in last.

"Let's fire this thing up, Mustard!"

Moments later the furnace was at 1400F and heading towards 1600F.

"Do you think that's what hell will feel like, Chuck?"

"I reckon so, Mustard. Maybe a touch warmer."

"Hmm, not looking forward to that."

"It appears we ain't got much choice. Based on our work the past 20 years, there's little chance we'd be mistaken for angels."

"True," sighed Mustard.

"Hey, I brought a cooler of beer. Would you like a cold brew?"

"Any chance you brought something to eat also?"

"Pretzels."

"Sounds good to me."

For two hours they sat watching the smoldering crematorium, while knocking back a half-dozen beers and a large bag of salted pretzel sticks.

During the two hours, they talked about everything from baseball to politics. And, being men, they talked about women.

While talking about women, Mustard brought up the look Marcia and Mike shared at yesterday's meeting.

"Did you by any chance, Chuck, see that look Marcia gave Mike when Brett made that remark about her 'persuasive powers'?"

Chuck, lying, responded, "No, I didn't. What kind of look was it?"

"I don't know. Maybe she was looking for backup."

"Backup? What the hell do you mean?"

"The remark Brett made wasn't too cool. It offended her. It seemed she looked to Mike to stand up for her. Now why would she do that? I'm wondering if they got something going on."

"Well, I'm with one or the other daily, and I have seen nothing."

"Yeah, well, I'm betting Mike's bedding her whenever Brett's not."

"Hey, Mustard, don't be mouthing off about that. If it made its way back to Brett, he'd have them both killed."

"I won't say nothing. Don't worry. I'm just surprised you haven't picked up on anything."

"It ain't none of my business and it ain't none of yours either. Let sleeping dogs lie, Mustard."

"I knew it! You know something! Don't you?"

"Now why would you say that?"

"Because of what you said."

"Which was?"

"It ain't none of your business."

"Well, it ain't!"

"Yeah, but you know he's banging her, don't you?"

Chuck was a lousy poker player. It was much too easy to read his eyes and discern the cards he was holding.

"Like I said, Murph, let it go. Stay away from this. What they do, they do. They know the consequences."

"Yeah, they do, but you do too, Chuck. If Brett finds out you knew and you didn't tell him, he'll have you put down like a mangy dog."

"Would you be the one to do it, Murph?"

"It isn't something I'd want to do, but I would."

"I suppose you'd throw me into that oven like I was a dead dog, wouldn't you?"

"I suppose I would."

"Are you going to tell Brett?"

"No!"

"Then there's no difference between my knowing and not saying anything and you knowing I know, and you not saying anything."

Mustard pondered on Chuck's proclamation for a moment, then responded, "It's best we forget about Mike's and Marcia's affair, Chuck. It's best we be like those three monkeys: deaf, dumb, and blind."

"Agreed," said a wary Chuck.

Mentally, Chuck started going over his plan.

CHAPTER 31
Norman Lincoln

WEDNESDAY - OCTOBER 2, 2019 12:15PM

He was a 2014 graduate of the UNC at Chapel Hill, having majored in computer science. His current job had him working in the Horry County Tax Assessor's office as their computer guru.

During his five years of employment, he had not received recognition in terms of pay or status.

Depressed and resentful, he felt undervalued, making him Marcia's perfect target.

His name was Norman Lincoln.

Six-foot and weighing a slender 165, Norman thought himself a stud, but he was wrong. The women he worked with thought of him as a geek. After all, he wore dark-rimmed glasses, had a white pocket protector tucked into his shirt's pocket, and wore black and white sneakers.

Norman was no stud.

It took Marcia one day of walking the halls of the Horry County Municipal Building to find the perfect foil. A blind man would have had no trouble picking Norm.

He had all the signs: a loner, bad posture, and the all-to-obvious geek qualities.

She caught his favor at a Jersey Mike's, where he ate lunch every weekday.

Holding a drink in one hand and an Italian sub in the other, she approached his booth, asking, "Do you mind if I sit with you?"

Looking up at the unexpected voice, and seeing a woman of such intense beauty, startled him.

"You want to sit with me?" he asked, taken aback by the request.

"If you don't mind?"

"Er, no, no, not at all. Please, sit."

"Thank you. My name is Marcia."

"I'm Norman. Norm Lincoln."

"I've seen you in the municipal building. Do you work there?"

"Ahh, yes, I do. I'm a computer specialist."

"Oh, and what does that entail?"

"I'm responsible for the software."

"Software?"

"Yes, ma'am, that's…"

"Please. Call me Marcia."

"Okay, Marcia. As I was saying, the software is the code that runs the business. I wrote many of the programs."

"Besides good looks, you also must be very smart, Norm."

"Thank you for the compliment, Marcia, but you wouldn't know it by what happens in there," he said, nodding his head toward the building where he worked.

"What does that mean, Norm?"

"They don't even know I exist. I haven't had a raise since I started, and no promotions, of course."

"What's your pay like, Norm?"

"It's okay. I make about $45k a year."

"Yikes! That's downright disgraceful. I bet you could use some extra bucks from time to time. Yes?"

"Almost every week to tell the truth. I bought a new car, and the payment is killing me."

"Maybe I could help you out."

"You? How?"

"Well, I need a favor."

"What kind of favor?"

"I have an ex who's trying to bleed me dry."

"That's a unique reversal, isn't it? The husband bleeding the wife."

"Yes, it is, but I'm the successful one in the pairing. He's a bum."

"I see. So he wants a share of your... portfolio?"

"That's about right, Norm. He's hired a lawyer to look into properties I own. He hopes to get his hands on them, sell them, and leave me high and dry."

"The guy sounds like a prick to me."

"He's a big one, but his isn't, if you get what I mean."

Norm, somewhat embarrassed by the woman's admission, gave a polite nod.

"What can I do for you?"

"I own a warehouse on Oak Street that I don't want his lawyer to find. I've stored many of my valuables in it, and if he gets access, I could lose everything."

"Okay, but where do I fit in?"

"Could you delete that property from the computer files?"

"Well, yeah, I could, but if my boss found out, I'd lose my job, and could go to jail."

"I'll pay you $100,000."

Norm's jaw dropped to his chest, or so it seemed.

Staring at her in disbelief, he said, "Did you say, $100,000?"

"I did. Is that too little? I'll go $125,000 if you say yes, right now."

"Y..ye...yes!"

"Just to show good faith, I'll give you $50,000 now and the rest after you've deleted the records. Is that okay?"

"Ahh, yeah, sure. You have that kind of money with you?"

"It's in my car. Wait here. I'll be back in two minutes."

He watched her rush out the door and disappear around a corner. Her absence allowed him to give thought to what she asked him to do. Deciding it would be much too reckless, he made up his mind to tell her no when she returned.

A moment later, she reappeared across from him.

"Look," he blurted, "I've given this some…"

She opened a bag and tipped it toward him. Inside he could see five packs of $100 dollar bills in wrappers marked $10,000.

"Take it. It's yours," she said. "Please, do what I asked. I'll meet you back here at 5:00 with the other $75K."

While he sat staring at the money, he began thinking.

What she wants done will only take a minute. A few keystrokes, a push of a button, and the record disappears forever. For a minute's worth of work, she'll pay me $125,000.

"What's the address?"

Smiling, she replied, "It's 604 Oak."

"I'll see you at 5:00. If you're not here, I'll reset the record to active."

"I'm not here to screw you, honey. I'll be here with the money. Bring me proof you deleted the records. Once I'm convinced you've done your part, I'll hand over the $75,000."

"What if I want more?"

"Are we getting greedy, Norm?"

"I'm not talking money," he said, as his eyes fell to her extensive cleavage.

Following his eyes, she smiled, saying, "Now that has possibilities."

"Really! How?"

"Instead of meeting in the parking lot, why not meet me in my hotel room?"

He wondered why a hotel room.

Someone with this kind of money would own her own home, he thought.

His sudden erection pushed whatever doubts he had, away.

Money and sex, he thought. *Damn if it ain't Christmas!*

"What hotel? What room?"

Marcia, expecting such a request, had booked a room at the DoubleTree Hotel.

"Do you know the DoubleTree?"

"Yes!"

"Room 316. I'll be waiting."

"I should be there by 5:15."

"Yes, I believe you will," Marcia said, with a knowing smile. "I'll see you then, Norm. Please, don't make a lady wait too long."

She rose from the table, and never having touched her drink or sandwich, left the restaurant.

Norm, giddy with excitement, took his bag of money, Marcia's untouched sandwich, and left two minutes later.

Thursday – October 3

It was 11:50am when a maid unlocked the door to room 316. When opened, she would find, lying between the room's two double beds, the nude body of an unidentified man. Someone had slashed his throat and left him to bleed out.

An autopsy would reveal the deceased, within the past 24 hours, had consumed two sub sandwiches, one a meatball, the other an Italian.

Robert Edge, based on the unique mixture of oils and vinegar, determined it was a Jersey Mike's sub.

Police showed photos of the victim at area Jersey Mike's shops. It took less than a day to locate the shop where Norm Lincoln had eaten his last meal.

Employees of Jersey Mike's identified the victim as an everyday customer who worked in the Horry County Tax Assessor's office.

"Yeah, he came in Monday through Friday. He always ordered a meatball sub," said a female employee. "Weird fella. Never said much."

"We think he may have also eaten an Italian sub," said the interrogating officer.

"I don't know about that, detective, but the woman ordered an Italian sub."

"Woman? What woman? Describe her for me."

"Kinda pretty. Blond. Blue eyes. She wore glasses. They sat in that booth," she added with a pointing finger.

"Did they talk?"

"She did most of the talking. Although she didn't look like a pro, it seemed they were making some type of arrangement, if you know what I mean. He seemed amazed about whatever she told him."

"Amazed how?"

"Shocked face. Enormous eyes. Mouth fell open. You know. I'm thinking it was going to be the first time he got laid. Just saying."

"Anything else?"

"She left for a few minutes. She came back with a bag and gave it to him."

"What kind of bag?"

"A plain white shopping bag like you get at a grocery store."

"Then what?'

"She left without taking her food. The weirdo waited about two minutes, got up, and taking the white bag and her Italian sandwich, left."

The police would never find a blond-haired, blue-eyed woman wearing glasses. Marcia, a black-haired beauty, had brown eyes, and had no need for glasses. Knowing people would take notice of her constant presence, she wore disguises. One for the sub shop and another while roaming the halls of the Horry County Municipal Building.

After further investigation, police listed Norm's death as a probable "John" set up by a prostitute.

It would be weeks before the truth came to light.

CHAPTER 32
Turnover

TUESDAY - OCTOBER 8, 2019 3:00PM

"Boss. Got a minute?"

"Yeah, Luiz, what do you need?"

"It's been 22 days since we changed shifts."

"That's pushing it."

"Yeah, that was my thought, although this group has been super-productive."

"So you told me a couple of weeks ago."

"It's been 11 days since we last spoke. During that time, they've been averaging about $90 mil every 4 days. I'm guessing we have about $900 million to go."

"Which calculates into how many days, Luiz?"

"If we can continue at that pace, I'd say 40 days, give or take."

"That's mid-November!"

"Don't get too excited, boss. You don't know what you're going to get when we change crews. They might be a herd of sloths. This crew we have now is doing over $22 mil a day. Previous crews averaged about $13 mil a day."

"What's the feeling about this current crew, Luiz?"

"I can see they're getting tired, but they could go another week. The pace may decline, but not to where it was with previous crews."

"Okay, so let's keep them one more week."

"Good idea, boss."

"Have we collected all the money?"

"The last bins came in yesterday. We have about 75 totes to separate."

"Damn, that's a lot of totes."

"When you think we started with about 325, it doesn't seem like too many, boss. They're doing two-and-a-half bins a day. At that pace we should finish it up around the middle of November."

"Driscoll made a lot of money for us, but he was a dumbass about taking care of it."

"No arguments here, boss."

"Listen, Luiz. When you call for the next crew, tell them I don't want any married couples. Just men."

"May I ask why?"

"No, you cannot."

CHAPTER 33
Options

"Nothing?"

"Not a damn thing, Jim," responded Ron.

"It's amazing this is happening right under our noses and we haven't a sniff," said a displeased Braddock.

"We checked every warehouse within a 50-mile radius, Jim," said Tim. "That's all we had to go on."

"It also amazes me there's not a word on the streets," said Braddock.

"It has to be a small group," suggested Ron. "A leader, a couple of lieutenants, some muscle, and guards who watch the workers. No one leaves, so no one talks."

"Does anyone have an estimate on when they'll be fleeing the coup?"

"I'm guessing six, maybe eight weeks tops," said Ron. "But that predicated on our estimate of two billion."

"Maybe they're gone," voiced Tim.

"No, they're not gone, Agent Pond. Someone is still buying large quantities of gold every five days. In fact, the buys have increased the past three weeks from $60 million to $75 million."

"If that's the case, Jim, I'm guessing we have less than six weeks."

"You had FAFT follow up on our idea of 'following the gold', Jim. Anything come of that?" asked Tim.

"Nothing. They are using brokers all over the country. FAFT can't get a handle on it."

"We need to catch a break. I'm afraid they have already replaced 12 more workers."

"Yeah, it's been a month since we discovered the truck," Tim said. "If we're right about them doing a turnover every three weeks, then the current group has maybe two weeks before they're history."

"I wonder how they are bringing them in, Ron," said Jim. "Boat, air, bus, a caravan?"

"I doubt it's by boat. Air is a good bet, though. There are some private airstrips within a 75-mile radius. Most private airstrips don't keep records of who is flying in and out."

"I think transporting them by bus would be dangerous," said Tim. "They could walk off the bus and just disappear."

"They might, but I doubt it."

"What makes you say that, Ron?"

"I'm sure they're all living in fear of something."

"Like what?" asked Braddock.

"How about family they leave behind? Try anything and we kill your family is a most likely scenario."

"What about a caravan?" asked Tim.

"Possible, but there's always a chance of getting pulled over by a cop. What is it? A 2400 mile journey?"

"So you're saying they are coming in by air. Most likely a private jet."

"That's my best guess, Jim."

"Don't they have to file a flight plan?"

"They do, but they don't have to adhere to it. They are criminals!"

"Good point. So where do we go from here?"

"We can check private airstrips, but it would prove futile unless we were lucky enough to be there when the flight arrived."

"True," sighed Braddock. "Then what's next?"

"I don't know about you, Jim, but for us, it's lunch."

CHAPTER 34
Lunch Break

"Where are we going for lunch, Ron?"

"I'm hungry. Let's go big."

"By big you mean…"

"A lot of food."

"But of course! Any ideas?"

"There's a new sports bar on 501. It's right near the turn into the Legends."

"What's it called?"

"Walk In? Walk On? I heard they have excellent food and sizable portions."

"I'm game. Let's go."

Twenty minutes later, they entered the Walk On restaurant. It had two tiers of seating. The upper area, where the bar was located, had tables scattered in a seating area where floor to ceiling windows monopolized one side of the room.

The bar area was typical of sports bars, where it seemed every inch of wall space was covered with TVs.

The lower seating area was a long and wide aisle. At one end of the aisle was the entrance to the kitchen.

Booths occupied both sides of the aisle with 4-seat tables splitting the middle. Dozens of televisions, all showing sporting events, were mounted on the walls.

Given a table, they sat and perused the menu.

"Nice looking place," said Ron.

"The music is a little too loud for my taste."

"You have taste?"

"Yeah, I have a taste for music, and this crap ain't it."

"Touchy little butthead, ain't you?"

"Look at your menu…"

"Hey, fellas. Nice seeing you here. Mind if I join you?"

"Captain Bill Baxter!" shouted Ron. "Haven't seen you in about three weeks. Where have you been hiding?"

"Been busy, Ron. How about you guys? Are you making any headway with those mass graves?"

"Not a damn bit, Bill," snorted Tim. "We have a better chance of finding Jack-the-fucking-Ripper, than of locating the cartel's warehouse."

"Sorry to hear that, fellas. What are you having for lunch?"

"Haven't decided yet. Do you come here often?" asked Ron.

"This is my third or fourth visit. Everything is damn good, and if you can eat it all, well, you're just a damn hog."

Ron ordered a cheeseburger with fries and a milkshake, while Tim went with the large garden salad. Baxter had the cheeseburger sliders.

While they waited for their food, Ron asked, "So you've been busy. What with?"

"Some strange goings on, fellas. Two weeks back, a couple disappeared off a golf course, golf cart and all! Just vanished! Poof! Add to that, a property owner and his dog also disappeared. Not a trace."

"Did this happen on the same day?"

"Yes, Tim, it did."

"Is there a connection?"

"None that we can determine. The couple, not married, played golf every day, weather permitting."

"What golf course, Bill?" asked Ron.

"Prestwick."

"Tough course. Nice, but real tough," quipped Tim.

"If you say so, " replied Baxter, a non-golfer.

"What about the neighbor?"

"Guy went out to walk his dog at dusk. Never came home. Vanished."

"Names?"

"The couple was James Henry and Margie Horth. The neighbor was Dale Lozier."

"Dale Lozier! We play golf with Dale!"

"Not anymore, I'm afraid. Sorry, Ron, but we have nothing to go on."

"Tim! Why didn't we know about this?"

"Our busy schedule prevents us from doing a lot of things, Ron, including, it appears, reading the paper or watching tv."

"When did this happen, Bill?"

"Two weeks ago. It was the first of the month."

"Two weeks! Damn!"

"You said you had something else, Bill?"

"Yeah. We found a city employee, name of Norman Lincoln, in a hotel room with his throat slit. Makes no sense at all. The city cops are attributing it to a prostitute. Seems the guy was talking with some woman in a Jersey Mike's. The employees said she looked like a high-class pro. They had an exchange of words. She left, he left. The next day a maid finds him dead."

"Why doesn't it make sense, Bill?" asked Tim.

"People who knew the victim, describe him as a nerd. Had no friends, shied away from people, ate alone."

"Is this Jersey Mike's a place where prostitutes look for Johns?"

"Not at all, Ron."

"Where did this Lincoln guy work?"

"He was the computer guru for the Tax Assessor's office."

"Bill, what was the name of the guy who vanished off the golf course?" asked Tim.

"Henry. James Henry. Why? Does his name ring a bell?"

"It sounds familiar. What did he do for a living?"

"He was into real estate, Tim. Owned a lot of buildings around town. He wasn't a Burroughs and Chapin, but he did well."

"That's it! Ron! We checked out a bunch of his warehouses. I think he had three. They all came clean, of course."

"Maybe we missed one, Tim."

Opening his jacket pocket, Tim extracted a list.

"I have the list right here. Let's see… Henry. James Henry. Here it is, Ron. I was right. He has three warehouses, a bunch of condos, and about a dozen homes."

"We'll need to check out those homes and condos."

"Okay, Ron, but they don't fit what we believe is the operation."

"We still need to check them out, partner."

Turning to Bill, Ron said, "Tell me what you know about what happened at the golf course."

"There's not a lot to tell. The couple shows up to play golf around 3:30."

"That's somewhat late to get a round in. When did the sun set that night?"

"I'm not sure."

"I'll look it up on my phone, Ron," said Tim, keying in some words. "7:00. Sunset was 7:00."

"Figuring two hours for nine holes, they would have been on the 13th or 14th hole by 7:00."

"No, Ron. They started on the back side. Henry gave the starter a $20 tip to let him go off the back."

"That means they were on the 4th or 5th hole at 7:00."

Baxter's face turned a noticeable ashen.

Ron, seeing the change of expression on Baxter's face, asked, "What is it, Bill?"

"Lozier lived behind the 5th green."

Ron's eyes darted back and forth as he put the pieces together.

"What are you thinking, Ron?" asked his partner.

"Describe to me, Bill, if you can, the area around the 5th green."

"It's wide open on the right. There's a restroom to the left of the cart path. There's also a large stand of trees between the cart path and the nearest house."

"It sounds like a suitable spot for an ambush," Ron mumbled.

"What's your theory, Ron?" asked Tim, seeing his partner's spaced out looking face. "I know that look. It tells me you have a theory. Spit it out."

Ron was about to discuss his thoughts when the waitress appeared with their lunch orders.

"Damn! That's the biggest freakin' hamburger I've ever seen."

He ate it and every French fry in ten minutes.

"Check, please," he called to the waitress.

Tim, about halfway through a salad that would choke a horse, objected.

"I'm only halfway done, Ron."

"I still have a slider left, myself, Ron. We eat our food, not inhale it. Tell us your theory while we finish up."

"Okay. Here's what I'm thinking. Henry was to meet someone at the fifth hole, but it had to be dark when they met. That's why he asked to start on the backside."

"Makes sense, but who was he meeting?"

"My guess? The cartel."

"Why?"

"Don't know the answer to that. I think they were covering their tracks."

"Covering what tracks, Ron?"

"The tracks which would have led to their operation."

"We checked his warehouses. They were all clean."

"Did we?"

"What's that supposed to mean?"

"If Norman Lincoln were alive, he could tell us."

"What the hell are you talking about, Ron!"

"How is Lincoln mixed up in this?" asked a perplexed Baxter.

"What's the easiest way to have a piece of property disappear?" responded Ron.

Tim, seeing where this was heading, answered, "Remove its record from all files."

"Lincoln had access to the tax files, property files, whatever files. The woman bribed him with money and sexual favors. When he went to collect…"

"They killed him," murmured Baxter.

"And Lozier?" asked Tim.

"What time did Lozier walk his dog, Bill?"

"His wife said it was right around 7:00."

"It's just conjecture, but I'm guessing he heard or saw something… investigated and wound up dead."

"What now, Ron?" asked Tim.

"We find that deleted property."

CHAPTER 35
"The poison of choice..."

TUESDAY - OCTOBER 15, 2019 6:00PM

"Amigos! Bienvenido a la fiesta!" shouted Luiz.

Watching from a glass-enclosed office were Chuck and Murph. They would perform the cremations later that night.

Brett insisted they be in attendance because of the tight window between the disposing of the departed and the arrival of their replacements.

"What did he say, Chuck?" asked Mustard, who was eating a package of Ho Hos and drinking coffee.

"Welcome to the feast."

"Hmm, it seems it's more like welcome to the last supper."

"Don't be blasphemous," said Chuck, then noticing Murph eating Ho Hos, asked, "Damn, do you carry those things around in your pocket?"

"No, but I have a few packages in the cupboard," answered Murphy, while pointing to the cupboard where they kept coffee supplies.

Chuck just shook his head, while muttering, "I can't imagine what your blood-sugar levels are."

They watched the 12 workers take seats at three 8-foot picnic tables, placed end-to-end, with each covered with a snow-white tablecloth. Red roses adorned each table.

Twelve bottles of José Cuervo tequila, four on each table, stretched the length of the 24-foot table. Eight men, four each, occupied the end tables. Four women, two per side, sat at the center table.

Drinking began as soon as all had taken a seat.

"This is a first for me, Chuck."

"It's my second. Believe me, it's not anything you want to experience more than once."

"Is the tequila poisoned?" asked Murph.

"No, just the main course," answered Chuck.

"It would be a shame to poison good tequila."

Chuck, waving off Mustard's heartless comment, muttered, "Brett believes he's showing compassion."

"Oh? How?"

"He's of the opinion, the heavy drinking makes the dying less painful."

Murph raised an eyebrow at Chuck's reply, then asked, "What's the main course?"

"Fajitas, burritos, tamales, tacos, and the fixin's."

"Which entrée have they poisoned?"

"All of them."

"What about the dessert?"

"They won't make it to dessert."

"What do they use?"

"The poison of choice for tonight, is cyanide. They've used strychnine in the past, but it takes too long."

"Cyanide is nasty stuff."

"That it is, Murph. It prevents the body from using oxygen. The brain and the heart using the most oxygen, are most affected. All those people will die from convulsions."

The workers drank and danced to piped-in Mexican music for a half-hour before the serving of the soup and salad course.

"Is that…"

"No. The main course is the culprit," answered Chuck, without hearing Murph's full question. "The smells from the food hide the almond smell and taste."

Fifteen minutes later, servers placed steaming platters of fajitas, burritos, tacos, and tamales on the table.

"Looks good," said Murph.

"Yeah, right," snorted Chuck.

The soon to be ill-fated workers piled two and three of the entrees on their plates, before adding rice and beans from two large bowls.

Laughing, good-natured shouting, and hi-jinks carried on for 10 minutes before they felt the deadly effects of the cyanide.

Mustard, a veteran killer of more people than he could count, watched in horror as the men and women suffered horrific convulsions.

He watched the convulsive workers spill out onto the floor, grasping their throats and chests. He saw death fill their eyes as they strained in agony to hold on to life.

It was over in minutes.

Chuck, rising from his chair, glanced at his partner, and seemed taken aback by the look of revulsion on Mustard's face.

Hmm, I never saw this soft side of him before.

"C'mon Murph. The new crew arrives in two hours. They can't see this. Let's get these poor folks in the truck and get them cremated."

"That was god-awful," muttered Mustard. "There's no compassion in what we witnessed. Damn! A headshot is far more compassionate. It's quick and painless."

"Yeah, but we work for a guy who likes a show," noted Chuck. A glance across the warehouse floor glimpsed the man of whom Chuck spoke.

Brett was holding a glass of brandy and smoking a cigar. A smile creased his face as he watched one of his men hoist a dead female up into the truck.

Chuck heard him say, "Good job, Luiz."

Disgusted by what he heard and saw, Chuck decided he would make a call.

CHAPTER 36
Angie Jones

TUESDAY - OCTOBER 15, 2019 4:30PM

Two hours before the cartel would serve the death feast, Agents Lee and Pond stood in the office of Angie Jones, the Horry County Treasurer.

They had arrived almost three hours earlier with warrants to access the county's property tax files and were now reviewing the results of their findings with the treasurer.

"Are you telling us, Ms. Jones, Norman Lincoln wiped clean every single file pertaining to Mr. Henry's properties?"

"It appears so, Agent Lee."

"What about backup files?" asked Tim.

"No records on any of our three backup files either," she answered. "It seems Mr. Norman Lincoln knew what he was doing."

"They paid him at least $50,000 to do what he did," said Tim. "He deposited $50k in a checking account on the same day he wiped the files clean."

"It was also the day he took his last breath," added Ron.

"Well, whoever 'they' are, they got their money's worth," replied Angie.

"What about paper documents?" asked Ron. "He had to fill out documents with his signature."

"Absolutely, sir, but we have been scanning those documents and putting them on disk for years. The last I heard records completed all filings through 2017. If Mr. Henry purchased property in the past two years, it might still be in our paper records."

"What the hell are we waiting for! Let's check it out!"

"Special Agent Lee! Do you realize the amount of paper documents stored in our facilities?"

"Facilities, ma'am?"

"I'm afraid so, Agent Pond. We have files in about a half-dozen locations. All together they number in the thousands."

"Thousands?" questioned Ron.

"Ever buy a home, sir?"

"Yeah. About five to be exact."

"Do you recall what you did at the closings?"

"I signed a ton of documents."

"Yes, you did. How about the documents you signed before you arrived at your closing?"

"I must admit, there were a few."

"Right. Now, combine all those documents and multiply them by a few thousand. Wait! Make it tens of thousands. Then, sir, you might realize the amount of documents we will need to search, hoping to find something with Mr. Henry's signature. I'm afraid, Agent Lee, you have forgotten, Rome wasn't built in a day."

"So the point you're making is it might take a while. What's your estimate?"

"Anywhere from an hour to two weeks."

"Okay, Ms. Jones. Let us know if your people uncover anything. Thank you for your time."

"Will do, Agent Lee. Good luck to you fellas."

"Thanks. We'll take all the good luck we can get. We've had more than our share of no luck and bad luck."

It was nearing 6:45 when they returned to their office. Unbeknownst to them, the feast had started and people were dying.

"The day is about shot, Ron. I'm ready for a good meal and a drink or two. Let's go home, relax, and get a good night's rest. Maybe tomorrow, we'll catch a break."

"Sounds like a good idea, partner. God knows, we need a break."

"You'll get no argument from me, Ron."

"Do you know what's eating at my craw, Tim?"

"Go ahead, Ron. Spit it out. Get it off your chest. I'm listening."

"Do you know what I keep wondering about, Tim?"

"Are you going to keep asking me the same question, using variations of the same word? Just tell me what's eating at your craw."

"I keep wondering about those who have died we don't even know about. How many is it? A dozen? Two dozen?"

"It's screwing with my head, too, partner."

"I'm also thinking about the people who will die if we don't find the goddamn warehouse! Damn it, Tim! We need to find that son-of-a-bitchin' warehouse!"

"Tomorrow, Ron. Tomorrow is the day we catch the break we need."

The death toll was rising as they spoke, but Tim was right, a break was coming their way.

CHAPTER 37
Pedro Gomez

TUESDAY - OCTOBER 15, 2019 10:30PM

It was approaching 10:30 when Chuck pulled the truck into the driveway of what used to be the home of Tom Ledbetter.

Upon reaching the rear of the house, he backed the truck up to within ten feet of the front entrance of the crematory.

"I'll get the back door open, Murph, you fire up the ovens."

"How we gonna do this, Chuck?"

"We'll put five bodies in the larger chamber and one in the small. Figure two hours for each cremation. I'm guessing we'll be home, in our beds, by 4:00."

****

Pedro Gomez was a native of Chihuahua, Mexico. He was single, 24 years of age, stood at an even 6-foot, and weighed a solid 165.

Being the son of a Mexican father and an American mother, he spoke fluent Spanish and English. Both parents died in a car crash when he was 17 years of age.

Pedro's dream of becoming a police officer ended when he lost sight of his left eye during a training accident. He worked construction in Chihuahua, installing drywall, but when work ran out, he made his way to Juarez.

He arrived in Juarez just in time to receive a job offer in the United States. Told the job, assembly-line work, paid $30 an hour and included a room, clothing, and meals, he readily volunteered.

He completed all the application's information and answered all its questions, leaving out nothing except for one idiosyncrasy… he was a vegetarian.

****

"Amigos! Bienvenido a la fiesta!" shouted Luiz.

Pedro, like all the others rushed to the table. Sitting next to his close friend Emanuel, at the end seat of the third table, they drank the tequila and danced. He danced twice with a young girl named Maria who he fancied. He hoped when they finished the job and returned to Mexico, he might see more of her.

When they served the soup and salad, Pedro ate both his and Emanuel's salads. Knowing he wouldn't be having any meat servings, he sought anyone who passed on their soup or salad.

When the entrees came, not wanting to offend anyone, he took his plate and dutifully filled it with tacos and burritos.

He continued to eat his salads while the others, including Maria, who kept looking his way, enjoyed the entrees.

Then, as they were staring at one another, Maria's face changed. A look of excruciating pain filled her eyes. Pedro stood to go to her aid but stopped when Emanual stood and vomited across the table.

Pedro realized, upon seeing his co-workers tearing at their chests and throats, all while trying to rise from their seats amid the horrid vomiting, someone had poisoned their food.

They were being murdered. If he were to survive, Pedro had to pretend the poison had also affected him.

Bending over, he feigned staggering while putting his finger down his throat to make himself vomit. He watched the others. They were convulsing, their bodies quivering while they clutched both chest and throat. He mimicked them as best he could.

As he staggered, he bumped into Maria. Their eyes met, hers horrific, his alarmed. He grabbed her arm and together they fell to the floor like those around them.

Maria landed on top of him, her face looking into his. She took a last breath and died.

Pedro, seeing the others collapse, remained still. After another minute of retched moans had passed, all went silent.

Then a voice barked, "Check 'em out, Luiz. Make sure they are all dead before loading them in the truck."

He watched Luiz, moving from one body to the next flash a small light into the eyes of each victim.

Pedro closed his right eye and held his breath as all went dark.

A moment later, Luiz stood above the entangled couple. Bending, he lifted Maria's head upward so he could see her eyes. A second later, Pedro felt her head flop against his chest.

The small flashlight was now beaming its light into Pedro's left eye. He couldn't see it, but he knew. An excruciating moment later, he felt Luiz step over him and move on to another body.

Seconds later, he heard Luiz announce, "All dead, sir."

He heard the reply, "Good job, Luiz."

Next he heard Luiz say, "Get 'em loaded, boys."

Moments later, he felt Maria being lifted from his body, and daring to crack open his right eye, he watched two men carry her away.

Seeing two men approaching him, he took an unseen deep breath. One man grabbed his two arms, the other his feet. They hoisted him up, carried him across the room, and lifting him, handed him to two men standing inside the truck.

They carried him a few feet and placed him on the floor.

A body lay to his right. Two more bodies followed and laid to his left.

A moment later, a man working inside the truck called out, "We have twelve, Luiz."

He heard Luiz respond, "Okay, Chuck, they are all yours."

Darkness overtook the truck's interior as they closed and latched the cargo doors.

The darkness, however, was momentary.

Once the truck's engine turned over, a half-dozen interior lights switched on.

He remained inert to ensure no one else - alive, that is - occupied the truck's interior.

Waiting two minutes and hearing nothing, he sat up and looked around.

He knew what to expect, but seeing the bodies stretched out alongside him, still left him appalled.

Seeing Maria's body left him wondering of what was not to be.

Then his mind switched to survival mode.

✳✳✳✳✳✳✳✳✳✳✳✳

It was 6:00pm, Pacific Time, in Gales Creek, Oregon when Sheila Evans knocked on Lisa Cardone's office door.

"Come in."

"There's a call for you on line one, ma'am."

"I told you, no calls."

"I know, but the man says it's important. He says he has something you should know."

Picking up the line, Lisa snapped, "Talk."

Sheila, who had not left the room, noticed, as Lisa listened to the caller, her facial expression changing from irritated to angry to enraged.

Only a half-minute passed before Lisa, slamming the phone down on her desk, screamed at Sheila, "Find out when the plane can fly to Myrtle Beach."

"Yes, ma'am," replied a frightened Sheila.

Ten minutes later, Sheila returned saying, "Hank said the plane will be ready at 2:00am."

"Eight hours from now! What's the holdup?"

"Something about the landing gear, ma'am."

"Where is Ramon?"

"I believe he's in Portland."

"Call him. Tell him to meet me at the plane at 2:00am."

"Yes, ma'am."

"Call Hank back and tell him if the plane isn't ready at 2:00am, he's as good as dead."

I wouldn't want to be Hank, thought Sheila as she left Lisa's office.

CHAPTER 38
Inspections

WEDNESDAY - OCTOBER 16, 2019 2:45AM

Ron bolted from his bed. He had been lying awake, looking up at the ceiling since midnight. He glanced at his clock. It read: 2:45.

Something lingered in his mind, like a name he knew, but couldn't remember. It kept gnawing at him, keeping him awake.

Someone had said something. But who? And what?

Two hours he laid there, trying to recall who said what. He racked his brain, replaying every minute of the past 24 hours.

Then he remembered! It was the words spoken by Angie Jones, the Horry County Treasurer.

How about the documents you signed before you arrived at your closing?

He called Tim.

Tim's phone rang a half-dozen times before he heard a groggy, "Damn it, Ron, I thought tonight was our night for a good night's sleep."

"We've been looking at this from the wrong angle, Tim!"

"What the hell are you talking about, Ron?"

"We need to cross-check the sellers of warehouses to Henry. Lincoln couldn't have erased those documents. The buyer's name would be on those documents!"

"True, but couldn't this have waited..."

"Oh, and one other thing, Tim. Inspections."

"What about inspections?"

"Buyers always have the property inspected. There's an inspector who inspected a piece of property for Henry. We find him, and we find the missing property!"

Total silence endured for about ten seconds.

"Tim? Are you still there?"

"Yeah, I'm here. I'll check it out first thing in the morning."

"Good! What time will that be?"

"8:00."

"Make it 7:00."

"Damn, what a friggin' taskmaster you are."

"I could have said 6:00."

"Is there really such an ungodly hour?"

"Oh, and Tim, don't…"

"Yeah, yeah, I know. Don't forget the donuts."

A few miles away, someone else was shouting out orders. Orders to kill on sight.

CHAPTER 39
Cremation Miscount

The rear doors of the truck swung open, and a man climbed inside. He took a half-dozen steps, bent down, grabbed a body by the feet, and dragged it to the open door. After pulling the body forward until its legs dangled over the side, he returned to the next body in line, to repeat his actions. He did this twice more before a second man appeared.

"Murph, take two of these bodies inside. I'll get the final two in position."

"Okay, Chuck. I'll take the skinnier ones."

"Are the ovens hot?"

"Got any marshmallows or s'mores?"

"Not funny, Murph."

Chuck retrieved another body and placed it in the space Murph had left vacant.

As Chuck was sliding the sixth body toward the truck's opening, Murphy reappeared.

"I have one on the slab, Chuck. I'm thinking, it might be best to do four bodies in the big oven and two in the smaller one."

"Well, let's get these five inside, and then we'll figure out what's best."

****

They plan on burying us, Pedro thought to himself. *This is the truck they used to haul the pallets of money. I know its cab can only accommodate two men. I can deal with two men.*

Deciding it best to be the last body in line, he stood to go, but stopped when he noticed the gap between the bodies where he had been lying.

They might notice, he told himself.

He shifted the last three bodies, before moving to the rear.

While sitting next to the first body placed in the truck, his friend, Emanual, Pedro worked on his escape plan.

Glancing at his watch, he saw it was 10:20. He felt the truck slowing and making a left turn.

"We've been driving for almost an hour," he whispered. "I wonder where they are taking us?"

They answered his question ten minutes later when he heard the truck slow, make a right turn, stop, and then back up and come to a complete stop. They cut the engine, and the cabin went pitch dark.

A few seconds later the rear doors swung open. A man climbed inside.

****

Using the cover of the darkness, Pedro turned his head to the left, giving his right eye a view of a man dragging bodies toward the truck's open doors.

Moments later, he heard a conversation between the two men which made his blood run cold.

Cremation! He silently screamed. They are going to cremate us!

Pedro watched the man drag body after body to the doorway, while the second man carried bodies away.

He watched as the man in the truck climbed down to join his accomplice. Each man grabbed a body, threw it over his shoulder, and disappeared, only to return minutes later to fetch two more corpses.

Minutes later, a man returned to carry off the last body. Pedro, checking his watch, waited ten minutes before he moved. Standing, he crept toward the opening. Reaching it, he peeked around the frame to see a small building.

Inside there were lights. A pungent odor, he didn't recognize, filled the air. It didn't take a genius to figure out what it was.

He stepped down from the truck and ran. He ran until he could run no more. Stepping off the road, he found a tree, sat against it, and cried until he fell asleep. It was 12:30am.

****

"I think we've cooked this batch long enough, Chuck. They've been in there almost two and half hours."

"You have a way with words, Murph. You talk about these poor folks like they're the Thanksgiving turkey."

"Let's see how we did with the big batch," said Murph, pointing at the oven where they had enclosed four bodies.

Chuck opened the door and together they pulled out the table.

"Not bad," exalted Mustard. "A partial skull, and a bunch of teeth, are all that remain. This damn thing is a winner, Chuck. This was a great idea you had."

"Yeah, thanks, partner. Let's sweep the ashes into this pail."

"Before we do any cleanup, Chuck, let's look inside the little cooker."

Murph, after opening the door and looking inside, said, "Nope! Still cooking. I'm guessing we shouldn't have tried to cook two at a time. Next time, we'll keep it at one. Hey, live and learn. Right?"

"Yeah, I guess so, Murph."

Twenty minutes later they were out at the truck gathering the remaining bodies. Chuck, once again, dragged the bodies to the doorway, while Murph carried bodies inside, one at a time.

While reaching down for the fifth body, Chuck realized there wasn't a sixth. He dragged the fifth body to the doorway and waited for Murph to return.

He was staring at the three bodies he had slid to the opening when Murphy returned.

"How many of these bodies have you carried inside?"

"Two. Why?"

"Are you sure you only carried two?"

"Yeah, I'm sure. Why?"

"Two plus three is five," mumbled Chuck.

"Nothing wrong with your math, Chuckie."

"Yeah, but we should have six. The truck is empty. Where is number six?"

"Maybe we did seven the first time?"

"No. We did six. Three men and three women," Chuck replied with certainty. Pointing at Maria's body, he said, "She's the fourth woman. We're missing a man."

"Well, unless he's the second coming of Christ, he didn't just walk off."

"Didn't he? Get the flashlights out of the truck, Murph!"

Moments later the two men, with flashlights blazing, were walking the property.

" I don't see any of the brush disturbed, Chuck."

"If I were him, I'd run straight down the road, which I'm sure he did."

"How did he pull this off, Chuck?"

"I'm guessing he hid at the head of the line. Once we carried off those initial six bodies, he made like a scared rabbit. I'm thinking he has at the very least, a three-hour head start. He could be anywhere by now."

"What are we going to do, Chuck?"

"Put the remaining bodies in the ovens, Murph. I'll wait in the truck."

"Do you think Brett will blame us?"

"There's no reason to, Murph. We did nothing wrong. However, I wouldn't want to be Luiz."

****

Entangled in lust, Brett and Marcia lost the moment when they heard the doorbell.

Brett, angered by the interruption, after putting on a robe, answered the door.

Marcia, however, staying in the bed, felt saved by the bell. Her heart was with Michael.

Opening his villa's door, he saw Luiz.

"What the hell is it, Luiz? It's 1:30 in the morning!"

Knowing Brett was entertaining Marcia, Luiz, in a hesitant voice, said, "Sorry to disturb you Brett, but I thought you should know."

"Know! Know what?"

"I was talking with a guard. He mentioned something about a worker we sent off today."

"Look, Luiz. I don't give a rat's ass about a dead worker."

"I think you should hear me out, Brett."

"Okay, what was it the guard told you about this dead worker? It better be good, Luiz, or else I'll have your ass."

"He said the guy never ate meat."

CHAPTER 40
"...make him dead!"

Brett stared at Luiz, digesting what he had said.

"Are you telling me he's a fucking vegetarian?"

"It appears so."

"And nobody said anything until now?"

"The guard in question came on two weeks ago. He wasn't aware, until tonight, about the going-away dinner."

"But the rest of you. How did you miss it? He was here for almost four weeks, Luiz! How could his not eating meat go unknown to any of you?"

"I'm sorry, Brett, but I never gave a thought to monitoring their eating habits."

"You checked the bodies to make sure they were dead. Right?"

"I checked all twelve bodies, Brett."

"How did this guy pass the eye test?"

"It turns out he's blind in his left eye. It must have been the one I checked with the light."

"You weren't aware of that either?"

"No."

"How do you know it's true?"

"The guard told me. He noticed it while the guy was working on the line. It seems while working, he always tilted his head to the left."

"This guard, he's quite the observer, isn't he?"

Luiz nodded, while saying, "Yeah, I guess he is."

Brett's phone rang.

"I wonder who's calling at this hour, Luiz?" said a sarcastic Brett, as he made his way to the phone.

"Hello!"

"Mr. Cardone, this is Chuck. Bad news, sir. One worker wasn't dead. He escaped while Mustard and I were cremating the first batch."

"You're right, Chuck. It is bad news, but not unexpected. Luiz just told me the guy was a vegetarian. What are you doing about it?"

"I'm afraid the guy has a three-hour head start. We're going to ride the roads, hoping to spot him, but he could be halfway to Mexico by now."

"It would be a blessing if he were halfway to Mexico."

"Yeah, I guess it would," agreed Chuck.

"Do what you can, Chuck. If you find him, kill him. I'll call you back in about two hours."

Hanging up the phone, Brett turned to stare at Luiz. Although disgusted by the sight of the man, he remained calm.

"What do we know about this guy? Does he have a name? What is his history? Does he know anyone who lives in the immediate area?"

"His name is Pedro Gomez. He's ex-army, 24 years old. No known family, either in Mexico or here."

"Take four men, drive to the crematory, and search the area. Find this guy, Luiz, and make him dead!"

****

It was nearing 2:00am when Pedro awoke to the sounds of an approaching vehicle. He knew by the sound they had discovered he was missing. It wasn't a car making its way toward his position. It was the sound of the truck.

Standing, he made his way 10 yards deeper into the woods and stood behind a large pine.

The truck approached. It wasn't speeding; it was almost in crawl mode. The two men scanned the woods as they drove the road. When they reached the area where he had fallen asleep, the truck came to a halt.

Fear gripped his throat. He pressed against the tree so hard he thought, maybe hoped, it would swallow him.

He heard them talking.

"Shine your light over there, Murph. I thought I saw something."

Pedro could see the beam of light hunting its way through the trees surrounding him. Then it stopped, as did his heart, or so it felt.

The fluttering beam held still just yards from where Pedro, pressing ever harder against the pine, stood frozen and breathless.

Hearing a crashing of brush, and knowing they were coming for him, he was about to run.

But they weren't coming. It had been a deer, frightened by the dancing beam of the flashlight, making the now silenced thrashing noises.

"Just a deer, Chuck," said the man named Murphy.

The truck began moving again, but ever so slowly.

Pedro, not realizing he had held his breath during the entire ordeal, gasped for a lungful of air. Only then did he realize his bladder was screaming. He relieved himself for a full two minutes.

Peeking around the tree, he could see the truck's taillights only 100 meters up the road.

Remaining behind the tree, he tried to recall the route the truck had taken to where they were cremating the bodies. His escape would require he reverse the incoming turns.

As he raced down the driveway, he remembered the truck had made a right turn into it. Reaching the end, he made a left onto a gravel road. His mind flashed ahead to the previous turn.

They had made a left off a major road onto a paved road. The paved road turned into this bumpy dirt road after...what... two miles?

Then, talking aloud, he whispered, "There were no further turns until we turned into the driveway."

I remember, he thought*, it taking twelve minutes from the time the truck made the left turn off the major highway to the driveway. Now, if I assume the truck slowed to... let's call it 40 miles-per-hour, then I'm guessing we traveled seven or eight miles on this road.*

"I'm estimating I've covered at least four miles before stopping," he said aloud.

How much further is it to the paved portion of the road?

"If I'm right, the paved portion is about two miles away. The highway should only be two miles further," he said aloud.

Stepping from the trees, he made his way to the dirt road, and followed the taillights of the truck, now a half-mile ahead.

He assumed the truck would search until it reached the main road, then turn and reverse its route until returning to the old house.

****

It was nearing 3:00am when Luiz and four others made the turn onto Ledbetter Road. They hadn't gone a quarter-mile when they came upon the slow-moving truck.

Recognizing the truck as their own, they stopped. Luiz, who was driving, rolled down the driver's window and said to Chuck, "Nothing?"

"Nothing. We've traveled this road for the better part of two hours. If he's deep in the woods, we'll never see him. It's too bad we got us a moonless night."

"How long a lead does he have?"

Glancing at his watch and seeing it was 3:00, Chuck replied, "My best guess he's been on the loose now for over five hours."

"Hell, he could have made it to the main road and waved someone down."

"I don't think so, Luiz. If so, this entire area would be crawling with badges. No, I think he's still on this road. He's exhausted, for sure."

"What makes you say that, Chuck?"

"He's done some drinking, and he's been running for who knows how long."

"Did you check the house?"

"No. I doubt he'd hide in the house. I wouldn't. We didn't check the road to the right of the driveway either."

"You might be right about the house, Chuck, but we'll check it out. How much further past the house does the road go?"

"Maybe two miles before it dead ends."

"Anything down that way?"

"Nothing but wildlife. But our runner didn't know that."

"We'll check out the house and the other end of the road," said Luiz.

"Hey, how's Brett taking it?"

"How do you think he's taking it? Not well. He's pissed."

"I figured as much."

"He told me to find this guy and kill him. I think he wanted to add, 'or else.'"

"Then I guess we better find him and kill him," said Mustard.

As the two vehicles moved in opposite directions, Chuck's phone rang. It was Brett.

"Hey, boss."

"Anything?"

"Sorry, but no."

"Have you seen Luiz?"

"Yeah, he just arrived."

"Chuck?"

"Yeah, boss."

"I never want to see Luiz again."

"Understood, sir."

"Chuck?"

"Yes, sir?"

"I want him to suffer…cook the bastard alive!"

Click.

"What was that about?" inquired Mustard.

"It was Brett."

"That, I figured. What did he say?"

"He wants us to put Luiz in the ovens… alive."

"Damn!" said Murph. "These cartel guys don't play."

CHAPTER 41
... snap.

WEDNESDAY - OCTOBER 16, 2019 3:30AM

The moonless night made it difficult to traverse the uneven gravel road, but the determined Pedro kept pace with the trolling truck.

He calculated he had walked a mile, maybe more, when his right foot stepped on pavement. After taking a few more steps, he stopped.

The paved road. Two miles to go, he thought.

Looking ahead, he saw the truck's taillights, a half-mile ahead, disappear.

There must be a curve ahead.

Feeling the paved road would be much more even, he broke into a trot.

I don't want to lose sight of the truck.

He had run a half mile when he saw beams of light rounding the curve, now just a few hundred yards away.

It's not the truck, he told himself. It's coming too fast.

Leaving the road, he ran 20 yards into the woods and hid behind a large oak.

The speeding car squealed to a stop at almost the exact spot where Pedro had abandoned the road. He heard doors opening and slamming shut. Flashlights beams danced all around him.

A voice exclaimed, "I swear Luiz, I saw something running into the woods."

"Spread out! Check behind every tree! If you see him, kill him!"

I'm doomed, he thought. *I can't run, they'll see me.*

Looking to the heavens, he prayed. However, he cut the prayer short when, because of a passing beam of light, he saw the outline of a low-hanging branch.

Turning, he reached up, trying to find a branch. Finding one, Pedro began climbing. He was 20-feet up the tree when a man passed underneath. Standing motionless on a good-sized branch, he waited, breathless.

The man moved on.

Minutes later he heard the voice of Luiz.

"If it was him, Phil, he's long gone. We'll never find him in these woods."

"Maybe we should wait here until daylight, Luiz," suggested another man. "He has to come out sometime."

"Yeah, but if it wasn't the escapee Phil saw, then we'd be wasting time. Let's make sure he's not hiding in the house. It's also possible he ran toward the other end of the road."

The team moved toward the car but stopped when they heard, *snap*.

Swiveling, Luiz called out, "Spray the area!"

All five men, carrying AK-47s, cut loose a volley of gunfire back and forth across the woods for a distance of 50 yards.

"Cease fire!" yelled Luiz.

The sounds of gunfire ceased, and dead silence filled the air.

Moments later, the silence ended when two raccoons exited the woods, scurried across the road, and disappeared into the woods.

"How in the hell did we miss them!" exclaimed a laughing Phil.

A pair of approaching headlights interrupted his laughter. It was the truck. It stopped behind the car parked in the middle of the road.

The truck's doors flew open and Mustard and Chuck jumped out, weapons in hand.

"What the hell was all the gunfire about?" screamed Chuck.

Luiz explained the situation, to which Chuck replied, "What the hell were you thinking, Luiz. You had better hope no one else heard it. If so, we could have unwelcomed visitors."

"Brett said to kill the son-of-a-bitch!"

"Yeah, but he didn't want half the free world to know it," replied Chuck, while giving Murphy a slight nod.

While Chuck and Luiz continued a back-and-forth conversation, Mustard made his way behind Luiz, and knocked him out with the butt of his gun.

"Hey, what the hell is going on, Chuck?" asked Phil.

"Don't ask questions, Phil," ordered Chuck. "I suggest the four of you check out the house and the stretch of road beyond it."

"Sure thing, Chuck."

After watching the four men drive off, Murph and Chuck carried Luiz to the back of the truck and threw him inside.

"You'd better get in there with him, Murph, in case he comes to."

"I will," said Murphy, begrudgingly, "but this prick ain't coming to for quite a while. I gave him a good knock."

"Yeah, well, if I were him and knew what was coming, I'd rather you had killed me."

Pedro, still high in the oak, could hear every word. Even though he knew Luiz's probable fate, he felt no pity.

CHAPTER 42
"Bad karma."

After the truck pulled away, Pedro remained in the tree for another half hour, climbing down at 4:30. Afraid to move any further, he stood at the base of the tree for 15 minutes before venturing out to the road.

After assuring himself the road was clear both ways, he took off running, reaching a major highway twenty minutes later. Seeing a road sign, he approached it and saw Ledbetter as the name of the road he had traversed. The name of the highway was Route 17.

Remembering his arrival by plane from Mexico, he recalled the van taking them to the warehouse had traveled south on this highway.

Wanting to get as far away from Myrtle Beach as possible, Pedro headed north.

****

Driving the truck to the rear of the house, Chuck parked next to the crematorium.

Leaving the cab, he moved to the back and opened the doors.

"Has he come to yet?"

"No. He's out cold."

"Murph, I saw your reaction to the poisonings."

"Yeah, so?"

"Let me ask you, how do you feel about this?"

"I'll admit I don't feel too good about it, Chuck, but we have always followed orders."

"That's true, Murph. However, putting a bullet in someone's head is one thing… burning someone alive, well, that's something else."

"I'll admit, it's over the top."

"It's inhumane."

"Are you suggesting we shoot him before we…"

"I guess I am. Brett will never know."

"True."

"So, are you with me on this?"

"I've always followed orders, Chuck."

"So have I, Murph, but burning someone alive isn't what we do. Together we aren't worth a shit, but damn, we're better than this!"

Mustard paused before answering.

"Okay, Chuck. We'll do it your way."

****

While checking out the house, Phil received a phone call.

Wondering who could be calling him at this early hour, he answered, "Hello?"

"This is Brett Cardone, Phil. Anything on the escaped worker?"

"Nothing, sir. We've scoured the entire area. It's heavily wooded. He could be anywhere."

"I was afraid of that. Where's Luiz?"

"Strange you should ask, sir, but Chuck and Murphy have him. They knocked him out."

"Then what?"

"I don't know, sir. Chuck sent us off."

There was a pause, then Cardone said, *"Listen, Phil. I want you to find Chuck. I told him to burn Luiz alive. Make sure that's what gets done. Report back to me as soon as it's over."*

Phil, disturbed by what he heard, replied, "Yes, sir."

As Cardone hung up, Phil, taken aback by Luiz's impending fate, looked out the window to see the truck parked at the rear of the house.

Watching from the window, he saw Chuck walking to the rear of the truck and open its doors. He observed Chuck and Murphy as they engaged in a conversation. He couldn't hear what was being said, but it looked serious.

A moment later, he witnessed Murphy put a bullet in Luiz's head.

****

5:55AM

An hour had passed since a weary Pedro started walking north on Route 17. His legs, feeling lead-like, had taken him only three miles and change.

During the hour, only a handful of vehicles, mostly trucks, had passed his way heading north. Each time one of those vehicles approached, he cringed, thinking it might be one of them.

The sun's rising was an hour away when he heard a vehicle approaching. This time, however, it appeared to be slowing as it neared.

Fear filled his throat when the small SUV stopped next to him.

I'm dead, he thought.

"Hey, fella! Need a ride?"

It was a woman driver, but visually, something was wrong.

She was driving on the wrong side of the car!

Seeing his quizzical look, she said, "My name's Kelly. Kelly O'Shea. I deliver newspapers, which requires I drive on this side. I'll ask you one more time. Would you like a ride?"

Pedro initially guessed she was in her late forties, maybe early fifties. But upon closer examination, her gray hair and wrinkled skin changed his assessment closer to sixty. She wasn't overweight, but nor was she skinny. He guessed her height at five-foot two. Aggressive best described the tone in her voice.

"Yes, yes, very much so!"

"Well then, get your ass around in the passenger seat. I'll take you as far as the town of Southport."

Hearing the town's name, Pedro remembered it being where the plane had landed.

"That would be fine."

"Where are you headed?"

"As far north of Myrtle Beach, as possible."

"Oh? May I ask why?"

Pedro thought about telling the woman, but thinking she might freak out, he decided against it.

"Bad karma."

"Bad karma, eh? How bad?"

"Scary bad."

"What's your name?"

"Pedro."

"Mexican?"

"Yes."

"You speak pretty good English."

"I had an American mother."

"That explains it. What were you doing in Myrtle?"

"Working."

"You don't believe in long answers, do you?"

"The less you know, the better."

"Are you in trouble?"

"Not with the law."

"Then who?"

Pedro didn't answer.

"Look, my husband is a retired North Carolina State Trooper. If you need help, I'll take you to him. You tell him who or what has you so scared. He'll help you."

"I doubt anyone can help me."

"Okay! That's it! I'm calling my husband."

"No! I cannot have you mixed up in this. They'll kill you too."

"They? Who are they, Pedro?"

With undeniable fear washing over his face, he answered, "The Juarez cartel."

CHAPTER 43
... crawling with badges...

WEDNESDAY - OCTOBER 16, 2019 6:45AM

Ron was about to walk out the door when his phone rang.

Seeing it was Braddock, he answered, "What's up, Jim?"

"Just received a call from the North Carolina State Police. They report a retired trooper's wife picked up a guy walking north on Route 17."

"And?"

"The guy claims he escaped from the Juarez cartel just before they were about to cremate him."

"Holy shit!"

"My words, exactly. They are bringing him here."

"How soon before he arrives?"

"He'll be here by 7:30."

Hearing that, Ron replied, "Jesus Christ! I'll be there in fifteen minutes. Call Pond!"

****

Phil watched as Chuck and Murphy removed Luiz's body from the truck and carried it into the structure housing the crematory.

Although he couldn't see what they were doing, it didn't take a genius to figure it out.

Five minutes later, puffs of smoke from a roof vent told him all he needed to know.

Leaving his window perch, he made his way downstairs and out to the crematory. He wanted to thank them for not following orders.

As he entered the crematory, he saw Chuck and Murphy sitting on small stools, watching the smaller oven.

"I wasn't Luiz's biggest fan, but I think you guys did the right thing. Your secret is safe with me."

Startled by Phil's entrance and shocked by his statement, Chuck asked, "What the hell are you talking about, Phil?"

Understanding their need for denial, Phil nodded his head, saying, "Brett called me and told me what he ordered you to do. He asked that I watch and make sure you do it. All I can say is, I'm glad you didn't."

"So, you're going to tell Brett we followed orders."

"Yes. I couldn't have stood by and watch you put Luiz in the oven alive. He didn't deserve to die like that."

"Okay, Phil," said Chuck. "We appreciate your silence."

"No problem."

"Look, Phil, we still need to catch our runaway. Have you guys completed checking the road to the right?"

"We have about a mile remaining."

"Get out there and finish the job. When you're done, come back here, and clean this oven. Dump any remains, teeth, and bones, out in the woods."

"What about you and Murph?"

"We're driving the truck to the end of the road. I'm going to park somewhere on Route 17 where we can watch the intersection. If he's hiding in the woods and thinks we're gone, he might make a break for it. If he does, we'll get him. When you finish up here, come join us."

"Okay, Chuck. We'll see you in about an hour."

They watched Phil scurry out the door in search of the others.

"Can we trust him, Chuck?"

"Our runner has been in the wind for six plus hours, Murph. I'm guessing he's told the law where we are and they are on their way. We need to move!"

"What about Phil and the others?"

"I suspect this place will be crawling with badges within the hour."

"But you told Phil to meet…"

"I know what I told Phil."

"Oh, I see. You expect the law to eliminate Brett's canary."

"Get in the truck, Murph. We need to move."

✱✱✱✱✱✱✱✱✱✱✱✱✱

"Is he here yet?"

"Not yet, Ron. They're ten minutes out."

Ron, checking his watch, saw it was 7:16.

"What do you know, Jim?"

Before Jim could answer, Tim came through the door, asking, "Is he here yet?"

"Look around the room, partner. Do you see any Mexicans?"

"No donuts for you, smartass."

"You stopped for donuts?" asked Braddock.

Tim, looking like a deer caught in the headlights, responded, "Are you kidding, Captain? Do you think I'd stop for donuts when something this important is happening?"

Ron smiled at Tim's double-talk where he neither denied nor admitted he had stopped. Although he agreed with Braddock's assertion of non-professionalism on Tim's part, deep down, he hoped Tim had picked up a couple of éclairs.

Braddock's phone rang.

Answering the call, he muttered, "Bring him to my office." As he hung up the phone, he said, "He's here."

CHAPTER 44
... closed caskets."

WEDNESDAY - OCTOBER 16, 2019 7:30AM

He looked as if someone had dragged him through the mud when they brought him into Braddock's office.

Dried blood, from scratches he gained from bushes and tree limbs while scrambling through the woods, marked his face and arms. He may have been 24, but the past 12 hours made him look more like 40. Looking drawn and haggard, like he hadn't slept in days, he limped to a chair and sat.

Ron, scrutinizing the man from head to toe, noticed the smallest sign of a facial tic. It was not an uncommon trait when a person has had a traumatic ordeal.

Braddock, sitting across from Pedro, said, "Tell us what happened, amigo."

"I speak English," was the man's reply.

"Good," responded Braddock. "What can you tell us?"

"I can tell you the location of the crematory."

"Where!" shouted Ron.

Startled, Pedro turned his head toward the abrupt voice to his left. The man asking had leaned toward him. His eyes were full of fire.

"It's about eight miles down Ledbetter Road. There were six men looking for me when I escaped."

"Where's Ledbetter Road, Tim?"

Before Tim pulled his phone from his pocket, Pedro said, "It's north off of Route 17."

Ron looked at Braddock.

Braddock said one word: "Go!"

Ron and Tim scrambled to their Tahoe, with Tim taking the wheel. The vehicle shot out of the FBI parking lot and headed north on 17. Within 30 seconds, Tim had the SUV, with lights flashing and siren wailing, coursing up Route 17 at 75 mph.

Ron dialed in Ledbetter Road on his phone's GPS but got nothing!

"It doesn't show, Tim!"

"What state did you enter?"

"Damn, I'm an idiot," screamed Ron as he reentered the road name and changed the state to North Carolina.

"Shit! It's 24 miles on our left. I'll call the state troopers and have them block the entrance."

Waiting until Ron finished his call, Tim asked, "What's happening with the revelation you had in the middle of the night?"

"Damn, I forgot about that. I'll call Heather."

A moment later, Heather answered, *"Ron?"*

"Listen Heather, I want you to call Angie Jones, at the Tax Assessor's Office. Ask her to crosscheck sales or leases where James Henry was the buyer, not the seller. Once you have the list, crosscheck it against the list we have of his known properties. Call me with the addresses which are not on our list."

"Anything else you need, tiger?"

"Yes, there is!"

"Ooh là là, and what might that be?" she asked with an unseen smile.

"I want you to call all licensed property inspectors. Ask them if they have ever worked for James Henry. If they have, ask them for addresses of the properties."

"Okay..."

Ron hung up.

Taking a glance at the speedometer and seeing it reading 98, Ron asked, "How much further?"

Tim, checking the trip odometer, replied, "Four miles."

"How long?"

"ETA… about two-and-a-half minutes."

Tim's estimated arrival time was 15 seconds off.

A half-dozen North Carolina State Troopers were at the scene with two of their cruisers parked in a wedged position at the entrance to Ledbetter Road.

Ron, leaving the Tahoe, asked, "Who is in charge?"

"That would be me, Sergeant Nichols," answered an approaching mountain of a man.

"Has anyone tried to leave, sergeant?"

"No, sir. One of my guys arrived about a minute after we got the call. So he's been in position for 17 minutes. The rest of us arrived within five minutes of him."

"Okay, here's the deal, sergeant. We believe there are six heavily armed men down this road where a crematorium is located."

"I know it, sir. The county named the road after the owner. He's the only inhabitant on the road. I'd say his place is seven, maybe eight miles. The house sits on the right."

"Then we'll drive seven miles and stop. No lights, no sirens. We'll go the rest of the way on foot. In case someone slips by us, leave two officers at the seven-mile mark. Also, call the Sheriff's Department and ask them to maintain this roadblock."

"Yes, sir," said the sergeant.

"Do you have any snipers in this crowd, sergeant?"

"I have Corporal Oliva. He's not an official sniper. But the boy can shoot."

"We'll take the lead, sergeant. Have your man follow us. If we run into this crowd, some may try to escape to the woods. Tell the corporal not to let it happen."

"Yes, sir."

As they returned to the Tahoe, Tim asked, "Are you positive you want us to take the lead?"

"Not really, but we are... the F-B-I. We can't look weak. Bad for our image."

"Do you know what else is bad for our image, Ron?"

"What's that, Tim?'

"Bullet holes in our bodies, or worse, our heads."

"Why worse?"

"If our heads get blown off ... closed caskets."

"Good point. If we get into a shootout, keep your head down."

"I'll do better than that," said Tim. "I'll hide where nobody will see me. Behind you."

"We'll rehash that comment come annual review time."

CHAPTER 45
"...easy pickin's."

After reaching the seven-mile mark, they abandoned their vehicles and, leaving a pair of officers behind, continued on foot.

There were seven of them; Ron, Tim, Sergeant Nichols, Corporal Oliva, and three other troopers.

As they walked, Ron received a text from the County Sheriff's office saying they had four units at the entrance to Ledbetter Road.

"Fellas, I don't know what might be waiting for us up ahead. But, if possible, I'd like to take someone alive."

Ron had no sooner finished speaking when they heard a vehicle approaching. The road curved a 100 yards from their location, preventing them from having a visual.

"Take positions on either side of the road, gentlemen," barked Ron. "Agent Pond and I will remain here."

"Damn, if you don't have some screwy ideas, Ron. Another bad image for us is getting run over by a car."

"Draw your weapon, Tim, and if they don't stop, riddle the windshield."

"Sure thing, partner. I'll also riddle the gas tank as the car is passing over my crushed body."

As the car exited the curve, the driver, seeing two men with weapons drawn standing in the road, slammed on the brakes, and spun the vehicle to his left.

The car came to an abrupt dust-filled halt with its right-side facing the posse of FBI agents and North Carolina State Troopers.

Its' four occupants scrambled from the vehicle's left side and took defensive positions behind it.

"FBI!" shouted Ron. "Drop your weapons and step out from behind the vehicle."

"How many are there?" asked a now sweating Phil.

"I see seven," answered one man.

"Have you got a clear shot?"

"Those two assholes standing in the road look like easy pickin's."

"Then take the bastards out!" screamed Phil.

Raising up with his AK-47, the man took dead aim at the two FBI agents. He never had a chance of pulling the trigger. Corporal Oliva sent a high-velocity bullet his way which took half his head off.

"Nice shot, Corporal," said Ron. "We owe you one."

"I'm thinking it might be a good idea to abandon the road, Ron."

"Not a bad idea, partner. After you," said Ron, nodding toward the left side of the road.

"Damn!" hissed Phil.

"Hank! Red! We can't stay here," said Phil to the remaining two men. "We need to get to the woods. I'll make a run for it while the two of you provide covering fire. If I make it, Red and I will provide cover for Hank. Then we'll both provide cover for Red. Got it?"

Both men nodded they understood, but neither looked as if they approved of Phil's plan.

Seeing the doubt in Red's eyes, Phi shouted, "What? Would you rather stay here and shoot it out against all their firepower? Our best chance is to get into the woods and hide."

"We could surrender, Phil," replied Red.

"Surrender? If you surrender, the cartel will kill you and everyone in your family. Go ahead, surrender. But wait until I make it into the woods. Okay?"

"We won't surrender, Phil," voiced Hank. "You go. I'll be right behind you."

As Hank and Red provided a blanket of cover, Phil made a successful run for the woods.

Once the cover firing ended, Corporal Oliva, seeing an opportunity, took aim at one target and fired. The bullet passed through two car windows and struck Hank in the chest, killing him instantly.

Red immediately threw his gun over the car and into the road, yelling, "I surrender! Don't shoot! I'm coming out."

Phil, who made it safely into the woods and hearing Red surrendering, put himself into position to send a burst from his AK-47. Four bullets ripped into Red's body as he was walking around the car with his hands up.

"Surrender, hell!" muttered Phil, as he ran deep into the woods.

"One got away!" yelled Sergeant Nichols.

"Get the bastard!" yelled Ron. "Alive!"

"I've called for a chopper, Ron, and dogs."

"Good thinking, Tim."

Phil had run 200 yards into the woods before stopping to catch his breath. He thought for a moment about the direction he was running and correctly calculated he had run south.

"Chuck and Murph," Phil hissed. "Those bastards left us hanging out to dry. Odds are, I'm a dead man, but those two pricks won't be around much longer either."

Pulling his phone from his pocket, he called Brett.

"Hello."

"Brett, this Phil."

"You sound winded."

"Yeah, that's because the law showed up. All our men are dead. I'm guessing the runaway told them the crematory's location. I'm hiding in the woods, but if they get dogs, I'm done."

"What about Luiz?"

"That's what I'm calling you about. Chuck and Murph killed Luiz and put him in an oven. Then they left us behind. I think they wanted me dead because I knew what they did with Luiz."

"Are you telling me they didn't burn him alive?"

"Yeah. Mustard shot him and then they cooked him."

"Is that so? Hmm, I guess I need to…"

Sounds of gunfire interrupted Brett's reply.

"They're on me!" screamed Phil.

Brett, thinking on his feet, screamed into the phone, *"Hang up and get rid of the phone!"*

Phil, although under heavy fire, did what he was told. Hanging up, he tossed the phone and ran.

He hadn't run over 20 yards when he heard footsteps closing in from behind. Phil turned to fire, but three shots turned his head into hamburger. He was as dead as Grandma Moses before hitting the ground.

"Damn, Tim," said a late-arriving Ron, "we needed this prick alive."

"Couldn't help it, partner. He was about to spray those two troopers with his AK-47. It was him or them. I chose him."

"You made the right decision," confirmed Ron.

"I thought so," agreed Tim, "and I'll bet a dollar to a donut, the troopers would agree."

"No bet," replied Ron. "Now that they know we have the runaway worker, they'll try to retreat to Mexico. Our problem is, we don't know from where."

"Let's head back to the office. Maybe our worker knows more than he thinks."

"Yeah, and maybe we've heard from Angie Jones."

They were about to leave when one of the troopers saved by Tim's marksmanship approached.

"Agent Lee?"

"Yes."

"I saw that fella tossing something away. I searched the vicinity and found this phone."

"Good job, trooper. What's your name?"

"Corporal James Benton, sir."

"I'll put a word in to your captain, Benton."

"Thank you, sir."

Ron nodded and turning to Tim, said, "I wonder who our dead guy was calling?"

"Hit the call back button, partner. Let's see who answers."

The phone rang twice.

"Phil! Are you okay?"

"I don't think Phil's up to talking right now," answered Ron. "Half his face is missing. With whom do I have the honor of speaking with?"

"Who's this?"

"I'm Special Agent Ron Lee of the FBI. I'm guessing you represent the cartel. Yes?"

Click!

****

While Ron and Tim stood in the woods talking on Phil's phone, two situations were about to unfold. The first had Chuck and Murph heading to Brett's office. The second situation had two passengers, Lisa Cardone, and a hitman, who people in the business called Mr. Clean, debarking from a private plane at the Myrtle Beach airport.

Death was in the wind.

CHAPTER 46
"...some parting words..."

Hearing the unexpected knock on his villa door, a shaken Brett yelled, "Come in!"

Murphy, followed by Chuck, entered looking guilty.

Chuck, seeing Brett's face, sensed something was wrong.

"So? How did it go?"

"The runaway is in the wind, Brett. If he hasn't hooked up with the law, you can bet it won't be long. I suggest we clear out of here as soon as possible."

"Excellent advice, Chuck. I've already taken steps in that direction. What about Luiz? Did he suffer?"

"He did," answered Murphy.

"In the fire?"

"Yep. Just like you wanted. We cooked him alive. I ain't never heard screams like that before."

"What about the other four men?"

"They were scouring the woods to the west of the house when we left. They should be along in about an hour," suggested Chuck.

"What do you need us to do, boss?" asked Mustard.

"Chuck, go to the warehouse and supervise the removal of the remaining cash."

"Where is it going?"

"Back to a half-dozen selective storage locations."

"Does Juan Pablo know the situation?"

"No, Chuck, he doesn't. I'm going to call him tonight when Beltrán arrives. Together we can decide about the rest of the money."

"What do you need me to do, boss?" asked Murphy.

"I have a job for you, Mustard. We have a problem needing immediate attention."

"I'll be on my way if you don't need me, Brett."

"Okay, Chuck. Keep me posted on the progress of getting our money back into storage."

"Oh, before I go, what about the workers?"

"We'll release them into the general population."

"Good," agreed Chuck as he left.

Brett poured himself a drink but didn't bother to offer one to Murphy.

"Okay, boss. Who needs outing?"

"I spoke with Phil just before you came in, Murph."

"Oh? He's back?"

"No, neither Phil nor anyone else I sent with Luiz is coming back, Mustard. They are all dead."

"Damn!"

"Phil had some parting words though."

"Oh?"

"Yeah, he said he saw you shoot Luiz and then throw him in the crematorium. Is that what happened?"

Mustard's tongue couldn't move. He became fidgety. Standing, he paced in circles around the room.

Brett let him sweat before saying, "It wasn't your idea, was it?"

"No! No, no, it was… Chuck. He didn't have any problem killing Luiz, but…"

"He didn't want to fry him alive?"

"Yeah. He didn't. He talked me into going along with him. I shot Luiz in the head, and together we tossed him into the oven."

"What about Phil?"

"He saw me shoot Luiz. I'm guessing he knew we were supposed to throw Luiz in the fire alive, but he sided with our decision and he promised not to spill the beans."

"He probably wouldn't have, but you, knowing the law would show up, left him hanging."

"Yeah, it was Chuck's idea. He didn't feel comfortable about Phil knowing the truth, but he didn't want to kill him. He figured if the law showed up, they'd do the job for us."

"Chuck was right."

"Now what? Are you going to kill me?"

"Kill you? No way! But I want Chuck out of the picture."

"When?"

"As soon as you kill two FBI agents who will probably be here soon."

"Soon? How soon?"

"Good question. I don't think the runaway can direct the FBI to the warehouse. However, the FBI is on to us. They could show up in the next hour, or it could be a week. I'm thinking we need to disappear within 24 hours."

"So the plan you laid out a few weeks ago, it's how you want it done?"

"Yeah, and when it's done, put Chuck to sleep."

Mustard, halfway out the door, stopped and turning to Brett, said, "There's something you should know, boss."

"What's that, Murph?"

"It's Marcia."

"What about her?"

"Chuck told me she and Mike, whenever they get a chance, are spending afternoons at the DoubleTree."

Brett's face turned ashen. Hate filled his eyes.

Mustard, recognizing Brett's look, knew Mike and Marcia were all but dead.

CHAPTER 47
"... Mr. Clean?"

The plane, carrying just two passengers, touched down at the Myrtle Beach Airport just shy of five hours after leaving Portland, Oregon.

Both passengers disembarked and walked to a waiting car Sheila had reserved.

The man named Ramon drove, while Lisa sat in the backseat.

His name was Ramon Baez. His profession: Contract Killer.

With Brett taking the company's muscle with him to Myrtle Beach, Lisa, needing a substitute, hired Ramon.

Ramon had an impressive track record, including well over 20 kills, most on the west coast. Those kills, so efficient and deadly, earned him the nickname "Mr. Clean."

"Where to, Mrs. Cardone?"

"The address is 8500 Costa Verde Drive."

After entering the address into the vehicle's GPS, Ramon announced, "It's 10 miles away, Mrs. Cardone. The GPS says it's a 22 minute drive."

They arrived at 10:07.

"I don't know his villa, Ramon. Go inside and ask."

Minutes later, Ramon returned, saying, "Villa 865. It's the penthouse suite."

"Of course it is. Take me there."

Pulling up to a lavish-looking building, Lisa exited the car, saying, "Are you prepared, Ramon?"

"I am," answered the hitman, while patting his shoulder holster.

As they walked toward the entrance, Murphy, on his way to the warehouse, was exiting.

"Mrs. Cardone! What brings you here?"

Ignoring Murphy's question, Lisa says, "Murph, this is…"

"I know who he is, Mrs. Cardone. How are you doing… Mr. Clean?"

"I'm doing fine, Mustard. How about you?"

"It's been busy."

"So I hear."

"It's going to get a lot busier in the next 24 hours."

"Same here."

"All right, boys, you've had your back-and-forth. I need to see Brett."

"Catch you later, maybe, Ramon?"

"Anything is possible, Mustard."

Murph watched the pair enter the building, thought about following them, but decided against it and made his way to his car.

As he drove to the warehouse, his thoughts bounced around between how he would kill Chuck and wondering why Lisa had come to Myrtle Beach.

Lisa rang the doorbell, and a moment later Brett opened the door.

"Lisa! What in the world? Damn, it's great to see you, my love."

"Don't give me any of your bullshit, Brett. I hear you've been tapping Marcia, and god knows who else, while enjoying your time in this so-called paradise."

"What!" cried out Brett. "Where did you get that idea?"

"A little birdie told me. Someone who you shouldn't have trusted."

"Well, they are lying. In fact, Murphy just told me Marcia and Mike are having daily conjugal meetings."

"I bet that news pissed you off. I wouldn't doubt you're having thoughts of having them killed. Well, don't concern yourself about Marcia. I'll take care of her."

"I see you brought Ramon."

"Oh? You know Ramon?"

"I do. Do you have business here in Myrtle Beach, Ramon?"

"Matter of fact, he does, Brett," announced Lisa. "He's here to put a bullet in your head."

"You're kidding!" said a seemingly unconcerned Brett. "Are you saying you came all this way to kill me?"

"You've been banging my so-called best friend. How long has it been, Brett?"

"Oh, I must admit, it's been quite some time now. But would it matter, Lisa, if it were a day or a year?"

"No, I guess it wouldn't. You disgust me. Kill this bastard, Ramon!"

Ramon didn't move.

"What are you waiting for? Kill him!"

"I like Ramon's nickname," said Brett. "Mr. Clean. It has a nice ring. Don't you agree, Lisa?"

Lisa whipped around to face Ramon.

"Sorry, ma'am, but long before you hired me, Mr. Cardone hired me."

"What!"

Turning to Brett, she screamed, "You son-of-a-bitch! I'll kill you myself!"

Brett, laughing at her, replied, "One of us is going to die, Lisa, but it won't be me."

"Oh, really. Let's see about that!"

Pulling from her purse an engraved dagger Brett had given her for a 10th anniversary, she charged with the weapon held high.

Brett's laughing demeanor turned to rage. Grabbing Lisa's raised arm, he pulled it down and behind her back.

The dagger slipping from her hand, fell to the floor, and came to rest under a coffee table.

Lisa screamed in agony as he pushed her arm upward, almost to the point of snapping it at the shoulder.

Brett, his eyes flaring, his teeth clenched, grabbed Lisa's hair, ran her across the room, out onto the balcony, and threw her over the railing.

Her screams lasted for nine floors, before halted by a poolside table umbrella.

Brett and Ramon watched from above as people gathered around the impaled woman.

As they stepped back inside, Brett said, "Thanks for the call, Ramon."

"The woman was a bitch, Brett. She killed a couple right in front of the workers because the husband was stealing about an ounce of cocaine a week and selling it. She was a heartless bitch who loved the power you gave her."

"Believe me, I know."

"She was capable of anything."

"Almost anything," corrected Brett. "It seems she couldn't fly."

CHAPTER 48
"We have a body."

WEDNESDAY - OCTOBER 16, 2019 - 10:55AM

When they arrived at the scene, Myrtle Beach detectives Ken Phillips and Avery Calhoun saw, to their collective relief, the area cordoned off with the proverbial yellow crime scene tape.

The detectives estimated seventy-plus people stood outside the tape gaping at the impaled facedown woman, whose innards, much like a tangled hose, dangled from her waist.

Dripping blood soaked the torn umbrella, and had covered most of the table's top, with some puddling on the poolside macadam.

The woman's open eyes had retained in death a crazed look of horror, and her wide-open mouth appeared as if it were emitting silent screams.

A Sergeant Rush approached the detectives, saying, "I have men checking all rooms above the crime scene area, detectives."

"Did anyone see what happened?" asked Calhoun.

"No such luck, I'm afraid. Witnesses said they heard screams and then, 'thud' and there she was."

"Did you find any identification?"

"None."

"Cameras?"

"We're locking those down as we speak, detectives."

"Excellent work, sergeant," said Calhoun.

A call came in on Rush's mic.

"Found something on the floor in the penthouse villa, Sarge."

"Talk to me."

"It's a dagger. It has an inscription that reads, 'Lisa, I'll love you always. Happy 10th. Brett.'"

"Print the body and the dagger," instructed Phillips.

"Suicide?" asked Avery of his partner.

"Not a chance, Ave. Look where she landed. If she had jumped, she would have landed closer to the building. No, someone, I imagine, very strong and pissed off, threw her overboard. I dare say, we have us a murder, partner!"

Rush's mic sounded again.

"Sarge."

"Yeah, officer. What is it?"

"We have a body."

"In the penthouse?"

"No. Seventh floor. Villa 720."

****

30 Minutes Earlier

Leaving the penthouse suite, Brett and Ramon made their way to the elevator. After stepping into the elevator car, Brett pushed the button for the 7th floor.

"We need to make this stop, Ramon."

"The cops will be here soon, Brett."

"I know. This shouldn't take long."

The elevator doors opened and the two men made their way to Villa 716. Brett knocked. Hearing no reply, he knocked again. Again, no answer.

"She's not here," he muttered. "Let's see what's happening in room 720."

A knock on Villa 720s door brought a quick reply.

"Yeah, who is it?"

"Brett."

The door opened and Mike said, "What's up, boss?"

"Where's Marcia?"

"Marcia? I don't have a clue where she is. Did you check her room?"

"Yes, but there was no answer. I thought she might be with you."

"Why would you think that, Brett?"

"It was just a hunch, seeing the two of you work together."

Seeing a man standing to Brett's right, Mike asked, "Who is this guy? What does he do?"

The two men stepped inside with Ramon closing the door behind him.

"This is Ramon."

"Hello, Ramon."

Ramon answered with an ever so slight nod.

"I've been told, Mike, you and Marcia have been having an affair. Is it true?"

Mike, normally unflappable, fell into desperate denials.

"It's a lie, Brett!"

"Is it, Mike? So you're denying playing 'hide the wiener' with Marcia at the Doubletree?"

Mike's eyes told all. They couldn't hide he was lying and, in concert with knowing what was to come, they also expressed his impending doom.

Brett, seeing Mike's reaction, said, "I thought so. I'm very disappointed in you, Mike."

"Brett, I'm sorry, but…"

Holding up his hand, Brett said, "Say no more, Mike. You asked what Ramon does. I'll let him show you."

Turning toward the door, he gave Ramon a slight nod.

Ramon stepped forward, removed a silenced weapon from his holster, pointed at Mike's head and pulled the trigger twice.

The impact threw Mike's body ten feet backwards, with large portions of his brain going yet another ten. Stopping only when splattering against a wall.

"Now we can go, Ramon."

"What about the woman?"

"We'll find her and when we do, I'll kill her myself."

It was nearing 10:40 when they left the hotel and walked to Ramon's rental car. They were opening its doors when two police units, with lights flashing, pulled into the hotel's parking lot.

They watched the officers leave their vehicles and rush into the hotel's lobby.

As Ramon drove from the parking lot, Brett sighed, saying, "Ahh, yes, it's true. Timing is everything."

CHAPTER 49
"Do I hear a drumroll?"

WEDNESDAY - OCTOBER 16, 2019 - 11:30AM

"What the hell is taking so long?" bellowed Ron. "We asked for that information hours ago!"

"Take it easy, Ron. They have a lot of files to search."

"Bullshit! It's only a ten second job for a damn computer."

"You're right, Ron, but I'm guessing they are checking the document archived files."

The phone rang.

Ron, moving like a gazelle, answered the phone with a thundering, "Tell me you found something!"

"What the hell? I wasn't even thinking of calling you, Ron. But I just received a call from a pair of Myrtle Beach detectives and thought you'd be interested."

"Bill? Baxter?"

"Yeah, it's me. I take it you were expecting someone else?"

"Yeah, we were. Sorry, Bill, what do you need?"

"Nothing, but I have something for you."

"Spit it out!"

"Someone tossed an unidentified woman from the penthouse floor at the Oceanfront Villas, this morning."

"Ouch, that had to hurt," responded Ron.

"Oh, no doubt about that, Ron. In fact, her landing made a big mess in the pool area. Her fall ended with her being impaled on an umbrella which, if you can imagine, makes opening the umbrella very difficult."

"Funny, Bill, but why is this important?"

"Be patient, Ron. There's more to tell."

"Well, don't make this a fucking novel, Bill. Get to the point."

"They found a dagger in the penthouse. Fingerprints on it matched those of the fallen angel. It had an inscription that read, 'Lisa, I'm yours forever, Love Brett.' We figure her name must be Lisa."

"Now that there is cracker-jack detective work," muttered Ron.

"You're an asshole, Ron."

"Why thank you, Bill. It was nice of you to say so."

"Oh, and they found a man, identified as Michael Carter from Portland, Oregon, shot to death in another villa."

"Are we going somewhere with this, Bill? It sounds to me like you have a love triangle gone wrong. So why call me?"

"It's not a love triangle, Ron. Hotel records show the guy in the penthouse, a Brett Cardone, leased five villas through December."

"When did he check in?"

"June first."

"I'm listening, Bill."

"The names attached to the other villas are, Michael Carter..."

"Your dead guy?"

"Yep!"

"I'd say we have a definite connection. Who else?"

Baxter continued, "... *Marcia Cole, Luiz Patrone...*"

"Hold it for a second, Bill," yelled Ron. "Tim, didn't our runaway mention a Luiz?"

"He did," agreed Tim.

"Coincidence?" asked Ron. "I think not. Sorry for the interruption, Bill. Please continue."

"The other two names, Chuck Delgato and Murphy Bortelli, are in our database. They are contract killers who do most of their work on the west coast."

"Pieces are coming together, Ron," voiced Tim.

Baxter continued, saying, *"Now cameras caught the woman being thrown off the roof, but they couldn't identify the guy doing the throwing."*

"Damn it, Bill, where are you going with this?"

"I'm getting there, Ron, but I need to build a foundation."

"Then get on with it!"

"Okay, here goes. Although the penthouse shot was too fuzzy to make a clear identification, the cameras in the lobby and parking lot gave us clear photos of two men."

"Do I hear a drumroll?"

"One is Ramon Baez."

"He's a contract killer. Why is he in town?"

"Don't hold my feet to the fire on this, Ron, but maybe he's here to ply his trade."

"And you dare call me an asshole," said Ron with a hint of sarcasm. "What about the other guy?"

"I can't say for sure, but we're thinking it's this Brett Cardone guy. He might be your well-kept secret cartel fella."

"Send us a photo, Bill. We'll match it against descriptions our runaway gave us. Did you capture a photo of the car plate?"

"We did. They found the vehicle parked near the convention center. No prints."

"Yeah, well, that's to be expected. Before we hang up, I want to apologize for being so belligerent."

"I expected nothing less."

"Screw you, Baxter. Send me the photos."

"You got it. Keep me posted. Goodbye."

Tim, having heard the entire conversation, asked, "Does any of this crap we're dealing with make sense to you, Ron?"

"You know, partner, from day one, it's been like trying to put puzzle pieces together in the dark."

"With the pieces upside down as well." added Tim.

"True. Everything we knew, was pure supposition. But, with what Bill told us, things are making sense."

Without a knock, their office door opened, and Heather entered the room. Holding up a large envelope, she said, "Someone from the Tax Assessor's office just dropped this off."

Ron leaped from his chair and grabbed the envelope from Heather's hands like it was the last éclair on earth.

Tearing open the envelope, he extracted a single sheet of paper. He read the handwritten note aloud.

"Special Agent Lee, here are all the addresses of properties sold to Mr. James Henry in the past 15 years. Yours, Angie Jones."

"How many, Ron?"

"It looks like two dozen, give or take. Where's our list of the properties we checked out?"

Tim, opening his desk drawer, removed a sheet of paper.

"Start calling them out, Tim."

Five minutes later Ron's list had all addresses checked off but two.

"We have two, Tim."

"Where are they?"

"One is in Little River and the other is on Oak Street."

"Oak Street, downtown Myrtle Beach?"

"Yeah, 604 Oak Street."

"Would they be crazy enough to operate in downtown Myrtle Beach?"

"Crazy is sometimes mistaken for shrewd, Tim."

"Okay, so which one, if either, is the right one?"

"If this Cardone guy is leaving town, he's going to make sure whatever money is remaining, doesn't get stolen or lost."

"I'm sure Juan Pablo would expect nothing less," added Tim.

"Agreed," said Ron. "They found the rental car near the convention center, which is much closer to Oak Street than to Little River."

"I Googled it, partner. It's 1.3 miles from the convention center."

"That nails it, Tim. I say you and I check out Oak Street. We'll send another team to Little River."

"Sounds like a plan, Ron."

"Let's mount up. Be sure to wear a vest. These guys won't go down without a fight."

CHAPTER 50
"You're so predictable..."

Just about the time Mr. Clean was ending Michael Carter's career, Murph walked into the warehouse office. Seeing Chuck drinking a cup of coffee, he asked, "Any coffee left?"

"Plenty," answered Chuck. "I just made this pot."

"Good! I'll have a couple of Ho-Hos with mine," said Murphy, as he opened the office fridge and removed a 2-pack of his favorite snack.

"How many Ho-Hos have you eaten today?"

"These will be my third and fourth."

"How do you stay skinny eating all those calories?"

"Must be all the exercise I do."

"I've never seen you exercising, Murph."

"I exercise when you're not looking."

"Sometimes you're hilarious, Murph. Tell me, why did Brett ask you to hang around?"

"Oh, he wants me to take care of Phil when he gets back," lied Murphy, as he consumed a Ho-Ho in two bites.

"That shouldn't be too difficult, being Phil is most likely dead already."

"Those were my exact thoughts, Chuck."

"Hmm, what else did you two talk about?"

"He wants us to stick around and take care of those two FBI agents he mentioned a few weeks ago."

"I hope he doesn't want us to carry out his lame-brain plan he went over at the meeting a few weeks back."

"Sorry, but he does."

"Ain't no FBI agent going to fall for that dumb-ass ploy, Murph."

"I agree. Do you have any better advice?"

"Yeah, I do. If you're fond of sleeping with both eyes closed, I recommend you not kill an FBI agent. Otherwise, their buddies will hound you to your grave, but only if they don't kill you first."

"That sounds like the same thing, Chuck," said Murph, after finishing his second Ho-Ho, and washing it down with a gulp of coffee.

"I guess you're right," replied Chuck.

"Well, if we don't kill those agents, and Phil won't need killing, I'll need to move on to Brett's third order."

"Which is?"

"Killing you," answered Murph, while extracting his Glock from his shoulder holster and targeting Chuck's chest.

"Why does he want me dead?" asked Chuck with an outward calm.

"Because we didn't fry Luiz alive."

"Did you tell him?"

"No. It seems Phil called it in. I guess he thought we betrayed him."

"How come you're getting a pass?"

"I don't think I am."

"How's that?"

"Mr. Clean is in town."

"Ramon? Here?"

"Yep. I ran into him and Mrs. Cardone as I was leaving the hotel."

"Lisa's here already, eh?"

"What's that supposed to mean? You don't sound surprised."

"I'm not. I made a call to a friend. Told him Brett was screwing every broad he came in contact with. He passed it on to Lisa."

"Damn, she's here to kill Brett."

"That was the idea."

"Well, to make things even, I gave Brett the lowdown about Marcia and Mike."

"Why did you do that, Murph! That's a death sentence for them both!"

"I thought it might gain me some favor."

"Damn," sighed Chuck. "I hope Lisa kills Brett before he has Marcia killed."

"Why do you seem so laid back, Chuck? You're about to die."

"Oh, I'm just waiting for it to kick in. It should be any moment now."

"For what... to... kick... what the ... hell..."

"Hey, Murph. You don't look all that well," said Chuck, with feigned concern. "Is something wrong... partner?"

Murphy, dropping his gun on the desk, clutched his throat, saying, "I... can't ... breathe."

The eaten Ho Hos, soaked in coffee, erupted from Mustard's mouth, across the desk and onto the floor. He staggered to a stance and lunged toward Chuck who remained seated, drinking his coffee, while smiling.

"You... poisoned... me!"

"I did, Murph. It was the Ho Hos. You're so predictable. I knew if you had a cup of coffee, you'd eat those things. I warned you they would kill you some day. But wait, Murph, Don't die yet. I have a surprise ending."

Murphy, now convulsing, collapsed to the floor, holding his throat, gasping for air.

Chuck stood, put down his coffee cup, took a few steps around the vomited Ho-Hos, and took a stance over the dying Murphy.

"Here's a taste of your own medicine, Mustard."

Drawing his muted weapon, Chuck took aim at Murphy's right eye.

"Slight difference though, Murph. I'm doing the first one while you're still alive."

Chuck pulled the trigger and Murphy's right eye turned into an erupting red hole while a pool of blood appeared from under his head.

Although Murphy was already standing in a line in hell, Chuck addressed his dead partner with, "Here's another, you sick puppy!"

The Glock popped and Murphy's left eye disappeared.

Now at peace with himself, Chuck was straddling Murph's body, unscrewing the silencer from his weapon, when the office door swung open and a screaming Marcia yelled, "Chuck! What the hell have you done!"

CHAPTER 51
"... Mr. Cardone's bidding."

"You need to disappear from here, Marcia."

"Why?"

"Brett plans to have you killed."

"What are you talking about?"

"Murphy told Brett about you and Mike."

"Omigod! I need to warn Mike."

"You can call him, Marcia, but I doubt he's in any shape to answer."

"What's that supposed to mean?"

Chuck, ignoring Marcia's question, said, "Let me get you out of here before... oh, shit! Too late."

Turning around, Marcia sees Brett and a man she didn't recognize entering the building.

"Who's the man with Brett?"

"They call him, Mr. Clean. His actual name is Ramon, and he, like me, is a contract killer. He's here to kill us both, although I would think Brett wants to kill you himself, for obvious reasons. I'm guessing Mike is already dead."

"You think he killed Mike!"

"I do. Mike was in the hotel. I doubt they would have left without killing him. I'm assuming, since she's not in the immediate picture, they have killed Lisa as well."

"Lisa? Is she here?"

"Murph, before I killed him, told me he saw her and Mr. Clean at the hotel."

"Why would she come to Myrtle Beach?"

"To kill Brett."

"Why would she kill Brett?"

"Because, I informed her Brett was humping every woman he could."

"Including me?"

"I'm afraid so."

"What should we do?"

"I'll meet them and try to lead them away from the office. Once you see I have them distracted, slip away."

"How?"

"Make your way toward the front door by hiding behind pallets. When the opportunity presents itself, exit the building and never look back."

"What about you?"

"Have you ever seen the tv show, Gunsmoke?"

"Yes."

"Well, I'm hoping to be Matt Dillion. He never lost a showdown."

Chuck, moving to the desk where Murphy had sat, picked up Murphy's weapon and handed it to Marcia, saying, "Do you know how to use this?"

Marcia, shattered after hearing of Mike's probable death, lied, and said, "Yes," then whispered, "Good luck, Chuck, and thank you."

Leaving the office, Chuck turned off the lights as he went, making it near impossible, from the outside, to see anything inside the darkened office.

Brett and Ramon were talking with a guard when Chuck approached.

"Chuck! I was just asking Randy where you were."

"Just getting some pallets near the rear of the building moved upfront, boss."

"I'd like you to meet…"

"I know who Ramon is. His reputation precedes him."

"Glad to see you again, Chuck. I ran into Murphy earlier today. He said you guys have been busy."

"We have had our share. What's your business here?"

"I'm here to do Mr. Cardone's bidding."

"Hmm, and how much bidding have you done so far?"

Brett interrupted, saying, "Have you seen Murphy?"

"Can't say I have, boss."

"I see his car parked out front."

"Maybe he went for lunch. There's a place at the end of the street he likes. It's just a two-minute walk."

Brett, peering toward the office and seeing it dark, asked, "How come the office lights are out?"

"Damned if I know. I've been running around this warehouse ever since I left the hotel."

"Let's look," said a suspicious Brett. "Lead the way, Chuck."

As they approached the office, Chuck knew Brett had marked him for death. Once they stepped into the office, Ramon would execute him. Somehow, he couldn't let it happen.

He was getting desperate as each step brought them closer to the door. He determined his only option was to shoot them before Ramon shot him.

I need to be Matt Dillon; he thought. *Fast on the draw.*

Chuck was right. Brett, upon seeing Mustard's body, would order Ramon to shoot Chuck.

They were three steps from the office door when they heard, "FBI! EVERYONE DROP YOUR WEAPONS AND GET ON THE GROUND!"

CHAPTER 52
... rat-a-tat-tat...

WEDNESDAY - OCTOBER 16, 2019 - 12:30PM

Marcia, seeing the three men approaching, retreated until her back was flush against an office wall. After removing the safety, she used both hands to raise Murphy's Glock to a firing position.

Her intentions were to blow Brett's head to smithereens as soon as he walked through the door.

She wasn't sure whether it was to her chagrin or relief that he never passed through the doorway.

For reasons she didn't understand, they broke rank and took off running in all directions. Something had spooked them.

She took a step toward the door but stopped when hearing the distinct rat-a-tat-tat sound of machinegun fire.

Tim, carrying a submachine gun, was the first agent through the door. Ron, armed with a 12-gauge shotgun, was only a step behind.

Dozens of pallets, all loaded with 6-foot high containers, lined either side of the door, and like the cars of a freight train, extended throughout the warehouse.

After barging through the warehouse entrance, Ron and Tim found cover behind a container.

Three other agents, all heavily armed, followed, with two making it to cover.

The last man to enter, Agent Al Lambert, wasn't as fortunate.

Randy, the guard who Brett had spoken with just moments earlier, must have thought he needed to impress his boss. He open fired on the incoming agents, striking Lambert in both legs, before Tim's response almost cut him in half.

"Brody," yelled Ron to one of the FBI agents, "get Lambert outside. Call for an ambulance."

Two guards made the mistake of trying to gun down Brody. Ron's shotgun sent one to hell. Tim's machine gun sent the other.

Seeing the FBI's deadly response, the remaining guards dropped their weapons and fell to the floor with their hands tucked behind their heads.

Brett, standing behind a pallet some 20 feet from the office door, had his silver-plated .45 in his hand.

Seeing the guards throwing down their guns, he screamed, "Pick up your fucking weapons and take those bastards out!"

Not a single guard took his advice.

Enraged, Brett, seeing one guard lying just 15 feet away, shot him in the head. Then repeated his command, adding, "I'll kill you all if you don't pick up your weapons."

A guard, seeing Brett's work, made the mistake of grabbing his machine gun and coming up to a stance. He fired off a small burst before being torn apart by a fuselage of FBI fire.

No others tried to imitate the dead guard's foolish and irreversible decision.

Brett, knowing the others would no longer do his bidding, began looking for another way out.

Looking to his right, he saw three Mexican workers, their eyes filled with fear, huddled against a nearby pallet.

Brett, pointing his pistol at them, growled, "Come here!"

One worker shook his head and with a forceful tone of defiance, said, "No, senor!"

Brett shot him in the jaw, removing most of the man's face.

Another stood and ran, but he couldn't outrun Brett's bullet. The .45 slug ripped a hole in the man's back, killing him.

Seeing his two co-workers gunned down, the remaining worker, seeing Brett's gun trained on him, nodded, and with great reluctance, made his way to Brett's position.

Putting the gun to the man's head, Brett whispered, "You do exactly as I say or I'll blow your brains all over this warehouse. Comprender?"

"Sí, sí ," said the man, so overwrought with fear, his bladder failed him.

CHAPTER 53
"... priorities have changed."

WEDNESDAY - OCTOBER 16, 2019 - 12:40PM

"Who the hell is firing, Ron, and who are they shooting at?" asked Tim.

"The shooter is behind the container sitting just outside the office. Who he's shooting at is open for debate," answered Ron, "but it sure isn't us."

Almost on cue, two men, one short, one tall, and locked so close together they appeared almost as one, emerged from behind the container.

"Well, well," remarked Tim, "it appears we have a new situation."

Cardone was using the worker as a human shield. He had his left arm wrapped around the Mexican's neck while his right hand held a gun to the man's temple.

"I'll blow this man's head off if I have to. If you want him to live, stay clear of me as I walk out of here. Once I'm away, I'll release him unharmed," lied Brett, who thought nothing of taking a human life for little or no reason.

"What do you want to do, Ron? They could be in cahoots."

"I think not, Tim. I'm guessing the guy with the gun to his head is one of the money counters. Look at his eyes. He's scared to death."

"I see a better clue, Ron. Look at the front of his pants. He's wet himself. The guy is either genuinely scared or a hell of a method actor."

"My money is on the former," said Ron, then adding, "I believe the guy with the gun is Cardone."

"That means Ramon Baez is somewhere nearby," added Tim. "He, in case you need reminding, has nothing to lose."

"Agreed, partner. I don't think we'll be taking him alive."

"I hope to be alive when we don't," quipped Tim.

"Have I ever told you, your witty replies are a comfort during stressful times like these?"

"Thanks, Ron. I'll bring it up at my annual review."

"You should always hi-lite your strong point."

"You mean points."

"I said what I mean."

"We'll talk about this later, Ron. Now, how about informing this Cardone fella what his options are."

"You're not leaving the building, Cardone!" shouted Ron. "If you kill the hostage, you won't be far behind."

"Damn, Ron, I bet those words made the hostage feel all warm and fuzzy."

"I guess I could have been less direct. Chances are though, he no hablo inglés."

"Either I leave or this man is dead," responded Brett. "Your choice, Agents Lee and Pond."

"He knows us, Ron. What's up with that?"

"Good question. Let's try to find out."

"I take it you're in charge of this operation, Brett. I doubt Juan Pablo will be happy with your work. Did he tell you to kill us while you were here?"

"He did, but he didn't make it a priority," answered Brett. "However, priorities have changed."

"I don't think the odds favor you, Cardone. It would be in your best interest to free the hostage and surrender."

"I don't see it that way, Agent Lee. I'm not alone."

"You're looking kinda alone to me, Cardone," cracked Tim.

Cardone, losing his composure, screamed, "I want you chickenshits to get up off the floor and earn your fucking money!"

None of the floor-hugging guards twitched a muscle.

"It looks like the chickenshits are just that, Brett," said a snickering Ron. "Those boys have thrown in the towel. You, and all others hiding behind these containers, might consider doing likewise."

"Ain't gonna happen, Agent Lee."

"If that's so, your only option is death. It's not much of an option, in my book."

"I'll take my chances."

"You have two chances, Brett. Living or dying."

"If I die, then this little fella will die too."

Brett and his hostage were creeping at iceberg speed toward the door, when behind them the office door opened and Marcia emerged. She made her way toward Brett, who was unaware of her presence. Closing to within a dozen steps of her prey, Marcia raised her weapon and pointed it at the back of Brett's head.

A moment later, all hell broke loose.

CHAPTER 54
Matt Dillon

Ramon and Chuck scattered to the left of the office when the FBI announced their arrival.

Chuck had moved behind a container twenty feet from a container where Ramon, his weapon drawn, now stood.

When the office door opened, both men diverted their eyes from Brett's hostage-held trek to the office doorway.

As the door opened wide, they saw Marcia, armed with Murphy's Glock, exit the office with a look of deadly determination.

Chuck, seeing Marcia's face, knew her intentions.

So did Ramon. Raising his weapon and aiming it at Marcia, Ramon yelled, "Behind you Brett!"

Chuck, seeing Ramon was about to shoot Marcia, shouted, "Nooooo, Ramon! Marcia, get down!"

Ramon, hearing Chuck's warning, pivoted, but today it wasn't Chuck who Ramon had to face down, it was Matt Dillon.

Everyone knows Matt Dillon doesn't lose.

Chuck, with his weapon pointed at Ramon's chest, fired three booming shots, hitting Ramon in the chest, throat, and head, killing him.

Today was my Matt Dillion day, thought Chuck.

Marcia, ignoring Chuck's warning, continued toward Brett, who, hearing Ramon's alert, wheeled around to see the looming Marcia just a few steps away.

Brett abandoned his grip on the hostage, leaving the worker to break away and run in a direct line toward Ron and Tim.

Tim yelled at the freed hostage to get down, but the Mexican, not understanding a word of English, kept coming.

With the Mexican worker blocking his view, Tim and the equally obstructed Ron could only watch the scene taking place 30 feet away.

As Brett swiveled, Marcia fired a shot which caught Brett's left elbow, shattering it.

Marcia, never having used a handgun, didn't realize the kickback of the powerful Glock. Thrown backward, the jolt resulted in her falling with the gun spinning from her hand and skidding across the concrete floor.

Brett, staggered by the blow, regained his footing, and took dead aim at Marcia who was scrambling to pick up the dropped firearm. He was about to pull the trigger when out of the corner of his eye he saw Chuck taking aim at him.

Brett rotated to his left, but Chuck peeled off three rounds before Brett could pull his trigger. All three found their mark and Brett was dead before his body hit the floor.

Ron and Tim saw the woman knocked to the floor, but with the ensuing gunshots they ducked behind their container.

"C'mon," yelled Chuck.

Marcia, raising herself from the floor, ran to Chuck, and the two of them disappeared behind the pallets.

Hearing only silence, Ron and Tim emerged from behind their container and rushed toward the fallen Brett.

Brody and McNair arrived seconds later.

As they stood around the body, Ron caught movement out of the corner of his eye. A guard rising from the floor was reaching for his weapon.

Raising his shotgun waist-high, Ron fired. The blast caught the guard flush in the chest, knocking him out of his shoes and sending him flying backward ten feet or more.

"Everyone stay glued to the floor with your hands behind your heads," warned Ron. "If anyone else moves, they'll be just as dead as that fool is."

"Damn! I forgot all about those guards," whispered Tim.

"We got lucky," said Ron in a low voice.

CHAPTER 55
Ho Hos

Ron, looking at Brett's body, said to McNair and Brody, "Nice shooting. Which of you two nailed this guy?"

One looked at the other, both shook their head, and replied in unison, "It wasn't us, Ron."

"Well, it wasn't us, and Agent Lambert," said Ron, pointing at the door, "is lying outside."

"Maybe the woman?" asked McNair.

"Hey, where's the woman?" asked Tim.

"Tim, McNair, look behind the containers," said Ron, "but be careful. Ramon is in here somewhere. Brody, look in the office. She may have ducked back in there."

McNair made his way to the nearest container and stepped behind it. Seconds later, they heard McNair yell, "We have a man down, back here!"

When Ron and Tim reached McNair, he was kneeling next to Ramon's body. As Ron knelt beside him, McNair said, "I'm guessing this man took out Cardone."

"Possible," said Ron, "but who took him out?"

"There were warnings yelled," said Tim. "One at the woman, and one at Cardone."

Ron, having picked up a weapon lying next to Ramon's body, said, "There's a silencer on this gun, and there are only two bullets missing from the magazine. Cardone took three dead center hits. This guy wasn't the shooter, but whoever put him down is no amateur."

"Then where is he? And where's the woman?" asked Tim.

"Gone," said a loud voice coming from near the doorway. It was Agent Lambert. Earlier, Brody had dragged his wounded partner outside and propped him up against the building just outside the doorway.

Rushing outside to Lambert's position, Ron asked, "Al, what did you say?"

"They're gone."

"Gone! Gone where? When? How?"

"I watched a half-dozen people pour out of the doorway. They took off in all directions."

"Did you see a woman wearing black slacks and a green jacket, run out?"

"Yeah, I did. A guy had her hand. I took them for workers, although in hindsight they looked much different from the others."

Ron rushed to the street and looking both ways saw no one.

As he stood in the street, multiple law enforcement vehicles showed up along with an ambulance.

Stepping back inside, he told Brody and McNair to round up the guards.

"Let's have a look inside these totes, Tim."

"I already did. They are all filled with cash. I'm guessing there's 500 million or more."

"Oh, I can hear Juan Pablo crying all the way from Mexico."

As Tim and Ron talked, Brody approached, saying, "Ron, you need to come to the office."

As Ron entered the office, the first thing he saw was vomit. The second was Murphy.

"It looks like our eye shooter got away," said Tim.

"I wonder what this was all about?" asked Ron. "This guy certainly died before we arrived."

"Do you think the woman may have shot him? She walked out of this office," said Brody. "She was in here with him."

"Not a chance, Brody," said Tim. "Hell, the kick of the Glock knocked the pure crap out of her. I'm betting it's the first time she ever fired a gun."

"It wasn't her," agreed Ron. "I see no powder burns on his face. Which means, someone stood above him and shot his eyes out. The woman couldn't have done that. I'm guessing the guy who took out Cardone and Ramon, also did this deed."

"What's the vomit about?" asked McNair.

"That is a brilliant question," remarked Tim. "It looks like chocolate cake mixed with coffee."

"I found a box of Ho-Hos in the fridge," said Brody. "It looks like the guy got sick after eating these."

"Let me see the box," said Ron.

Removing a 2-pack of the Ho-Hos from the box, Ron examined the pseudo-cupcakes. Spinning the pack in his hand, he brought the package closer to his eyes.

Finished with his examination, he handed Tim the 2-pack, asking, "Is that a needle hole?"

Tim, examining the package, nodded his head, saying, "It sure looks like a needle hole. You think someone poisoned these?"

"I do, but the coffee could also be in play."

Ron, scanning the scene, said, "Look at the coffee cups on the table and the desk. The cup on the desk, knocked over. The cup on the table…"

Tim, interrupting Ron's analysis, said, "… has coffee in it. Whoever was drinking this likes their coffee with lots of cream."

Ron, giving Tim an annoyed look, said, "Well, damn, partner, that narrows our list of suspects to about forty-million. Now, do you mind if I continue?"

"Oh, by all means, be my guest," answered Tim with a sheepish grin.

"Lying on the desk are Ho-Ho cellophane wrappers. I'm guessing we'll find needle holes in those as well. I'm thinking two guys, who knew one another, were sitting having coffee. For reasons we may never know, the guy sitting at the table poisoned the Ho-Hos, knowing the guy sitting at the desk would eat them."

"Well, he weren't wrong!" added Tim.

"No, he wasn't. Seeing there was a box of them in the cupboard, I'm guessing our man was a Ho-Ho junkie."

"Better than cocaine," said Brody.

"Irrelevant, but true," said Ron. "Now, the guy sitting at the desk, feeling the effects of the poison, vomits his Ho-Hos and coffee over the desk. Then, in his struggle to stand up, he knocks over the cup. He tries to make his way toward the table but falls to the floor."

"I see where you're going, Ron."

"Go ahead, Tim-o-thy. Finish it up."

"The guy sitting at the table, puts down his cup, stands up, walks around to the guy lying on the floor, straddles him, and shoots out his eyes."

"Good job, Tim. Let me add, no one in the warehouse hears the shots because the guy uses a silencer."

"So the guy who shot out this guy's eyes, also outed Ramon and Cardone?" asked Brody.

"That's the way it reads."

"So where does the woman come in?"

"That, I can't decipher, McNair. She must have had a serious hard-on for Cardone, seeing as she tried to kill him. But unless we catch them, we may never know."

"Well, we have plenty of evidence to help identify them," said Tim. "The cup will have fingerprints and possible DNA. We should be able to pull the woman's prints off the gun she used."

"True," said Ron.

"Oh, shit. Look who's here," said Tim, nodding toward the warehouse.

CHAPTER 56
Leroy

WEDNESDAY - OCTOBER 16, 2019 - 1:00PM

Ron looked out to see Jim Braddock standing in the warehouse talking with Agent Travis Coe. Together they headed toward the office with one of the arrested guards in tow.

A minute later, the three men entered the already crowded office.

"Damn," yelped Braddock, "this is a hell of a mess, Ron."

"You noticed, did ya?"

Braddock, not amused by Ron's sarcastic comment, said, "I heard some got away. How did that happen?"

"Poor decision-making," said Ron. "We didn't cover the door while responding to some shootings."

"Shit happens," voiced Braddock. "I may have some good news though. This man… what's your name?"

"Leroy Perkins."

"Leroy might fill in some blanks for you."

"We have plenty of blanks," conceded Ron. "What can you tell us, Leroy?"

"The man lying on the floor is Murphy Bortelli. He's a badass hitman man."

"Was," said Tim.

"Yeah, right," replied Leroy after giving the eyeless Murphy another glance. "Anyway, it looks like someone gave him a taste of his own medicine."

"What do you mean, Leroy?" asked Ron.

"They called him Mustard because he liked to embellish his kills by shooting his victims in the eyes after they were dead."

"This guy shot people in the eyes?" barked Ron.

"Yes, sir."

"Who killed him, Leroy?"

"Can't rightly say, but it was his partner who killed Mr. Cardone. I wouldn't want to be Chuck. The cartel will search under every rock and stone until they find him. And when they do….ugh!"

"Who's Chuck?" asked Tim.

"Chuck Delgato. He's a hitman. They call him 'The End' because if you're in his sights, it's the end for you. He and Mustard were Mr. Cardone's muscle."

"Is Chuck the guy who ran out with the workers?"

"Yep. He and Marcia…"

"Marcia? Who is Marcia?"

"She and Mike…"

"Mike? Who's that?" asked Tim.

"Let him answer about Marcia, Tim," scolded Ron.

"Her name is Marcia Cole. His name is Mike Carter. They worked for Cardone. Together they set up this place."

"Was it Marcia who shot Cardone?"

"Yeah. She left with Chuck."

"Why did she try to kill Cardone?"

"I don't know. Word is, Cardone had her on call whenever he wanted to get laid. Maybe he told her she was a lousy lay, and it pissed her off."

"Maybe he was the lousy lay, and it pissed her off," quipped Tim.

"That too," conceded Leroy.

"Where is this Mike, guy?" asked Braddock.

"He's dead, Jim," said Ron. "Myrtle Beach police found him shot to death in his hotel room."

"Why was he killed?"

"No clue, Jim," said Tim.

"How much money have we confiscated?"

"Tim estimates about $500 million."

"It's closer to $700 million," volunteered Leroy.

"This keeps getting better," said Ron, with a big smile.

"The workers finished packaging $65 million this morning," said Leroy.

"So what?" asked Braddock.

"That means the man will be coming tonight to pick it up. He comes every 4-5 days."

"What man?" asked Ron.

"Our foreman, Luiz Petrone, told me he was a very important man."

"What is the man's name, Leroy?" asked Ron, his face just inches from Leroy's.

Leroy, seeing the darkness in Ron's eyes, answered, "His name is Luiz Beltrán. Petrone said he was the big boss's financial advisor."

"The big boss?" asked Braddock.

Leroy's face turned pale, his mouth went dry, and his eyes widened with fear. He had said too much. He didn't want to mention the name. Too many times, people who spoke his name never spoke again.

"Who!" growled Ron.

"Juan… Pablo… Amarillo."

"Damn!" yelped Ron. "A link straight to Juan Pablo will be here tonight. What time, Leroy?"

"He comes at 7:00."

"Who is with him?"

"He comes in a big limo. Four men, all pros, packing heavy, accompany him into the building. The driver stays in the car. Beltrán goes into the office, speaks with Cardone for about five minutes, and walks out with two very heavy satchel bags. He gets in the car and they drive off."

"Thanks, Leroy. You've been a great help."

"What are you thinking, Ron?" asked Braddock.

"I'm thinking I'm getting weary of Juan Pablo sending hitmen to kill Tim and me."

"I'll second that, partner."

"This Beltrán fella knows more about the operations of the Juarez Cartel and Juan Pablo than most anyone else. We need to get this guy. Are you with me on this, Jim?"

"Whatever you need, Ron."

CHAPTER 57
"S-E-X."

WEDNESDAY - OCTOBER 16, 2019 - 2:30PM

Grabbing Marcia by the arm, Chuck pulled her behind the container, whispering, "Stay quiet and follow me."

They maneuvered between the containers until reaching one parked just a few feet from the doorway.

Huddled against a nearby wall were a half-dozen Mexican workers.

Chuck peered around the container and saw the two FBI agents running toward Brett's body.

Turning to the huddled Mexicans, he waved them to run. As they ran toward the open doorway, he and Marcia fell in with them.

Once outside, they ran down the alleyway leading to Business 17. Just before they reached the intersection, Chuck stopped in front of the Good Day Café where he and Mustard would often have lunch.

"Marcia, before we go inside, take off your jacket and toss it into the trash can."

After Marcia dumped the jacket, they stepped inside the café, and finding a table far from a window, sat down.

A waiter, recognizing Chuck, came to the table, asking, "Ahh, Mr. Chuck. Where is Mr. Murphy today?"

"He's having some eye irritations, Eddie. He couldn't see coming today. The lady and I will have a cup of coffee for starters."

"Here are two menus. I'll have your coffees in just a minute."

"Thanks, Eddie."

After waiting for the waiter to move on, Chuck whispered, "We need to disappear, Marcia. The FBI and the Juarez Cartel want our asses."

"Where can we go?"

"Somewhere far away from here."

"That's going to take money."

"Yes, it will. There's a lot of money in the warehouse. It's too bad it's all in FBI hands."

"Not all of it," said Marcia.

"What do you mean?"

"Luiz Beltrán is coming tonight."

"I know, but so what? His money will also be in FBI hands."

"His money, yes, but not Brett's."

"What are you saying, Marcia?"

Before Marcia could answer, Eddie had returned carrying two cups of coffee.

"Here are your coffees, Mr. Chuck. Can I get you something to eat?"

"I'll have a cheeseburger and a side of fries. Marcia, what would you like?"

Scanning the menu, she replied, "I'll have a tuna sandwich with tomato."

"We'll have those for you in just a few minutes," said Eddie as he gathered their menus.

Marcia waited until Eddie was away, then said, "Brett was skimming."

Chuck, not surprised, asked, "How much?"

"Two weeks ago, he told me he had $20 million hidden away. I'm guessing he may have added to the total since then."

"Where?"

"In the warehouse."

"Do you know where in the warehouse?"

"I do. It's in the office behind the fridge. He knocked out some wall and put in a safe."

"Any chance you know the combination?"

"I might. Don't most safes have a three-digit combination?"

"I think that's right," answered Chuck.

"Then there's a chance Brett used 19-5-24."

"How did you come up with that?"

"The only thing Brett loved more than money was sex. Those numbers are the numerical positions of the letters - s, e, and x."

"And if it doesn't work?"

"Do you have any safe-cracking skills?"

"Do you consider blowing things up, a skill?"

"Only as a last resort."

"Well, Marcia, therein lies the problem. We have but two resorts; your first and my last."

"How do you propose we go about getting to the money, Chuck?"

"If I were a betting man, I'd guess someone has spilled the beans about Beltrán's impeding arrival tonight."

"Which means?"

"Which means they will be setting a trap for him. They know if they capture him, he will have valuable information which could break the cartel."

"They won't be wrong."

"We'll have to watch to see what happens. When the FBI clears out, we go in and open the safe."

"Just like that?"

"Not exactly. We need to go shopping for a few necessary items. After we do that, we'll need to steal a van."

CHAPTER 58
"... playing dead."

"So, what's the plan, Ron?"

"We make the place look like normal."

"How do we do that?" asked Braddock.

"Leroy," said Ron, directing his question at the handcuffed guard, "how late did you work?"

"We started at 7:00am and worked until 9:00pm. We had a lunch break at noon and a dinner break at 6:00."

"Damn!" said Tim. "That's a helluva long day."

"Petrone worked them hard. He wanted them packaging $25 million a day," elaborated Leroy. "Their goal was to finish before Thanksgiving."

"How well does Beltrán know the employees?" asked Ron.

"Beltrán wouldn't give us the time of day. He only dealt with Brett and Luiz. Although, he might, emphasis on might, recognize me because I unlock the door to let them in, making me the first face he sees."

"That's good," said Ron.

"So what do we do, Ron?" asked Braddock, looking at his watch. "It's 2:30. We have five hours before Beltrán shows, if he shows up at all. Word may have gotten out we secured the warehouse, and Cardone is dead."

"That's true, Jim, but we will only have wasted a few hours if he doesn't show."

"Okay, Ron, so what's our next step?"

"Replacing the guards with our own people."

"What about the replacement workers, Ron?" asked Tim.

"We'll need Latinos as replacements for the workers," said Ron.

"Why is that?' asked Braddock.

"He may be personally oblivious to the employees, but I'm guessing either Beltrán or his bodyguards would notice if the workers were other than Latino."

"That is a good point," noted Braddock. "Anyone have any ideas how to resolve the issue?"

"I have a Mexican fella who does my yardwork," stated Brody.

"And?" asked Tim.

"He has a crew of a half-dozen guys, all of whom are Latinos. I'm thinking if we offered monetary considerations, they'd be willing to play the part."

"Jim, how do you feel about citizens getting involved?" asked Ron.

"I'll get the money, Brody. You get your guy. Offer him a hundred a man."

"Okay, sir, but I have a question."

"What's the question?"

"How are we going to guarantee their safety, sir?"

Braddock, dumbfounded by Brody's question, said, "That's a damn good question. I wish you hadn't asked it."

"If there's trouble," stated Ron, "it will happen in the office area. We'll keep the workers in Beltrán's view, but as far away from him as possible. Once we have secured Beltrán and his henchmen in the office, someone can take the workers outside, out of harm's way."

"Good plan," said Braddock, giving Ron a thank you nod. "Go ahead, Brody. Get your yard crew."

"I want Leroy too, Jim. We'll give him an inoperable weapon. We'll need him to open the door. If Beltrán sees a familiar face, it will put him at ease."

"Who will play Cardone?" asked Tim.

"Cardone will play himself. The only thing is, he'll be playing dead."

CHAPTER 59
"... more a mannequin."

The limo arrived at the warehouse at 7:00pm. Four men of bodybuilder caliber, all dressed in dark suits, and each armed to the teeth, stepped from the limo.

Three stood outside their car doors, scanning the area for any sign of trouble.

The fourth moved toward the warehouse door and knocked three times. The door swung open, and the man stepped inside to scrutinize the warehouse activities. Seeing nothing irregular, he stuck his head out the door and satisfied all was well, gave a nod.

The man closest to the limo's back door opened it. A moment passed before a distinguished older looking gentleman stepped out.

He wore a gray suit and vest, and a blue shirt with a matching tie. His right hand clutched an unnecessary walking cane with a gold-plated handle. A mustache added another touch of dignity, as did a pair of bifocals attached to a gold chain which fed into a vest pocket.

As he made his way toward the door, a bodyguard held it open. Two bodyguards preceded his entrance while the other two followed.

Entering, he noticed Leroy but didn't acknowledge him. He saw a half-dozen workers counting money near the back of the warehouse. Guards, carrying AK-17s, mingled around the warehouse floor. None looked his way.

It seems quieter than usual, thought Beltrán.

The group moved toward the office. As they closed in, they could see Brett Cardone, his back to them, sitting at the office desk. They could also see the usual two large bags lying on the table to his right.

One bodyguard opened the door and Beltrán entered, saying in a boisterous tone, "Brett! How are we doing, my friend?"

Only a second passed before Beltrán realized something was wrong.

Beltrán, stepping toward the chair, whirled it around only to see the dead eyes of Brett Cardone.

"Grab the moncy and get me out of here!" Beltrán screamed.

The four henchmen encircled him while extracting machine pistols from under their jackets.

"Get the door, Lou," ordered Moe, the senior bodyguard and Beltrán's most fearless soldier.

Lou, opening the door, met death with a bullet to the head. His blood and brains splashed Beltrán and both men standing behind him.

Tim, hidden in the warehouse's upper rafters with his sniper's rifle, moved his scope to the next front man but didn't pull the trigger.

"Mr. Beltrán," came a booming voice over the warehouse's speakers. "Welcome to Myrtle Beach, sir. As I'm sure you know by now, we have been expecting you. This is Special Agent Colonel Ron Lee of the FBI. I need you to know, we have your driver under arrest, and we have driven away the limo."

"Mother…" hissed Beltrán.

"As you can see, Mr. Cardone is no longer functioning as a human being. I'd say, he's more a mannequin. Wouldn't you agree?"

"You are clever, Agent Lee," whispered Beltrán.

"We raided the warehouse today, and in doing so, Mr. Cardone lost his life. Now you, and your remaining three men, can join him, if you wish. We can and will accommodate you if that's your decision. Or you can surrender and live. It's your choice, senor."

"Turn out the lights!" ordered Beltrán.

Upon seeing the office go dark, Braddock said, "I'm guessing it's a sign he won't surrender."

"Yeah, I think you are correct, Jim. But, I didn't expect him to just lay down."

Ron got back on the mic, saying, "Mr. Beltrán, I don't think turning off the lights will protect you. Our snipers have night-vision and can see your every move. Do I need to give you a demonstration or will you surrender?"

"What would you have us do, senor?" asked Moe.

"How many are out there?"

"Well, I believe every so-called guard we saw when we walked in, including the workers in the background, are all FBI. That makes at least a dozen, but the count is most likely closer to 20. Plus they have snipers in the rafters."

Beltrán, considering Moe's assessment said, "We are out-manned, and they have us boxed in. It appears we don't have a choice."

"Beltrán!"

It was Ron again, talking through the speaker system.

"I'm giving you one more minute. Come out or die! This is your last chance."

"We're coming out, Agent Lee."

"Turn the lights back on!" ordered Ron.

"Moe, turn the lights on."

"No, senor."

"What?' Do you want to die, Moe?"

"I'm sorry, Senor Beltrán, but I have my orders."

"Orders? What orders?"

"Juan Pablo's orders, Senor Beltrán."

"He told you to never surrender?"

"No, he told me to never let you surrender."

"If we don't surrender, Moe, they will kill us all!"

"I have my orders. Juan Pablo does not want you to surrender."

"What happens if I am taken alive?"

"He will have my family tortured and killed."

"Wait!" said Beltrán as he removed his phone from a pocket. "Let me call Juan Pablo. I'll straighten this out."

"You have no need for that, Senor Beltrán," said Moe, taking Beltrán's phone and tossing it across the floor. "Like I said, senor, I have my orders."

Raising his weapon, Moe pointed it at Beltrán's chest, saying, "I'm sorry, senor."

Tim, watching the proceeding through his night-vision scope, called to Ron, saying, "It looks like one of Beltrán's men has turned against him. I think he's going to execute him."

"Take him out!" ordered Ron.

Tim lined up Moe in his scope and pulled the trigger. Moe's head exploded.

Seeing what happened to Moe, the remaining two men panicked and charging from the office, haphazardly sprayed the warehouse with their automatic weapons as they ran toward the exit door.

Machinegun fire from three agents took down the first bodyguard.

Hit by eight high-caliber projectiles, he appeared to jitterbug across the floor, before falling in almost the exact spot where Cardone had fallen earlier in the day.

A hail of various caliber bullets took down the remaining bodyguard, but not before he killed Agent Travis Coe.

Coe, while taking cover behind a container, caught a ricochet from the haphazard firing of the bodyguard. The bullet punctured his chest and blew out his heart.

Ron and two other agents, seeing the bodyguards were no longer standing, rushed toward the office. Busting through the door, they found Beltrán, wounded but alive, huddled against the wall, covered in Moe's blood and brains.

"I think we need to talk, Senor Beltrán."

"Bastard!" screamed Beltrán.

"Now, now, Senor Beltrán, you are in no position to name-call. But I am. So get up, you lousy prick!"

****

Parked two blocks away, but with an unobstructed view of the warehouse, was a white van whose two inhabitants watched the ongoing activity with keen interest.

They had been there for over two hours, watching trucks hauling away pallets of money, and ambulances carrying away body-bags.

"It appears, Marcia, Beltrán's bodyguards didn't fare too well," said Chuck.

"That's the sixth body-bag they have carried out, Chuck. Beltrán only had four bodyguards."

"We heard the shootout, Marcia. I'm supposing there were FBI casualties too."

"What about Beltrán?"

"Hard to tell. I suppose he could have been in one of those body bags. However, I gotta believe the FBI would do all in their power not to kill him."

"Look!" shouted Marcia, "There goes the seventh body-bag!"

"Yeah, but why are they putting it in the back of that black Yukon?"

"Maybe they ran out of ambulances?"

"Maybe, but doubtful. Do you see those two guys getting into the Yukon? They don't look like morgue staff. The suits tell me they are FBI."

"What's your take, Chuck?"

Chuck went deep into thought, then pronounced, "I think they are hiding a witness. I'm guessing Beltrán is occupying that body-bag. The FBI will announce they killed Beltrán just so Juan Pablo doesn't send someone to kill him."

"But he'll send someone for us," muttered Marcia.

"Oh, yeah. You can bet on it."

"It looks like things are clearing out, Chuck. The trucks and ambulances are no longer coming and going. The police are moving out as well."

"We'll wait until midnight."

"How do we get into the warehouse?"

"Not to worry, my dear. I have a key."

CHAPTER 60
"... marked for death."

WEDNESDAY - OCTOBER 16, 2019 - 10:45PM

Chuck was no dummy. The FBI did indeed claim to have killed a high-ranking member of the Juarez Cartel.

Myrtle Beach news outlets reported, Luiz Beltrán, a high-ranking member of the Juarez Cartel, and four bodyguards died during an FBI raid on a downtown Myrtle Beach warehouse.

The FBI claims to have confiscated over $700 million dollars in cartel drug and extortion money.

As they extracted Beltrán from the warehouse office, he told Ron that Juan Pablo would never let him live. That's when Ron suggested they report him being killed. If dead, Juan Pablo would have no reason to look for him. And, in return for his cooperation, he would live in the Witness Protection Program.

"Have you ever lost anyone in that program?" asked Beltrán.

"Nooooo!" lied Ron.

Ron, having grilled Beltrán for the better part of two hours, left the interrogation room to ask, "Where are his personal possessions?"

Tim opened an office envelope and spilled its contents onto a table.

Ron, sorting through the various items and not seeing what he was looking for, asked Tim, "Where's his cell phone?"

"He didn't have one."

"What? Beltrán is near the top of the food chain, and he doesn't carry a phone! Is that what you're telling me! That's pure bullshit!"

240

Barging into the interrogation room like a bull in a china shop, Ron interrupted Braddock's ongoing questioning of Beltrán.

"Excuse me a minute, Jim. I have a question for Senor Beltrán."

Giving the prisoner a stern look, Ron asked, "What did you do with your phone, Luiz?"

"My phone? It was in my coat …"

Seeing Luiz hesitation, Ron snarled, "What?"

"I just remembered. Moe, the bodyguard who was going to kill me, took it from me."

Ron pressed an intercom button, saying, "Tim, look through the personal effects of the bodyguards. Luiz says one of them took his phone."

"Okay. I'll have a look."

"Don't bother," said Beltrán. "I remember he tossed it across the floor."

"Tim!"

"Yeah?"

"Check with the lab guys. If the phone was on the floor, they probably picked it up and bagged it."

"Will do."

"Okay, Senor Beltrán, it's getting late. You've been cooperative up to this point and we appreciate it. However, we have many more questions, and we know you have more to offer. We'll pick it up again in the morning. You'll be staying here, under tight security, tonight. I'll see you in the morning."

"You know, Agent Lee, Juan Pablo will never stop coming for you and your partner. You are both marked for death."

"Your asshole boss hasn't had much success so far, has he Senor Beltrán?"

"But he won't stop until you are both dead."

"No, I don't suspect he will," said Ron, as he prepared to leave. "However, if he keeps on sending guys like Cardone and yourself, I doubt we have much to worry about."

As the door closed behind Ron, Beltrán turned to Braddock, saying, "Agent Lee is a prick."

"Tell me something I don't know."

****

It was 11:35 when Tim called Ron to say the forensics lab didn't find a phone on the office floor.

Tim's call caught Ron getting undressed for bed, albeit it was only his left shoe he had taken off.

"I'm thinking it's still there, Tim."

"I suppose it could have slid under a piece of furniture, although I find it difficult to believe forensics wouldn't look everywhere."

"Yeah, you would think so. The phone needs finding, Tim. I bet it has a wealth of information on it we could use. We need to find it."

"I'm about a mile from home, Ron and I'm dead tired. The warehouse is 15 miles behind me. I'll stop by in the morning and check it out."

"Okay, partner, I'll see you tomorrow. Good night."

Ron, sitting on the edge of the bed, with one shoe off, did some serious pondering.

Two minutes later, at 11:49, the shoe was back on, and Ron was driving to 604 Oak Street.

CHAPTER 61
Lance and Helen

THURSDAY - OCTOBER 17, 2019 - Midnight

Chuck parked the van directly in front of the warehouse's front door and exited the vehicle. Moving to the door, he unlocked it and stepping inside, turned on the interior lights. He then joined Marcia at the rear of the van.

After opening the panel doors, they removed two large pails, brooms, mops, and cleaning supplies.

Leaving the front door open, they took the cleaning equipment into the office where they filled the buckets with soap and water.

Dressed in blue and white overalls, they both wore a baseball style cap that read, "Murphy's Industrial Cleaning Services." The lettering replicated the printing on the signs on either side of the van.

Marcia, having dyed her hair, looked nothing like the woman who tried to kill Brett Cardone in the building just 12 hours earlier.

Their plan was to make it appear someone sent them to clean the warehouse. To reduce suspicion, they would turn on the lights, leave the front door open, and actually clean, although in a limited capacity.

"I saw a big blood splotch on the warehouse floor, about 30 feet from the door. Take your bucket and mop and take a few swipes at it. I'll clean up in here."

Both pseudo clean-ups lasted only 30 seconds before Chuck made a move to the fridge to pull it away from the wall to reveal the safe.

He hadn't yet reached the fridge when they heard a car pull up.

"Get back to your spot, Marcia. Let me do the talking. Remember, if asked, your name is Helen."

Ron, already on high alert because of the open warehouse door, and lights being on, entered with gun drawn.

Scanning the now empty warehouse, he saw he wasn't alone.

There were two others.

Thirty feet away, he watched a woman, seemingly unaware of his presence, mopping an area of the warehouse floor where two men had bled out and died earlier in the day.

Inside the office, he saw a man stacking office furniture.

Approaching the woman, he saw the company name on the back of her uniform and noted it matched the name on the doors of the van.

"Excuse me, what's your name?"

Marcia, with her back to Ron, feigned being startled, answered, "Helen. Who's asking?"

Ron, holding up his badge, replied, "FBI. What's going on here?"

"You'll need to talk to my partner. He's in charge. All I know is somebody hired us to clean the office and various other spots throughout this warehouse."

"Okay, miss. What's your partner's name?"

"Lance. He's a pretty friendly guy. Go talk to him. He has all the answers."

Ron, cautiously at ease, made his way to the office. As he came through the door, he held up his badge, saying, "Special Agent Ron Lee of the FBI. Would you mind telling me, sir, your name and how it is you are here?"

"I'm Lance Taylor, and the lady is Helen Ellis. We work for Murphy's Industrial Cleaning Services. I received a call a couple of hours ago to clean the office and any spots needing cleaning in the warehouse. I take it, by all the blood stains I'm seeing, something bad happened here."

"Yeah, Lance, something bad happened here. How did you get in?"

"I used the key attached to the work order."

"Show me the work order."

"Sure thing. I'll go get it. It's in the van."

Ron, convinced there was nothing suspicious going on, stopped him, saying, "Never mind. I came here to find a phone. I need a minute to search for it. Give me a minute and then I'll get out of your way."

"There's no rush," said Chuck. "We have all night."

"Thanks," said Ron, feeling more comfortable with the situation.

"If there's anything I can do to help," offered Chuck, "just ask."

"Maybe there is. I'm looking for a cell phone someone dropped on the floor. Have you seen it?"

"No, but I was just getting started. I'm moving the furniture to one side, so I can clean. I saw nothing under the table or desk."

"Maybe it slid under the refrigerator."

"That's a reasonable possibility, sir. I'll look for you," volunteered Chuck, while dropping to the floor on hands and knees.

Peering under the fridge, Chuck saw nothing. Putting his hand under the fridge and sweeping it back and forth, found nothing but dust.

"Sorry, sir, but I see nothing and felt nothing."

"Help me pull it away from the wall, Lance. It may have slid further under."

Chuck, fearing this might happen, replied, "Sure thing, Agent Lee," while giving Marcia a slight nod.

Marcia, seeing the signal, pulled a gun from her basket of cleaning supplies, and made her way to the office doorway.

"Step back, sir, I think I can handle this," said Chuck. He grasped both sides of the fridge and rolled it away from the wall.

With the refrigerator pulled away, Chuck stepped into a position that prevented Ron from seeing the wall.

"Ahh, I think I see it, sir!"

Chuck reached down and retrieved the phone.

"Got it! Good call, Agent Lee," said Chuck as he stepped from behind the fridge and handed the phone to Ron.

As Ron inspected the phone, Chuck moved the fridge back into place.

"Thank you," said Ron.

"Glad to help, sir," said Chuck as he gave Marcia a shake of his head.

Marcia, seeing the signal, walked back to her bucket, returned the gun to her basket, and resumed mopping the blood-stained floor.

"Anything else we can help you with tonight?"

"No, no! This is what I came to find. You've been a great help. I'll leave and let you get back to work. Good night."

"Thank you, sir. Good night."

They watched as Ron exit the building. A moment later, they heard his vehicle start and pull away.

"Damn, Chuck, that was close!"

"That it was."

"Did you see the safe?"

"Yeah, I did. It was good Brett had it placed close to the floor. It prevented Agent Lee from seeing it."

"Let's open the damn safe and then get our asses gone!"

"Sounds like a plan, Marcia."

CHAPTER 62
"... mop-up work."

THURSDAY - OCTOBER 17, 2019

12:30am

Ron was heading back home on Business 17 when, out of curiosity, he called what he referred to as the FBI help desk.

"FBI. Your badge number and PIN, please."

Ron supplied both and waited.

Moments later, he heard, *"This is FBI responder Phillips. What is it we can do for you, Special Agent Lee?"*

"I have a question, Phillips."

"Yes, sir."

"Does the FBI specify who cleans up messy crime scenes?"

"Yes, sir, we do."

"Is there a specific agency in Myrtle Beach we assign to do such work?"

"There are two, sir."

"Is Murphy's Industrial Cleaning Services one of the two?" he asked as he turned onto Farrow Parkway.

"No, sir, they are not."

Ron, slamming on his brakes, pulled over to the side of the road in front of Warbird Park.

Having jotted down the license plate of the van, he passed it on to Phillips.

"Tell me," asked Ron, "has anyone reported anything about that plate number?"

"I'll check, sir. Give me a moment."

"Hurry!"

Ten seconds later, Phillips said, *"Someone reported the plate was stolen off a Buick Envoy yesterday at 4:30pm, sir."*

"Thank you, Phillips."

"Will that be all, sir?"

Ron thought about sending backup but thinking it might cause a major shootout where someone could get hurt or killed, decided against it.

"That's all for now, Phillips. Thank you."

Ron sat there for a moment, thinking.

Who are those two people? Why are they in the warehouse pretending to be cleaning it?

Another moment passed when he realized the couple had to be Chuck and Marcia! Now why would they come back? There has to be a reason. If he were a betting man, he would bet the reason was money.

Performing a U-turn, Ron blasted through the light at Business 17 and Farrow.

Being after midnight, traffic was light as Ron barreled north on 17 at speeds exceeding 80 mph.

A Myrtle Beach traffic officer, sitting in the parking lot of the Christmas Mouse store, seeing the speeding vehicle flash by, pulled out to give chase. As he did so, he radioed for other units to block the road ahead.

Ron, seeing the chasing patrol car, wasn't about to slow down or stop. That is until he ran into the roadblock set up in front of one of his favorite restaurants, the Villa Romana.

He came to a screeching stop just 20 feet shy of the two cruisers blocking the road. Seeing two officers crouched behind the hoods of their vehicles, pointing their weapons at his head, Ron raised his hands.

Realizing they might shoot him if he made any sudden moves, he yelled out his open window, "I'm FBI!"

The officer who gave chase had pulled up close to Ron's rear bumper to prevent any backward movement. The officer, hearing Ron's claim, moved toward him, with his weapon drawn.

"Let's see the ID!"

"Okay, officer. I'm removing my badge from the left jacket pocket with my left hand."

"Do it slow," ordered the officer, "using only your thumb and index finger. Keep your right hand on the steering wheel, sir."

"Fear not, officer. I know the drill."

Ron extracted the badge as ordered and held it out the window.

The officer removed it from his hand and seeing it was valid, holstered his gun, then asked, "What's going on?"

"Officer Daniels," said Ron, after seeing the man's nametag, "I need to get to 604 Oak."

"Oh? And what is at that address?"

"An empty warehouse."

"So what's happening at this empty warehouse?"

"That is what I'm trying to figure out, officer."

"What's the problem?"

"Why would the two principal players in a deadly shootout earlier today, return, under false pretenses, to the scene of the crime? The building is supposedly empty of anything of value. So what's the draw?"

"Who are they pretending to be, sir?"

"Janitors," said Ron, knowing he now sounded ridiculous. "Don't ask! Please move those damn cars out of the way!"

The officer motioned to have the cars moved.

"Thank you, officer."

"Does the FBI need our help in apprehending the pretend janitors, sir?" asked the grinning officer.

Ron, realizing how the whole thing sounded, smiled, saying, "No, I think I can handle it. It's just mop-up work."

The officer, smiling at Ron's sarcastic retort, said, "Touché!"

Seconds later, Ron was once again barreling down Business 17. The dashboard clock read 1:02.

12:45am

Chuck moved the fridge out a second time, and Marcia stepped behind it. Squatting, she turned the dials to 19-5-24, and the safe clicked opened.

Pulling the door fully open, she saw stacks of money inside.

"Bingo!" she cried. "Give me the bag, Chuck!"

It took Marcia almost 15 minutes to remove the $20 million plus contents from the safe and stuff it into the duffel bag.

While extracting herself from behind the refrigerator, she hears Chuck say, "A vehicle just pulled up outside! Hurry, get to your bucket, Marcia! I'll move the fridge back."

A minute later, Tim, with his weapon in hand, walked through the door.

CHAPTER 63
"Hey, we're all friends here."

THURSDAY - OCTOBER 17, 2019

12:35am

    Tim, having made it home, had not yet exited his car. He sat there, parked in his driveway, thinking.

    I know Ron won't wait until morning. He'll go to the damn warehouse tonight.

    Resigning himself to the situation, he heard himself mutter, "I need to go back."

    Slamming the car into reverse, he burned out of the driveway and pointed the car toward Myrtle Beach.

    He had 18 miles to drive and he would curse Ron every inch of the way.

    Attired in her pajamas since 10:00, Wilma Pond was lying in bed watching a movie, while waiting for her husband to come home.

    Curious about the sound of screeching tires, Wilma left her bed and made her way to the window. Opening the blinds, she peered into the lamppost lit street, but saw nothing other than exhaust dissipating into the air.

    Disappointed Tim hadn't yet come home, she closed the blinds, returned to her bed, and continued to watch *The Godfather*. She wouldn't sleep until he was lying beside her.

1:00am

    As he approached the building, the first thing he noticed was its interior lights were ablaze. What he noticed second was the absence of Ron's car.

    Slowing as he approached, he saw the white van parked in front of the wide open front door.

Something ain't right, he thought.

Parking beside the van, he exited his car, pulled his gun from its holster, and approached the door.

Peering inside, he saw a slim man in a uniform and wearing a baseball type cap, mopping the floor.

"What the…" he whispered.

Tim walked to within a dozen steps of the man before stopping dead in his tracks. The man was actually a woman.

Again, Marcia, as she had when Ron approached, appeared startled as Tim advanced toward her.

"Who the hell are you!" she shouted.

"FBI," answered Tim. "Who the hell are you, and what the hell are you doing?"

Seeing the gun in Tim's hand, she said, "I'm Helen. Why do you have a gun?"

"It seems appropriate, and you're done asking me questions. I asked you, what are you doing here?"

"What does it look like I'm doing?" she asked, holding up the mop. "We're cleaning."

"We?"

"My partner, Lance, is in the office."

Tim, glancing toward the office saw a man mopping the floor. While trying to get a good look at the man's face, Marcia interrupted his concentration, saying, "You're late."

"Oh? How's that?"

"Your partner was here about a half-hour ago."

"Where is he now?"

"I would think, being the hour it is, he was going home. He came to find a phone. He found it, and then he left."

"Is there a problem, Helen?" asked a booming voice coming from the office doorway.

"No problem, Lance. It's just another FBI agent."

Chuck approached, saying, "Hi, I'm Lance. Your partner, Agent Lee, was it…"

"Yeah, Ron Lee."

"Yeah, he came looking for a cell phone. I found it under the refrigerator. He said thanks and left… oh, maybe, thirty, forty minutes ago."

"I'm guessing he asked what you were doing."

"He did."

"Do you mind telling me what you told him?"

"Why sure thing," replied folksy-sounding Chuck. "We work for a cleanup and restoration company."

"The company's name is right here on our caps," said Marcia, pointing at her head.

"Yeah, I see it, Helen. Thanks for pointing it out."

"Our boss called me around 8:00 to tell me to clean this place up. There was a shootout here today. Are you aware of that?"

"I am," answered a still wary Tim.

"It must have been one hell of a shootout, I reckon," said Chuck, acting overwhelmed by it all. "There sure is a lot of blood."

"Lots of blood is a recurring theme when multiple people get shot," said Tim.

"It makes sense," added Marcia.

"So are you and Helen partners?"

"Oh yeah," answered Marcia, "Chuck and I go…"

Tim's eyes lit up.

"I'm sorry," said Tim, looking at Chuck, "but I thought you said your name was Lance."

Chuck didn't waste a second. He pulled his gun, tucked in the back of his pants, and had it pointed at Tim's head in a blink of an eye.

"I'm sorry, Chuck, it just slipped out."

"It's okay, Marcia. No harm done. Isn't that right, Mr. FBI?"

Tim, still holding his gun, assessed the situation.

"Drop the gun."

Tim hesitated.

"Please, don't make me shoot you, Agent…I'm sorry, but I didn't catch your name."

Tim, dropping his gun, said, "It's Agent Tim Pond."

"Well done, Agent Pond. Now I'm going to tell you something you will appreciate."

"Oh, are you going to surrender to me?"

"Funny, but no. What I want to tell you is, I don't kill FBI. I've been told it's a dangerous habit. It seems you guys are as bad as the cartel when it comes to revenge."

"You heard right, Chuck."

"Now, after we tie you up, Agent Pond, Marcia and I will be on our way."

"Why are you even here? If I may be so bold to ask?"

"Tie him up, Chuck, while I answer his question," said Marcia, who had retrieved Tim's gun off the floor and had it pointed at his crotch.

"I saw your gunplay earlier, Marcia. I'm sorry, but it wasn't all that impressive."

"Yeah, well, now that I have experience under my belt, I wouldn't get too cocky, no pun intended, if I were you. Chuck might not shoot a Fed, but he doesn't speak for me."

"Well, would you mind lowering it a tad? I still have comprehensive plans for your current target."

"Well, from where I'm standing, it appears your 'plans' are more compressed than most 'plans' a lady would hope for."

"That was low, Marcia. Right now, I'm trying to keep my plan under wraps. When it's time, it will rise to the occasion, although I wouldn't classify it as a hi-rise."

"Just full of little quips, aren't you? Your partner wasn't funny."

"No, he takes this job way too serious. We call him 'Humorless Ron'… when he's not around and can't hear us."

"You must be a riot at a party, Agent Pond. Now, didn't you have a question?"

"Yeah, why are you here?"

"It seems Brett Cardone was skimming money. In the neighborhood of $20 million, we're guessing."

"That's heavy skim," said Tim.

"Agreed. Anyway, during another episode of terrible sex, he told me he had put a safe in the office, behind the fridge."

"I see, having both the law and the cartel nipping at your heels, demands that you disappear. But, to do so, you need cash. Lots of it! So you come back to claim Brett's $20 million. Under the circumstances, I can't say I blame you."

"I see why you're an FBI agent," said an admiring Chuck. "You, Mr. Pond, can put 2 + 2 together and come up with 4. Very talented, sir."

"Hey, well, thank you, Chuck, and please, call me Tim. We're all friends here."

"I love your attitude, Agent Pond."

"Why thank you again, Chuck. Tell me, what did you do with my partner?"

"Nothing. It was just like Marcia told you. He came, found, left."

"You're serious?"

"Yes! I told you, I don't do FBI."

"I might," said Marcia, stroking Tim's face. "You're cute."

"I'm sorry, Marcia, but you're not my type."

"Oh? And just what is your type, Agent Pond?"

"Women with brains."

"Why you son-of-a-bitch! I'll kill you!"

Tim froze when Marcia put the Glock to his forehead.

"No, you don't, Marcia," said Chuck, taking the gun from her hand.

Turning to Tim, he said, "Choose your words more carefully, Agent Pond. The next time, I may not be in the immediate neighborhood."

"I appreciate your help and your advice, Chuck."

"Yeah, well, maybe someday you can return the favor."

"You know, it probably won't happen, Chuck."

"Yeah, I know."

CHAPTER 64
"Correct...Lance."

THURSDAY - OCTOBER 17, 2019

1:12am

Ron turned off his car's headlights as he passed by the front of the warehouse. The traffic stop had cost him 10 minutes, but the van, parked at an angle, was still there.

"Unless they had a hidden car, they are still inside," he muttered to himself.

As he passed by the van, his heart sank when seeing Tim's car parked beside it.

"Damn! What the hell ever possessed him to drive back here," Ron whispered to himself.

Driving another 50 yards further, he pulled over and turned off his engine. Taking care not to slam the car's door as he exited, Ron made his way to the warehouse.

When he arrived, he noticed the rear panel doors of the van were open.

They're leaving. I wonder what they have done with Tim?

Ron moved to the doorway and peering inside, saw Marcia, still dressed in the janitor's uniform, standing outside the office door holding a large duffel bag.

A moment later, Chuck joined her and together they walked toward the exit.

He gave thought to waiting until they were almost upon him, then stepping out and dropping them both. Worried a miss might jeopardize his partner's life, if indeed Tim was still alive, he instead dropped back and waited for them to step outside.

Moving behind Tim's car, Ron knelt behind the hood. He was only eight feet the van's driver door. He couldn't miss.

As they exited the warehouse, Ron heard Marcia say, "Start the van, Chuck. I'll close the rear doors."

Ron, seeing Chuck reaching to open the driver's door, was about to confront him when from the rear of the van, Marcia screamed, "Chuck, he's gone!"

Before Ron could react, Chuck was rushing to the rear of the van.

Then he heard Tim's voice yell out, "She's lying, Chuck. Stay away! She's going to kill you."

Chuck, as he approached the rear of the van, heard Marcia say, "You worthless piece of shit. I should have killed both of you inside. Now die you fucker!"

Tim, lying bound on the van's floor, was now staring down the barrel of Marcia's Glock.

Realizing death was only a heartbeat away, Tim closed his eyes and waited for the inevitable.

His eyes sprung open when he heard two soft pops, and he saw Marcia's head obliterated.

"I told her, no FBI."

"She didn't listen very well, did she?"

"Greedy bitch, too. I guess she thought she needed all $20 million to get by."

"Drop the gun, Chuck."

Ron, having circled the van, stood but five feet away from the hitman.

He had his gun pointed at the back of Chuck's head.

"Agent Lee, I take it."

"Correct... Lance."

"Hey, it fooled you. We had Agent Pond fooled too until that stupid bitch opened her trap."

"Is he right, partner? Did they fool you?"

"Hello to you too, Ron. Chuck just saved my life for the second time in less than 20 minutes."

"Well, if he wants to save his own life, he best put down his gun."

"I'd do what the man asks, Chuck," suggested Tim.

"Hang on a minute, fellas. I'd like to review my options. Should I spend the rest of my life in jail, where someone working for the cartel can slit my throat, or maybe I should opt to have Agent Lee shoot me in the head? The second option sounds best to me. Quick and no pain. Would not the two of you agree?"

"Maybe we can offer another option, Chuck," said Tim. "Look, you saved me twice. I need to return a favor before you make a poor decision."

"I'm listening, Agent Pond."

"Put down the gun, first."

"Now, now, you know that ain't happening. Doing so would leave me with no leverage."

"Well, at least stop pointing it at me."

"That would be downright stupid of me, Agent Pond. Again, I would have no leverage. Let me hear this favor you're talking about."

"Well, first, I'm not worried, because you said, and I quote, 'No FBI.'"

"True, but I left off the addendum."

"Which is?"

"Unless I'm cornered like a rat."

"Hmm, now I'm concerned."

"Tim!" shouted Ron. "Get to the point. This gun is getting heavy and I'm afraid it might go off and kill someone."

"Don't worry, Chuck, Ron's always bitching about something."

"I'm growing impatient with you, Agent Pond. Do you have something to say? If not, then we have a situation."

"Yeah, I do. You worked for the mob. Right?"

"I did," admitted Chuck.

"Well, how about you flipping on them?"

"What will it get me?"

"Let me ask you something, Chuck," said Ron, interrupting Tim's reply.

"What is it?"

"Did you poison your partner and then shoot him in the eyes?"

"Yeah, I did. I watched that sicko shoot dead people's eyes out for years. I swore someday I'd give it back to him. You have a problem with that?"

"Not at all. In fact, for doing so, I'd be willing to recommend they take ten years off whatever they give you."

"Well, seeing they'll be giving me about a dozen consecutive life sentences, those ten years don't mean squat."

"True, but I thought it was a gracious gesture on my part."

"Now I see why they call you 'humorless Ron.'"

"What? Who calls me that? Pond, do you call me that?"

Tim, ignoring Ron, said to Chuck, "Would you be willing to enter the Witness Protection Program?"

"Would that be the same Witness Protection Program where, two years ago, a half-dozen guys in the so-called witness protection, including two in Myrtle Beach, were whacked by an Italian hitman?"

"Yeah, that's the one. But, hey, that was an anomaly."

"Hmm, I think not, but hear me out, Agent Lee."

"I'm listening."

"We spent some precious time on options one, two, and three. I am now going to provide some background for option four. This gun I'm holding against Agent Pond's head, has a hair trigger. Even if you shoot me, this gun goes off and kills your man. I'm ready to die, but I don't think Agent Pond wants to cash out just yet. Am I wrong, Agent Pond?"

"You're not wrong, Chuck."

"I didn't think so. So, option four is, Agent Lee puts his gun down or I shoot Agent Pond in the head. Or, Agent Lee, you can shoot me, but I still shoot your boy in the head. It's your choice. You have three seconds."

"Don't believe him, Ron. He's playing us."

"You're wrong, Tim," said Ron. "You're forgetting, partner, self-preservation is the first law of survival."

"You have an intelligent partner, Agent Tim."

"I'm putting my gun down, Chuck. Do nothing rash."

"Not to worry, Agent Lee. I'm under control."

Seeing Ron's gun on the ground, Chuck said, "The ankle gun too. Don't deny it, Agent Lee. I saw the gun while on the floor, looking for the phone you needed. Now, please, take it out and place it next to your other weapon."

Ron begrudgingly complied.

"Now, remove your jacket, Agent Lee, and turn around and raise your arms," ordered Chuck while never removing his gun from Tim's head. "Remove your cell phone and drop it on the ground."

Again, Ron complied.

Seeing Ron was weapons free, Chuck removed his gun from Tim's head, and cut free his leg bindings, but left Tim's arms bound.

"Get out of the van, Agent Pond, and stand next to your partner. Agent Lee, keep your arms well in the air. Now, I would like you both to walk inside the warehouse."

Reaching the door's threshold, Chuck said, "Please walk to the center of the warehouse and sit on the floor. Go!"

Chuck watched until the two men had sat, then he flipped the light switch, turning the warehouse into blackness.

"Agent Lee, I placed Agent Pond's weapons and cell phone in the backseat of his car. I'll put your jacket, weapons, and cell phone there as well."

"That's real nice of you, Chuck, but where are you going to place my dignity?" he heard Ron ask from somewhere in the dark.

"I must apologize, Agent Lee. You do have a sense of humor. Goodbye, gentlemen."

Closing the door, Chuck locked it and tossed the key. He then recovered Ron's weapons, phone, and jacket and, as promised, placed them in Tim's car.

Returning to the van, he closed the rear doors, climbed into the driver's seat, and drove off with a duffel bag filled with $22 million dollars.

****

1:50am

"This is embarrassing," said Tim, as they sat in the pitch darkness.

"You think?" said Ron with a hint of sarcasm.

"What's our explanation for this?"

"If it weren't for Marcia's body lying in the parking lot, we wouldn't need an explanation. Because neither you nor I would ever speak of this. The world, other than our boy, Chuckles, would never know this happened."

"If we get out of here before someone comes across Marcia's body, we won't need an explanation. But, in the meantime, I'll ask you once again. Have you, Mr. Brainiac, worked out a reasonable explanation of how we managed to get into this predicament?"

"Not yet," Ron replied.

"Okay, then let's try this for starters. We find the light switch."

"Then what?"

"You untie my hands. Then we look for a way out."

"That's your plan?"

"You have a better one?"

"Can't say I do."

"Which way is the door?"

"It's so dark in here, I can't tell. I cannot see my hand in front of my face."

"It's impossible for me too, but for a different reason. He tied my hands behind my back!"

"Let's find the light switch."

"Damn, that's brilliant, Ron. I wish I had thought of it. Why don't you lead the way?"

They bumbled and fumbled their way about in the pitch darkness for ten minutes before finding the door, and after a five-minute search, the light switch.

"I'm thinking," said Tim, "Stevie Wonder, himself, could have found the door faster. How many walls and support beams did you have us bump in to?"

"If you don't stop complaining, I'll leave you tied up and I'll turn out the lights."

Ron undid Tim's arm bonds, after which they set out searching for a way out of the building.

The search lasted only minutes, ending when Tim found the switch which opened the loading dock's overhead door.

Rushing out to the front of the building, Ron retrieved his coat, cell phone, and weapons from the backseat of Tim's car.

"Chuck is a man of his word," said Tim. "You gotta give him that, Ron."

"Okay, he's a man of his word. Let's call this in."

"Are you serious, Ron?"

"Call it in. We'll tell them the truth... make it a half-truth."

"And what's the half-truth?"

"We came to retrieve the phone. As we pulled in, we find half-a-head Marcia, check inside, and see an empty safe behind the fridge. We concluded someone got greedy."

"It sounds damn good, Ron. It's half-true."

"It's all true, Tim. We may have added some embellishments, but we evened it out by omitting minor details, so we wouldn't look like idiots."

"Minor details like Chuck getting the best of us?"

"That's the one, partner!"

"I'll make the call."

"Hey, Tim, I've been meaning to ask."

"What?"

"When you came back tonight, did you bring donuts?"

EPILOG

December 31, 2019

"2019 has been a long and tough year, Ron."

"Damn, if it ain't the truth, partner!" replied Ron as he savored his second éclair. "We had double jeopardy what with the damn cartel hit squad trying to kill us at the same time we had The Mamba attempting to off the president."

"Hey, at least those events brought you and Heather together. She's kept you busy."

"And then some!"

"Then we had the encounter with Mr. Sensitive."

"Not our finest moment, I'm afraid. He killed way too many people before we finally put him down."

"Yeah, and then we get suspended!"

"It was a nice paid vacation though."

"This last case put a dent in Juan Pablo's bank account, that's for sure."

"What was the final dollar amount?"

"Just shy of $682 million."

"A drop in the bucket," Ron replied as he answered a ringing phone.

"Ron. Bill Baxter."

"Hey, Bill, Happy New Year. What's up?"

"Do you remember a guy named Leroy Kincaid?"

"Yeah, he was a guard at the cartel warehouse. He gave us some good info that night. They put him in Witness Protection."

"Well, it appears it didn't help all that much."

"Oh, why's that, Bill?"

"Orlando police, responding to offensive odor complaints from neighbors, checked out the safe-house. They found the well-past ripe bodies of Leroy and his two bodyguards. I have a few specifics they provided me with as well."

"Please, Bill, let's hear the specifics," insisted Tim, who was listening in on the call.

"Well, for one, Leroy's balls were where his tongue should have been."

"Now that there was a specific I didn't need to hear," said Ron.

"They also informed me they riddled Leroy's body with forty-two bullet wounds, ten of them in the head."

"Seems like a little overkill to me, Bill."

"Not to mention, it's a terrible waste of ammo," added Tim.

"It seems to me you fellas just might need some Sensitivity Training."

"Anything else, Bill?"

"Not unless you can help with last night's sniper shooting."

"We can't help but tell us about it."

"There's not much to tell. A doctor was walking from his car to his house when a bullet ended his medical career. Someone shot him from a quarter-mile away. We have no suspects."

"Sounds interesting, Bill. Sorry, we can't help."

"Well, I thought you would want to hear the news about Kincaid. It appears keeping a secret from the cartel is difficult. They must have snitches everywhere. Okay, I gotta go. Good luck to you fellas in 2020."

"I doubt 2020 could be worse than 2019 was," said Tim.

"I hope you're right, but I don't feel so optimistic," said Baxter. *"There's always something in the wind."*

December 31, 2019 - Colorado Springs, Colorado

The lodge was high in the mountains surrounding the city of Colorado Springs. It housed one man and four bodyguards hired by the FBI to protect their most prized witness against the Juarez Cartel.

A winter storm leaving four-feet of snow the previous day, along with temperatures bordering around zero, provided an additional, if not permanent, layer of security in and around the lodge.

However, foul weather and four ex-military bodyguards were not enough to protect Luiz Beltrán from the wrath of Juan Pablo.

It was nearing 10:00pm when the lodge's front door blew open, and two men, armed with AK-47s, burst through the door. They took down a bodyguard before they themselves lost their lives in a hail of bullets.

Three more cartel soldiers replaced the two who had fallen. In an intense shootout with two bodyguards, they traded one of their lives for the lives of both bodyguards.

The remaining bodyguard and Luiz had barricaded themselves in an upstairs room.

The bodyguard, heavily armed, and hearing footsteps approaching the barricaded door, sent burst after burst of 9mm projectiles through the door and the surrounding walls while receiving no return fire.

His efforts did not go unrewarded.

His volley's had killed four more cartel soldiers.

Hearing nothing but silence, and thinking he had wiped out the intruders, the bodyguard stood and made his way to a doorway which his firing had reduced to splinters.

Peering through the splintered door was the bodyguard's first mistake. It was also his last.

From out of nowhere, a flashing nine-inch blade pierced the man's right eye and continued into his brain.

Luiz saw a hand extract the knife from the bodyguard's head. He watched in horror as the dead bodyguard slumped to the floor in a heap.

Luiz Beltrán was now alone.

January 1, 2020 - Juarez, Mexico

There was a soft knock on the door of Juan Pablo's office.

"Come in."

Jorge Ortiz entered the room, saying, "I just received word we have Luiz Beltrán in our possession, Juan Pablo. They are bringing him across the border tonight."

"Have them hold him in the dungeon under the stables. I will deal with him tomorrow."

"Si, senor."

"Has Ramon's brother arrived?"

"Senor Carlos Baez is five minutes away, senor."

"Good. Send him in as soon as he arrives."

As he waited for the assassin to arrive, Juan Pablo thought about what had happened to his empire since getting involved with the two Myrtle Beach FBI agents.

In his mind, he recalled the note which accompanied the return of Brett Cardone's body. It read:

Juan Pablo, don't send boys to do the work of men. Maybe, if you're man enough, you'd like to personally give it a try. Regards, Special Agent Ron Lee.

In the past two years they had killed his beloved nephew, wiped out an entire hit-squad sent to kill them, and captured almost $700 million at the raided warehouse.

268

The $700 million, however, was a minor financial thrashing, compared to the almost $2 billion in revenue lost because of Luiz Beltran's betrayal.

Tomorrow, before Luiz dies, he will watch his entire family pay for his betrayal. I will then take great pleasure in slitting his throat.

As his anger and fury reached the breaking point, he unconsciously snapped a pen he was holding, while muttering, "The American FBI bastards must die! I will see them die if it's the last thing I ever do!"

The voice of Jorge, saying, "Senor Carlos Baez has arrived, senor," interrupted Juan Pablo's incensed thoughts.

"Good. Send him in."

A moment later, a drop-dead image of Ramon Baez walked through the door and stood at attention in front of Juan Pablo's desk.

"Amazing, the resemblance!" harked Juan Pablo. "I would swear Ramon was standing in front of me."

"We were identical twins in every way, Juan Pablo."

"I did not know this."

"Ramon wanted it that way. He thought it would help keep us…mysterious."

"I'm sorry to hear about your brother, Carlos."

"Thank you, Juan Pablo."

"I want you to exact revenge on his killer."

"You know who killed him?"

"I do. An associate of ours, a Leroy something or other, disclosed the killer's name to us."

"I'd like to thank this Leroy, fella."

"That, I'm afraid, is quite impossible, Carlos."

Carlos, knowing the context of Juan Pablo's statement, no longer pursued the issue.

"An American hitman murdered your brother, and he also murdered my conduit in Myrtle Beach, Brett Cardone."

"I have heard of Brett Cardone. I understand he knew how to make money."

"Yes, but now he is dead. Killed by the same man who killed your brother."

"Who is this man?"

"His name is Charles Delgato."

"Where can I find him?"

"We don't know. All we know is he has a sizable amount of my money. I want you to find him, reclaim whatever money he hasn't already spent, and kill him. Make sure he suffers."

"Where should I start, Juan Pablo?"

"Start where he was last seen."

"And where might that be, Juan Pablo?"

"The bane of my existence for the past three years. Myrtle Beach, South Carolina."